CW00422225

TWENTY THIRTY FOUR

GRANT WILLIAMS

Copyright © 2021 Grant Williams

All rights reserved.

ISBN: 979-8-7218-8610-2

DEDICATION

This book is dedicated to all of those who fell firmly on the wrong side of the Government policies over COVID.

CONTENTS

Prologue   1

1   Chapter One: Charlie Wilson Monday 13th February   39

2   Chapter Two: Karam Shahid   67

3   Chapter Three: Sophie Hallam   102

4   Chapter Four: The Plan Begins   119

5   Chapter Five: Tuesday 14th February 2032   128

6   Chapter Six: Wednesday 15th February 2032   153

7   Chapter Seven: Monday June 19th 2034   224

    Epilogue   230

ACKNOWLEDGMENTS

Many thanks to the artist Keith for the cover design:
https://www.art-partnership.co.uk/

PROLOGUE

This story is set in 2032 and in many respects is the culmination of events that happened in the preceding 12 years. Without an understanding of the global events that occurred, the story might seem fanciful, almost impossible, but as we all know, nothing will ever be as it was. Life has changed for all of us. How did it happen and why did we let it happen?

The trade wars of the early 2020s were worrying at the time but everyone seemed to pull back from the brink. China and America seemed to have an understanding. Donald Trump, the US President seemed to know how far he could push, and President Xi JinPing understood that. Things worsened after Joe Biden won the 2020 presidency. He was not a natural negotiator and Xi knew this and saw weakness. Everyone had hoped a more conciliatory and diplomatic style would be good for relationships, but the Chinese ran circles around the new administration. It was the same when Truman took over from Roosevelt. Truman initially could not see what Stalin was planning and offered appeasement. Trump had seen only too clearly what President Xi and the Chinese were up to. Churchill had always known what Stalin was like, but his warnings were not heeded. America's belated response to the CoronaVirus pandemic of 2020 had isolated the USA. President Trump had started a new trade war with Europe, based around cars and digital firms but extending eventually to everything.

This escalated as these things often do. Under President Trump, the American administration had been genuinely concerned about cyber security, but it was the issue around Covid-19 that just would not go away. The Whitehouse had insisted on a full investigation into the origins of the CoronaVirus and insisted that China provide full disclosure. He tried to get the World Health Organisation to start a detailed investigation into the source of it and determine China's role in that, but the WHO constantly dragged their feet and China were obstructive. Fifteen months after the outbreak in Wuhan, the Chinese authorities were still preventing World Health Organisation investigators from entering the city where the pandemic had started. The change in Presidency in the US took the heat off the Chinese for a while but as the second wave increased the death toll, China became the focus once again.

The trade war continued to develop throughout the early 2020s even under President Biden and the Democratic administration. America struggled to recover from the impact of Covid-19 both economically and politically. The 2020 election had been incredibly divisive. President Trump and his team, mostly comprising family members, had refused to accept the result leading to the most extraordinary last sixty days of his Presidency. He had tried to settle old scores and became more belligerent towards enemies. By the time he finally left the Whitehouse, America was tearing itself apart. Trump supporters had stormed the Capitol and Biden talked of insurrection. This was the America that Joe Biden at 77, the oldest American President had inherited. It was a disastrous Presidency from start to finish. Anything that could have gone wrong certainly did and often it was the Chinese pulling the strings from afar. Crisis after crisis landed at the desk of the ageing Biden whose poor health saw greater involvement by his Vice President Kamal Harris who showed terrible inexperience. The Civil War that erupted briefly in twenty twenty-two was the death knell for Biden. Although brief, snubbed out at The Battle of Columbus, where three thousand from the newly formed militia, "For the Freedom of America" were annihilated by regular troops of the US Army, and another five thousand imprisoned for insurrection, it finally made clear the divisions that had been tearing America apart for decades. There were no pardons.

The War had been brief, lasting only twenty-three days. The rioting that occurred throughout Mississippi, Alabama, and Tennessee led to the formation of large groups of armed militias who raised the Dixie Flag above the Federal Buildings in Birmingham, Alabama. They tried to come together under the banner of The American Freedom Party, but in-fighting and disagreement meant they could not form a political agreement. However, they had thousands of followers who were just plain angry, and armed, and weren't prepared to wait. President Biden published a Proclamation ordering the insurgents to disperse. When they failed to do so, he used The Insurrection Act of 1807 to deploy the US Military. The rebels drove in a rag tag of privately owned vehicles singing and waving the Confederate flag. They met three divisions of the US Army, numbering 50,000 with armoured support. The rebels opened fire and what ensued over the next thirty minutes was a massacre, all played out on screens all over the world.

The images of blood running through the streets were indelibly marked on every American. The five thousand who were arrested, and corralled singing Dixie Land reverberated through all fifty states of the Union. More died that day than on 911, and all at the hands of fellow Americans. It was a public relations disaster for the Biden Presidency as it would have been for any incumbent President and is almost certainly what led to his stroke.

By 2024 the Democrats were in disarray, the American economy was in freefall and the Chinese were becoming more vocal about almost everything. Ivanka Trump pushed for the Republican nomination, and then at the last minute her father, the previous President threw his hat in the ring. Despite being impeached on the grounds of inciting violence which constitutionally barred him from office, Donald Trump had developed his digital media company during his time out of office and now had one of the most influential media machines in America. He ran on a campaign of the impeachment being orchestrated and against Democracy. After the Columbus massacre, it was not difficult to offer a credible alternative. On November 5th, 2024, Donald Trump won a landslide victory taking dominant control of both the Congress and the Senate. The collapse of the economy, the Civil War, and the rise of China played into his hands. The Democrats had been utterly discredited by his online campaign. It was the first time since Grover Cleveland in 1892 that a President had won a second term that was not back-to-back. Donald Trump was now 78, a year older than Biden four years previously, taking the unenviable title of the eldest American President appeared to be robust, much more so than his predecessor. His battles with China resumed, culminating in 2026 with the Export Control Act which had been used by Franklin D Roosevelt against the Japanese in 1940. Exactly like Roosevelt, the Act stated that "whenever the President deemed it necessary in the interest of National Defence, he could prohibit or curtail the export of any goods that might damage the interests of the United States." Under Roosevelt this has been primarily scrap metal, copper, armaments, munitions, and tools. But this was a vastly different world. Throughout the noughties and early 2020s the Whitehouse had tried to curb the appropriation of intellectual property and technology by the Chinese who had been manufacturing hardware for American companies for two decades. By 2026 Foxconn was the world's largest private company employer, manufacturing for Apple, with over one million workers. Donald Trump had tried everything to try and get manufacturing repatriated to the USA during his first Presidency and again now throughout 2024 and 2025, but to no avail. With the new Act he made it legally binding for Apple to bring all manufacturing back to the USA. President Xi of China immediately retaliated by seizing a Foxconn factory and its contents in a clear breach of International law. Foxconn was a wholly owned Taiwanese company who were making over 50% of all global consumer electronics. They immediately appealed to President Xi but were given short thrift. On April 9th, 2026, The Chinese Communist Party sent the army in overnight to all Foxconn factories on mainland China and secured them to the shock of the whole world.

Under the Taiwan Relations Act, the United States had an unofficial agreement to come to the aid of Taiwan in the event of Chinese aggression. The Act had always assumed this meant a Chinese military strike on Taiwan itself, in anticipation of annexation. The Chinese seizure of Taiwanese assets on mainland China complicated

things. Foxxcon was the major supplier of an American company Apple, which at $8tn was also the most valuable company in the world. Months were spent with public threats and private negotiations to try
and find a resolution, but none was forthcoming.

China had enjoyed huge economic development ever since the policies of Deng Xiaoping back in 1978 turned it into an economic powerhouse. Over the next 40 years many Western countries including America and the UK exported their jobs to China benefitting from a willing and cheap workforce. This led to a consumer boom of cheap products which disguised falling wages and collapsing productivity in the West. The benign presidency of Barack Obama meant China under Hu Jintao proliferated and stole a march on the USA. Donald Trump started to push back which led to increasing tensions, the trade wars, tariffs, tit for tat retaliations, and then the fallout from Covid-19 and Covid -22.

The Chinese desks at the Pentagon were producing data and statistics for the Whitehouse daily. The facts that jumped off the page were that China would lose 200m working age adults and gain 300m senior citizens over the next 30 years, that Chinese debt had ballooned eight-fold and was 400% of GDP at the end of 2026 and that since 2007 economic growth had more than halved and productivity has dropped by 15%. It was clear to the analysts that the Chinese wonder years were coming to an end. Like a wounded animal, China might lash out and do something rash.

Anti-China sentiment had grown. Nearly a dozen countries had suspended or cancelled participation in the Belt and Road initiative. Another sixteen including eight of the world's ten largest economies had banned or restricted use of Huawei products in their 5G networks and India had turned hard on China. Japan had ramped up military spending turning amphibious craft into aircraft carriers. The release of the Chinese film '800' in 2020, which had become the biggest grossing film in the world that year depicted 800 Chinese soldiers holding back a force of 20,000 Japanese from a warehouse in Shanghai. It was extremely popular in China and spawned a multitude of anti-Japanese movies. Tensions were rising everywhere, and it was the view of the Pentagon scenario planners that war may be inevitable.

By 2025 Donald Trump was becoming increasingly belligerent. His military team were warning him about Chinese military spending and their increasing capabilities. The Chinese seizure of Foxconn factories in April 2026 was portrayed as an act of war having a huge psychological impact due to the popularity of Apple products that Foxconn manufactured. The collapse in Apple's share price precipitated another dramatic fall on stock markets globally that had never really recovered from the Great Market Crash of 2021 and the ensuing global recession. The banking sector that had to be bailed out yet again was crippled and defaults had started to rack up. The Fed pumped yet more trillions into the global economy raising questions about the true worth of the greenback, dollar hegemony was being questioned. At the same time President Xi was pushing for the Chinese Renminbi to challenge the US dollar. China was able to use its sphere of influence in the South China Sea to promote its use and was encouraging the members of The Regional Comprehensive Economic Partnership to adopt its currency instead of the US dollar.

Donald Trump was already serving his two-term maximum under the 22nd Amendment of 1947 limiting any President to be elected a maximum of two terms. This Act came into force after Franklin D Roosevelt had been serving his fourth term having seen the USA through the Great Depression and then World War 2. It had been discussed since 1947 about changing it especially during the Presidency of Ronald Reagan, but as it stood, Donald Trump was due to stand down in 2028 and perhaps President Xi was sensing an opportunity. He probably felt it was very unlikely that another President would be as confrontational or stand up to China like Donald Trump had done.

Donald Trump went to Congress asking for the 22nd Amendment to be suspended and for his Presidency to be extended. He argued that the United States was already at war with China and that this was no time to be changing Presidents. He made a plea to the American people that he was the only strong and committed American politician who could take the Chinese on headfirst and restore American prestige. His approval ratings went through the roof, there were marches through all the major cities in support of Donald Trump, and the Chinese flag was burnt everywhere. Chinese businesses were attacked, and the American Chinese started to fear for their future and even their lives.

Donald Trump announced that anyone living in America for longer than five years or who had been born in America would be considered an American citizen. All others would need to apply for a special visa which needed to be renewed every six months. An exodus began, including the American Chinese who had lived in the USA longer than five years, fearing for their future. The violence of the 2022 Civil War and the sight of Americans turning on each other was still vivid in the memories, and they could see the writing on the wall.

Congress approved the suspension of the 22nd Amendment which allowed Donald Trump to remain as President indefinitely. With renewed confidence, the American President ramped up restrictions via the Export Control Act. The export of all kinds of technology, hardware, software, and intellectual property were severely restricted. The Chinese responded with similar restrictions, and very quickly the United States pressurised other countries to restrict trade with China. Over the next eighteen months countries found themselves in the unenviable position of being on one side or the other of the biggest trade war the world had ever seen.

The Chinese who left America in 2025/26 and had returned to China did not receive a hero's welcome. Like the Russians who had been captured in battle by the German Wehrmacht in 1942/43 they were regarded with suspicion upon their return. Many were held in detention centres for months, those who returned home to families had their papers stamped making them unemployable regardless of qualifications or skills, whilst some just disappeared completely. The Chinese leadership was paranoid about spies and 5th columnists infiltrating Chinese society and undermining from within. Once word got out about how tough it was to return to China, and what might happen to you and your family, Chinese nationals leaving the USA tried to find more welcoming countries spreading them all over the world.

In September 2026 things deteriorated. The previous two years had seen a ramping up of military spending and re-arming was unrestrained. Global resources were sucked into a vortex of military expansionism which happened in so many countries especially those in South East Asia fearful of what China might do. Most of this money was spent with the American industrial war machine under the agreement that America would come to their aid. The American military complex was working overtime and had been the most buoyant part of the economy for the previous five years.

The propaganda war was also building up. The United Kingdom as usual sided with the United States. Part of that meant emphasising the case against Russia who had been constantly portrayed as the enemy, friend of China, and risk to the West. Russia worried about its own borders with China, but the two had become inextricably linked by trade deals for oil, gas, and military expertise as well as The One Belt, One Road project that physically linked the two superpowers.

Europe was in crisis; the 2021/2 global recession had hurt Europe very badly. So many banks had gone bust that the European Central Bank struggled to cope. The International Monetary Fund was found wonting and the World Bank ineffectual. The ensuing disaster eventually led to full Fiscal Union with those members remaining giving up control of their own economies. It was either that or the break- up of what was left of the EU. The economic disaster had created the paralysis that allowed the European leaders to get their way, a fully economic and politically unified core of Europe but at what cost? Europe was bankrupt and looked to the United States for finance to prop it up, just as it had done after the Second World War. The United States was looking for allies to side with it against China. The thorn in the side was Germany whose economy and supplies of energy were so inextricably linked with Russia.

On September 16th, 2026, the unthinkable happened. The Chinese

People's Liberation Army invaded Taiwanese soil. China had made no secret that it considered Taiwan to be a part of China and the Motherland. Taiwan had been settled upon after the Chinese Civil War by the Kuomintang, also known as The Republic of China. A stalemate had pursued ever since with Taiwan and China settling into a mutually beneficial trading relationship, although China had consistently pursued a 'One China' policy with the aim of bringing Taiwan under its control. The invasion of some of the outlying islands belonging to

Taiwan was about to test the Taiwan Relations Act. This was the unofficial agreement between the United States and The ROC dating back to 1979 that said America would come to Taiwan's aid.

An amphibious armada had been assembled on the Chinese mainland over the previous week. Everyone knew what was coming. Satellite images were being watched around the world. Once again, the UN met to try and diffuse the situation but with China and the USA as permanent members of the Security Council it was an impossible situation. The UK and Russia both vetoed and the world was thrown into panic.

At 4am on the 16th of September, an armada of 200 vessels crossed the 2kms from Xiamen and landed on the island of Kinmen. This was part of Taiwan's territories and the site of the Battle of Kinmen in 1949 when the Republic of China soundly fought back the Communists of the PRC. The Taiwanese Armed forces put up some resistance firing at the Chinese from the other islands that they held, but they were quickly put out of commission by The PLA Air Force as well as support from the Navy.

The images beamed around the world were impressive. The island fell and the Taiwanese defenders surrendered the same day. The following day President Xi via The Apostolic Nunciature of the Holy See, one of the few nation states to have an Embassy on Taiwan, asked for the Government of the Republic of China to cede all control and bring Taiwan back to the motherland fulfilling the One China policy. An emergency meeting was held by the Government of Taiwan. The Taiwanese had been preparing for this moment for the last seventy years, but they knew they would not be able to stop the PROC without outside assistance. Parliament agreed not to respond until they had heard back from the Americans.

Donald Trump met with his military commanders and political advisors over the next few days. They were inundated with requests from the Government of Taiwan to come to their aid. Requests of clarity were also arriving from South Korea, Vietnam, and Japan.

American military spending had outstripped China's consistently for years. China still did not have a fully functioning blue water navy to match that of the USA. America boasted eleven aircraft carrier groups. China now had five, but they were untested. The concern for the military commanders was supply and support. There was infrastructure with a major naval base in Guam, but it was still a long way from home. China had significant manufacturing capability, access to raw materials and fuel from Russia, and a huge workforce that was under the autocratic control of Xi's party apparatus. The question everyone asked themselves at the Pentagon was 'would they fight?'. China had not been involved in any major military conflicts since the modernisation of its armed forces and was therefore unproven. The USA on the other hand had been on a permanent war footing ever since 1941 operating as the world's de facto policeman.

Should America show solidarity and respond militarily to the invasion of Taiwan? This was the question being asked. The President's advisors thought the American people would back military intervention. They had been sold the line of 'Making America Great Again' and this was the ideal opportunity to demonstrate that. The President wavered, and ten days went by. The Chinese Ambassador who had been called in daily by the Whitehouse, now asked for a meeting.

The Chinese Ambassador in Washington brought a message direct from Beijing. The Chinese Communist Party would respect all property ownership, and business ownership in Taiwan and would keep the Taiwanese Government as a semi-autonomous body in exchange for America recognising Taiwan as part of Greater China.

Whilst Donald Trump and his advisors deliberated, the Taiwanese cabinet protested arguing that it was just a delaying tactic by the Chinese Communist Party.

Donald Trump succumbed to China's proposal on the agreement that they left no more than 10,000 troops on Taiwanese soil. His military advisors felt they needed another six months to get the supply chains ready before a retaliatory strike could be considered.
President Xi revelled in the glory he received in China as 'The Great Unifier'. The American press, at least those supporting The Whitehouse called it 'extraordinary pragmatism by a leader for our times', others called it a sell-out and compared it to Neville Chamberlain's appeasement of Hitler in 1938.

Unsurprisingly the semi-autonomous government was not recognised. The most vocal anti-Chinese were arrested on trumped up charges of corruption. Some just disappeared, property was quietly seized, and life made difficult for anyone who did not sign up and join the Chinese Communist Party. Although China did limit the military to 10,000 on the Taiwanese islands, they brought in their own police force and Government officers to administer Taipei.

The armaments industry picked up a head of steam. America was not on a full war footing; the Pentagon did not want to spook the Chinese. On July 1st, 2027, the PLA marched into Hong Kong. The importance of the date was significant. It was July 1st, 1997 when Hong Kong was peaceably handed over to China by the British, it was significant. This had been coming for some time. The marching and rioting that had started in 2019 had never really gone away, China had made it abundantly clear that it was not going to wait until 2044 before it fully annexed Hong Kong. It gave the excuse for the imminent full annexation, that Hong Kong was ready and willing and did not itself wish to wait any longer. With no standing army, there was nothing they could do, the tanks of the PLA rolled down the streets of Kowloon.

Emergency meetings were called at the Pentagon and The Whitehouse. Diplomatic channels were buzzing globally as this was the most dangerous moment in world history since the Cuban missile crisis.

Donald Trump was being put on the spot for agreements made long before his Presidency, but equally he knew that the United States could not appear to be weak. This was the moment to demonstrate the power and resolve of the USA which they had failed to do over Taiwan nine months earlier.

The military strategists were laying out the options based on various scenarios. The Americans had been working very closely with the Taiwanese for years supplying them not only with hardware but expertise and training. They knew that they could work closely together if they decided to meet the threat posed by China. The question was if there was sufficient political will and popular support at home.

Donald trump knew that by suspending the 22nd Amendment, he was in effect putting the USA on a war footing. If he declined to get involved in this Asian crisis, the Democrats would raise the issue at Congress, already upset that the President had secured an extra term, in their view unconstitutionally.

Two days after receiving the plea from Taiwan, the Whitehouse gave China an ultimatum, to withdraw immediately from the Island of Kinmen, otherwise America would consider itself at a state of war with the Peoples Republic of China, Trump was calling Xi's bluff.

It had been sixty-five years since the world had been so close to war. President Kennedy and Nikita Khrushchev had diffused the tension then, and a hotline had been established to ensure a situation did not build up again. Unfortunately, relations between the USA and China had been in permanent decline over trade and intellectual property for years. The President of the United States called president Xi directly, hoping to reduce the tension and diffuse the situation.

Xi was adamant that the time had come to instigate the final part of the One China Policy and stated clearly that it was nothing to do with the United States who had been meddling in Chinese domestic policy for too long. From documentation later released, the telephone conversation was a dramatic put down for President Trump. He immediately called his Chiefs of staff and demanded a show of strength but held back against any kind of pre-emptive strike.

The Chiefs were split over what to do. Although the American military had a huge presence in the area and were fully supported by bases in Guam and other areas, re-supplying would be an issue in the event of immediate conflict. Some of the advisers advocated getting other countries on board not just for political support but also for practical reasons, logistics, bases, and refuelling. Then there was the issue of how this might look in the International community. Would America
be perceived as interfering in Chinese domestic affairs, or as the saviour of the free world supporting the independent nation of Taiwan and the will of the people of Hong Kong? It was complicated by the fact that only fifteen nations globally recognised Taiwan as The Republic of China.

On top of this there was the very real military risk. In the Taiwan straits, the carrier groups would be within one hundred miles of mainland China. Although American military intelligence did not believe that there were many, if any, ballistic missile bases on that seaboard, the majority being further south, it was not impossible. Carrier group defences were primarily designed on being attacked, and thus defended, in wide open water, not so close to a mainland.

It was agreed that the USA would sail the 7th and 11th fleets currently operating in the Malacca straights up to Taiwan to deploy between China and Taiwan. If the Chinese attacked, they would retaliate in a defensive role. If the Chinese did not back down, they would attack all mainland military complexes within striking distance. The two carrier groups had formidable firepower that had dominated the oceans and war zones for the last fifty years and had no peers.

It took two days to get the carrier groups into battle formation and a further four days to speed up to Taiwan, on constant alert from attacks on the Chinese mainland, all the while being tracked by Chinese Jets.

Once in position, and linking up with the Taiwanese defence force, a final ultimatum was made to the Peoples Republic of China. The Chinese responded by telling the Americans that they were trespassing in Chinese waters and that they must leave immediately or expect China to defend itself. The Americans responded by stating that they were in International waters.

Within minutes, four Chinese Sukhoi fighters were seen closing in on the American fleets. Nobody knew who fired first but what happened next was to change the world as we knew it. It was 2.45 in the afternoon, July 9th, 2027.

The Chinese had clearly been well prepared for this for some time, it was an ambush. The two carriers USS Ronald Reagan and the USS Nimitz were both attacked immediately by aircraft, submarine, and anti-carrier ballistic missiles, known as "Carrier Killers". These had been deployed much closer than the Americans had realised. With their hypersonic flight over such a short distance, the carrier group were fully occupied trying to stop the threat.

Missiles were coming in from every direction and all of this was being beamed back to the Pentagon in real time. Destroyers and cruisers were being hit and enveloped by Chinese aircraft. The aircraft carriers were getting planes up into the air who were dogfighting with Chinese fighters. Higher above, Chinese fighter bombers were now attacking the carriers.

There was an almighty explosion from the USS Ronald Reagan. It had been hit by a torpedo launched from a Chinese submarine. The weapons that the Chinese military were throwing at the American fleet were terrifying in their volume and accuracy. Planes were falling out of the sky, ships were burning and sinking, and all of this being watched courtesy of the ships cameras which had now been hacked and were being transmitted around the world via the internet. This was no CGI blockbuster movie; this was the pride of the US navy being butchered in a waterway miles from home.

The battle continued for six hours. Both aircraft carriers were hit. The Nimitz sunk within 15 minutes, the Ronald Reagan was crippled and listing heavily. There were still ninety aircraft airborne that had to land on Taiwanese soil. Thirty other vessels had been sunk or were now inoperative, the rest of the fleet headed for safety in port at Taiwan. By ten o'clock at night the pride of America had been slain. The Taiwanese in support had also suffered heavy losses. There had been no sight of the Chinese navy apart from two submarines that had been hit and sunk. The devastation was down to land-based missiles, thousands of them. This was no stroke of luck by the Chinese, they had played the Americans.

The remainder of the 7th and 11th fleets limped into Zuoying Naval base. The Pentagon was in shock. The American carrier fleets had been the undisputed show of strength for decades just as the Capital ships had been until World War 2, but they had been shown to be outdated against the latest in ballistic missile warfare. The Americans had lost over 9,000 personnel killed and both fleets crippled.

The Chiefs of Staff discussed their next move. Comparisons were made to Pearl harbour and the damage to the US Pacific fleet which at the time was not terminal. Many in the military felt they needed to retaliate; some even suggested the use of tactical nuclear weapons on the Chinese mainland. Options were discussed at Presidential level. Around the world, there was little support for the United States. Such was the global shock at the demolition of the American Navy that nobody was quite sure what to do. Staunch allies like the UK balked at the idea of trying to attack China in retaliation. America had requested the support of the UK's two carrier fleets but the British obfuscated and when asked outright, they declined. It was the lowest point in Anglo-American relations since the War of Independence. Within 24 hours of the battle, Russia had come out in full support of China against US aggression over Chinese sovereignty. Japan and Taiwan offered their support to the USA, but the Japanese were cautious. After the resignation of Abe in 2020 due to ill health, Japanese politics had returned to being very unstable. When asked if they would take part in a strike on the Chinese mainland they declined.

The US through diplomatic channels approached the Chinese to de-escalate. They offered to withdraw and not to attack if China recognised Taiwanese sovereignty. The Chinese declined and offered the United States Navy a window of 72 hours to vacate Taiwan and to be 200 miles outside of all Chinese waters. To make the point abundantly clear, an image was sent to Washington and copied to every other country of what Beijing believed to be Chinese waters. This included everything that had been in dispute for the last seventy years including the Spratly Islands, Paracel Islands, Scarborough Shoal and all the boundaries in the Gulf of Tonkin also known as the nine dotted line map. It was clearly a well-timed land grab. All the countries involved, Brunei, Indonesia, Malaysia, Philippines and Vietnam looked to Washington for support. An hour later, Japan received notice that China was seizing the Diaoyu Islands also known as the Senkaku Islands in Japan.

Scores of Chinese fighter bombers could now be seen in the skies above the American fleets moored in Zuoying naval base. An order came directly from the Pentagon not to engage.

The Taiwanese Government pleaded with Washington to stay and support their cause, but it fell on deaf ears. The shock to Washington and the American people was too great, and two days later what were left of the great carrier fleets were sailing south.

On the 12th of July, Taiwan officially surrendered and became part of The Peoples Republic of China. The reverberations were felt around the world, nobody knew what would come next. Would the Americans regroup as they did in 1942 and go on to victory?

The American military started to present cases to the President for a military strike to try and restore American prestige. Discussions were ongoing with many countries bordering the South China and East China Seas. Japan was put on a full war footing anticipating a Chinese invasion. President Xi addressed the Chinese people telling them about the American pre-emptive strike and how the Chinese PLA had defended itself, that finally, the world would recognise Chinese territorial waters and that China had proven that it could defend itself. This he said was a proud moment in the history of the Peoples Republic of China, that China was finally taking its rightful place on the world stage. He stressed that China was not interested in taking war to other countries but ominously said that China would soon know who her friends were.

In America, the Chief of Staff met and discussed options with the President. The assumption was that Donald Trump would push for immediate retaliation. Many in the Pentagon were wondering how they could keep his finger off the nuclear trigger but what happened next came as a surprise to them and their allies.

The military agreed that a strike on mainland China would achieve nothing militarily and would just be a demonstration of commitment. They discussed Roosevelt's Doolittle raid on Tokyo in 1942 as retaliation after Pearl Harbour but this was a different time and different circumstances. Pearl Harbour was a surprise attack, but what just happened, it was all agreed, was an ambush that had taken out the most powerful military ensemble the world had ever seen.

The use of tactical nuclear weapons was also broached, but immediately dismissed. China was a nuclear power and had just demonstrated the capabilities of its missile delivery systems.

Calls were going out simultaneously to allies to see what global response could be made, but it was clear that every country was in shock at the speed of the escalation and the sudden defeat of the American navy. Donald Trump had been right that so many countries had just been hiding behind America's perceived military might and spending power, especially those in Europe, but now that the American military had proven not to be invincible, their allies started to drift away.

All the countries bordering the South China and East China seas would not offer America their support to host American troops. They offered refuelling and some logistical support but nothing more.

On the 19th of July, news arrived at the Whitehouse that Japan had allied with China. It was a tremendous shock and something that had seemed unimaginable after all the support the United States had given to Japan since their surrender in 1945. This would never have happened under Shinzo Abe, but Japan had declined since 2020. Its attempts at encouraging immigration to offset its ageing population hadn't worked, the Japanese were too set in their ways to accept migrant workers, it just wasn't appealing for non-Japanese to go and work there.

Covid-22 had been a disaster for Japan with deaths amongst the elderly exceeding 500,000. The ongoing global economic crisis that had started in 2020 had impacted heavily on Japan's export dominated economy causing further problems. The trade wars between America and China had been very unwelcome for Japan who often found herself in a difficult situation. The Japanese Government felt they had no choice when they were approached by China. Despite increased military spending throughout the 20s, they knew there was little they could do against the might and scale of the Chinese military, and there was little appetite for war amongst the ageing Japanese population. The Prime Minister agreed a deal that would leave Japan essentially neutral but with leanings towards China. It was agreed that all American supplied military hardware would be sent to her or brought under Chinese control apart from a home defence force.

Losing America's closest ally was a gut blow for Donald Trump. The military spend alone was more than $50bn a year. On the 21st of July having had many discussions with his chiefs of staff, the President addressed the American people. He told them of the dark days ahead but stressed that he would not be supplying young American troops to come home in body bags to support countries that would not defend themselves.

America was no longer to be the world's policeman and would be withdrawing to a purely defensive role to maintain the integrity of the United States and its immediate interests. He acknowledged that the

USA was in a state of war with China and her allies. The wall with Mexico would now be finished to insulate the United States from other countries. A deal was signed with Canada to allow free movement of goods and people between the two countries, and America would extend its ring of steel to encompass Canada protecting it from Russia in particular.

The American people were shocked. America had been the dominant global military power for as long as anyone had lived. The disaster of the Battle of Taiwan as it was now known, was regarded as a temporary blip that the American military would bounce back from. In fact, there had already been over 80,000 applications for a commission in the military since it happened, but here was the American President saying they were not going to retaliate, at least not yet.

The rest of the world was equally shocked including the Chinese. Never in his wildest dreams did President Xi think the Americans would back down like they appeared to have done although he thought that they might be biding their time.

The diplomatic channels were buzzing as countries readied themselves for the next phase of events. All countries were put on full alert. South Korea prepared itself on the 38th parallel but also for a seaborne invasion. Vietnam steadied itself for a possible invasion, but it did not come.

China's Ambassadors started to call on countries on its borders declaring that China had no military ambitions in the region but making it quite clear that she would like to know who her friends were.

Once Donald Trump had declared that America was no longer the world's policeman, things started to escalate extremely fast. China made it publicly clear that it did not want to expand territorially but was looking for partners to work with. This was a veiled threat if ever there was one. One by one the countries of the East China and South China seas came out in support of China. They did not necessarily pledge allegiance or capitulate, but it was clear to see where the loyalties lay for North Korea, South Korea, Vietnam, Laos, Thailand, and Cambodia.

Other countries such as The Philippines, Malaysia and Indonesia appealed to America and the United Nations but to no avail. It was now quite clear what a role America had played for many years. This change in the balance of power was dramatic and caught so many nations off guard. There are Black Swan events that can be planned for, but America being defeated in battle and withdrawing was one that nobody had entertained.

That year passed with no other military action, just plenty of diplomacy. The world started to split into two distinct groups, those supporting China, or at least capitulating in fear of them, and the Rest of the World. America became an outlier, setting up a defensive line to protect what became known as Fortress America. She had been reducing commitment to NATO through 2019 and 2020 to get other NATO members to increase their own spending and commitment. This was now coming back to bite the members of the European Union who had taken Americas support for granted. Now the underinvestment and shortcomings of NATO were there for all the world to see. The European Union met frantically to discuss a unified policy response but the weakening of the Union ever since the UK departed in 2020 and the impact of the global recession meant that the EU was no longer the force it once was.

Europe had an emergency it could not ignore on its doorstep when Russia came out in support of China. The Baltic states were panicking wondering if Russia would make a land grab. The limited resources were rushed to the European borders with Russia, and America stepped up with some additional support. Russia regarded this as an act of aggression and moved personnel and hardware to the borders with Estonia, Latvia, Belarus, and the Ukraine. There was talk of a nuclear war, but nothing happened. Life continued as normal, supplies of certain things were disrupted but not too much, goods still travelled from China, it was a very strange war.

Back then, the whole world was waiting for someone to make a move. In early 2028, there was an outbreak of another SARS type virus in Angola that spread at an astonishing speed through The Democratic Republic of the Congo, and on to South Sudan and Ethiopia. At the same time there were civil uprisings in the Congo and Chad threatening stability in Nigeria. It was hard to prove, but the consensus was that the Chinese had planted what became known as Covid-28 to destabilise Africa as a continent. They also supplied arms, finance, and intelligence to disparate groups in countries that had weak Governments.

It later transpired that the Covid-28 virus had been man made and blended with the HIV virus making it highly transmissible. The rate of infection was exceedingly high, and the death rate catastrophic, it led to a mass exodus fleeing Civil War and the virus. Millions of Africans young or strong enough, began moving through the continent into Algeria and Libya, which had never recovered since Colonel Gaddafi was deposed and chaos ensued. Enormous camps grew as the flotsam of life arrived, fleeing and trying to make their way to Europe.

The number of new arrivals overwhelmed the authorities in Spain and Italy who pleaded for help from the EU. A decision was made that the threat from the African refugees was now the greatest crisis that Europe had ever faced. All member states introduced conscription for 18–21-year-olds of both sexes, and new armies were created to defend the southern shores. All of those who had been detained in camps were now deported and dropped back to Libya. Defences were created along the southern coast of Europe. Vessels of all countries were put into service to turn back craft coming from Africa. Initially this involved warning them to turn back, but after a few accidents and then coming under attack, they were ordered to ram the vessels and to fire upon them.

Human rights groups went crazy and lobbied the United Nations, but events were moving so fast that the UN had lost all credibility. The EU justified their actions by saying that China had weaponised the peoples of Africa by introducing a plague and destabilising many of the African countries. As time went on, the people smugglers found themselves in possession of high-speed torpedo boats and other military craft, all unmarked and of unknown origin, but the finger was pointed firmly at China and Russia.

The EU asked Great Britain for assistance as she had by far the largest Navy in Europe, but the UK had its own borders to protect and as the situation on the African continent deteriorated, larger vessels came to be used by the smugglers. In November 2028 HMS Dauntless was patrolling the English Channel fifty miles offshore when she came under attack from the NNS Aradu, a Nigerian Frigate. HMS Dauntless had asked the Aradu to turn around, but she opened fire causing some damage to Dauntless. The British destroyer opened fire and immediately sunk the Nigerian frigate. Over 400 people were pulled from the sea and just as many went down with the ship. Not long before there would have been public outrage, but now all people wanted to know was how those four hundred would be returned to Nigeria far away from the UK. Empathy had become a rare commodity.

The Dauntless docked and unloaded the survivors in a local detention centre, but then re-loaded everyone and returned to sea whilst the Government deliberated what to do next. It was considered moral hazard if the 400 survivors remained in the UK. Others would then see Britain as a softer touch than the rest of Europe, which might encourage more to try and make the perilous journey. The fact that one of Nigeria's most powerful vessels was used in the attempt and that it opened fire, steadied the Government's resolve. By an overwhelming majority it was agreed that HMS Dauntless would be re-supplied and take on board twenty dinghies with engines, each suitable for thirty people. The destroyer under the cover of darkness made its way to within 10 ten miles of the Coast of Benin adjacent to Nigeria, the dinghies were lowered, and the refugees were put in them. There was a struggle on board as some of the refugees refused, and two men were shot. It was not the crew of Dauntless's finest hour. Great Britain had always been recognised for its humanitarian posture and had often led the world in doing the right thing, but these were terrible times. Morality and taking the high ground were luxuries that could not always be afforded.

The dinghies headed towards the coast and HMS Dauntless quietly slipped into the night. There was no doubt the Nigerian military knew that the British vessel was there, they would have understood that this was just one small battle with many more to come.

In other times, the returning of refugees would have caused a public outcry, but they were not ordinary times. Although war had not come directly to the shores of the UK, everyone was aware of global events and knew that conflict could come at any time. A British ship being attacked in British waters suddenly felt too close to home. The people were generally in full support of the Government's tough stance. The news was filled with images from the Mediterranean and the Spanish and Italian coastlines, the barbed wire, minefields, anti-shipping defences. There were so many troops, all the seaside towns that British people had visited on holiday and used to have holiday homes before the war had become billets for the hundreds of thousands of troops defending the borders of Southern Europe.

China was fighting a proxy war, keeping the forces of Europe tied up in a defensive war they could never win. It was a clever and relatively inexpensive plan. China could not fight a physical war against Europe, the logistical challenges were too great, but equally, Europe as an enemy could not be left alone. As a collective she was too powerful and had great manufacturing capabilities to challenge China. China had been surprised by Europe's response to Covid-19, wildly above China's expectations. Covid-19 had been relatively small in terms of germ warfare, but the leadership was astonished at European Government's responses, especially France and the UK who had been prepared to crash their economies to save the lives of a few older people. This was an anathema to the Chinese, they had thought that the Liberal Governments of the West were weak, but this had come as a total surprise. The fear that Covid-19 spread throughout most of Europe planted the seed for a new type of modern warfare.

The Chinese leadership knew that war would come sooner or later.

They were ideologically opposed to many other countries, but critically wanted to restore China to its rightful position in the world. It seemed that they just bided their time until they were ready.

Covid-22 sought to prove what the Chinese had come to believe, that Western Democracies could not make the big painful decisions when it came to choosing between life and death for their own electorates. To try and make sure that it could not be blamed on them this time, the virus was started and spread in Bulgaria and blamed on a chicken farm. It quickly spread across Europe again. People were inoculated with the vaccines for Covid-19, but they did not work, this was a new more virulent strain. The drugs companies of the world united but once again it took almost eighteen months to produce a satisfactory vaccine by which time the already struggling economies and finances of Europe were in meltdown. Covid-22 did not spread globally as other continents had learnt many lessons from Covid-19. On this occasion Europe was regarded as a pariah. Even America managed to contain it with less than 10,000 deaths. Europe had a total of 500,000 deaths almost the same as the 520,000 deaths from Covid-19. The second Covid pandemic shook Europe to the core, wondering how it could have happened again, with just as many people dying. Had we learnt nothing from the previous experience?

The Chinese had looked on as though it was a simple laboratory experiment. The senior figures in the Chinese Government did not regard it in terms of life and death. Their attitude towards their own people was tied into the future of China, much more about the collective than the individual. They were far more interested to see how other Governments reacted, and whether they would make the big decisions and allow sufficient casualties. They got their answers.

The Liberal Governments were torn apart by the notion of sacrificing one group for the common good. The Chinese saw it as weakness, the European leaders regarded it is as humanity. This is how they differed, and this is what gave the Chinese the confidence to push for their greater goals. Virus warfare became a key part of military planning. It was not the military effectiveness of the weapon but the perception of it. The Western Democracies were in fear of the virus, and what they saw as its uncontrollable nature. The experiences of the two previous outbreaks had had a dramatic impact and seriously undermined the respect for Governments throughout the West. Populations were exhausted from the continuous lockdowns and disruption to their lives, finances, and wellbeing. The gap between the rich and the poor had widened even further, and Governments were perceived as being out of touch with their peoples. All the research showed that that the Virus was a socio-economic disease affecting the poorest the hardest, Governments were regarded as uncaring by many. The Chinese realised that if they could militarise the virus and commandeer a huge army from Africa, who did not realise they were being manipulated, they could tie up the military resources of the European Union without endangering a single Chinese soldier, not that they had the welfare of their own soldiers in mind, they were just protecting a valuable resource that could be used elsewhere.

By not committing their considerable military resources in a western sphere, they retained enormous strength in the Pacific and Indian Oceans, the threat of which kept the Americans at bay. With the capitulation of Indonesia, there were no buffers between China and iron ore rich Australia. Australia already had close trading ties to China who represented a third of all her exports. The Australian Government reached out to the USA and Great Britain for military assistance should China decide to invade. America refused to offer any troops or assistance other than selling more military equipment on a lend lease arrangement. The UK was pre-occupied with defending its own waters. There was talk of sending a carrier fleet in support, but it was considered too risky due to the distance and the logistics involved.

Australia had developed a close relationship with France developing joint military partnerships and asked France for their support. Like the UK, the French felt the distances and risks too great to send French forces. Australia was cast adrift; the Australian military was put on high alert. It had a very modern defence capability, having been the biggest importer of military equipment in the world surpassing Saudi Arabia in the early twenty twenties. Everyone wondered if the Australians would stand and fight. With a population of only twenty-five million against Chinas 1.2 billion it would be a David and Goliath struggle.

In January 2029 just before the start of Chinese New Year, President Xi offered a fig leaf to the Australian Government. They said that Australia could remain completely independent and would not be touched by China, that China had no Imperialist ambitions. All that China asked in return was a reduction in the size of Australia's military, by 50%. China also offered to keep all trade links open and guaranteed Australia that China was still willing to buy its goods but in Renminbi and not in US dollars. This was debated in the Australian Parliament and closely watched by the rest of the world. On the 3rd of February, the Sino-Australasia Peace Accord was signed. On the 7th, New Zealand also signed as did Papua New Guinea.

Westminster was aghast that Commonwealth countries with such close ties to the United Kingdom would succumb, but what were their options? They were dwarfed both militarily and numerically by China. They had discussed the impossibility of an offensive strike, having seen what had happened to the American fleets, the only option was a defensive guerrilla strategy, but what would that achieve apart from a show of resistance. How would the Chinese treat the Australian people? The Australian capitulation came as a mortal blow to both the Government of the UK and The Crown, but under the circumstances, she did not have much choice.

After the agreement with Australia, other countries realising that the cavalry would not be coming and signed peaceful accords with China. Myanmar, Bangladesh, Pakistan and finally India. India prevaricated, still having allegiance to The British Monarchy, but over the previous decade, China had become its biggest trading partner. As a nuclear power India could have declined. The deterrent would probably have been enough to deter any aggression by China, but once its lifelong allies drifted away, India felt abandoned. On February 23rd, the Sino – Indian Peace accord was declared.

Without firing a shot, China had signed extremely favourable agreements with nineteen neighbouring countries. China had also signed a military agreement with Russia who in turn had signed peace agreements with Kazakhstan, Uzbekistan, Kyrgyzstan, Tajikistan and all the countries on the Caspian Sea. President Putin had been in power for over twenty years. During the 2020s he had built closer trading ties with China but always remained wary of Russia's neighbour who dwarfed Russia economically. The Chinese had always been happy to wait, reflecting on the Chinese Proverb 'Patience is power, with time and patience the mulberry leaf becomes a silk gown'. Putin knew that China was biding its time, and that one day it would reclaim Vladivostok and much of Siberia that was ceded to Russia in the nineteenth century.

Putin was aware of his history. Stalin had signed an agreement with Hitler in 1939 to partition Poland to act as a pact of non-aggression. They had signed a Secret Protocol defining borders and spheres of influence which did not come out until The Nuremberg Trials. Putin knew that these agreements did not count for much. In 1941 Germany invaded the Soviet Union which led to the deaths of 17 million Russians. He was acutely aware of the danger that China posed, but for now it would be better to have them as an ally.

That was how the world lined up in the Spring of 2029. Armies were formed, defensive borders created, and yet not a shot was fired. South America universally agreed to remain neutral although the reality was that their economies were closely aligned to the United States and their currencies directly linked to the American dollar. China had made huge investments in many of the countries of South America over the previous two decades and there was a lot of trade which apparently continued unabated. It was war, and was known as World War III, but was not like any war that had been fought before.

The UKs first significant cyber-attack came on Black Friday September 2029. In a four-hour period, the credit card details of almost three million people were captured and farmed. The British banking system took a £70bn hit. For weeks it was considered the actions of a criminal gang operating out of Eastern Europe, possibly Russia but then on Christmas Eve, the National Grid and all associated infrastructure was attacked by a virus. The systems just shut down. Every time they were re-booted, they immediately closed down again. The nuclear power stations at Sizewell B and Torness both shut down and caused great fear for the surrounding people who were evacuated on Christmas Day. It took almost two weeks to get the National Grid operating again by which time it had caused a huge amount of damage both operationally and emotionally.

The Government was damned for being incompetent. Within a few days GCHQ had determined that the attack had come from a unit of The Peoples Liberation Army specialising in cyber warfare from addresses close to Shanghai. This was accompanied by a huge amount of dis-information through social media as well as infiltrating various blogs and comments sections in the national media. These tactics had been used before, the American election tampering of 2016 by Cambridge Analytica was a pre warning as to what could come and the efficiency of it. The gathering and manipulation of data had been discussed a long time ago with fears about the overarching power and influence of Facebook and Google, but all the while the Chinese military were gathering their own data and working out how to use it to their advantage. In a covert way they were leaps and bounds ahead of the West in the use of online technology to cause disruption. The joke of it all was that so many of their tech experts had been educated at American and British Universities who had willingly opened their doors for the extra fees that Chinese students would pay. As it turned out most of those fees were paid by the Chinese Government. By the time it became clear what was happening, it was too late. Tens of thousands of Chinese students had gone through STEM courses and were familiar with the way systems worked in the UK, useful knowledge if you were going to sabotage them a few years later.

The onslaught of false information led the Government to set up The Ministry of Information in February 2030. It had a wide-ranging remit of counter espionage but was separate to MI5 and responsible to a new Minister. It was not clandestine like MI5 but had a sinister aura about it. It was given extraordinary powers of intrusion trampling over all civil liberties under the auspices of powers drafted under the War Act of 2029. The Ministry could tap phones without any kind of warrant. Tracking people became standard practice, detention without arrest or even notification became commonplace.

The Cyber-attacks were becoming more frequent, it was not unusual for the phone network to go down for a day. On one occasion in 2033 they managed to interrupt the 7G network, considered to be the most secure system in Europe. All transport ceased to work, all telecommunications apart from the secure Government lines that were by then run on a system so secret nobody knew who ran it, went down. There was chaos throughout, all of it supplemented by a swift campaign of misinformation that populated every search on the internet. The Chinese became very adept at disruption and deception. This was the war that they were fighting, a war which slowly crippled its enemies by destroying the morale and cohesion of the countries it was fighting. What Bomber Harris had done to the German population with thousands of missions, bombing them into submission, the Chinese were doing silently from keyboards in Shanghai.

The only way for the Government to fight back against this was to make society more subservient, to reduce free speech and to counter it with the Government's own propaganda. This had all started back in 2020 with the Covid-19 outbreak. The constant Government announcements, the lockdowns, the removal of Civil liberties, it was all done under the auspices of battling the virus, but so many of the rules and regulations stayed in place after the virus had gone. The right to demonstrate was removed as a threat to Public Health. Although Civil Liberty groups pushed hard for it to be re-instated, the Government somehow managed to keep the law in place. There were a few minor demonstrations against the law stopping demonstrations, but they were broken up by the Police and some of the protesters arrested. By the end of 2021, all demonstrations had stopped, the population had acquiesced, and the Government subtly pushed through more laws that curbed freedoms.

By the time Covid-22 arrived, the country was in a permanent state of alert and quickly returned to the routine of lockdowns, masks, and social distancing. The people were exhausted but compliant. After the global crash and the economic disaster that followed, so many people became reliant on the state, over 60% by the time of the second outbreak. Inflation was rampant and the value of the pound was collapsing. Government borrowing had doubled to over £5tn, but the printing presses just kept it all going. On the positive side, the Governments push to renewables really took off, generating lots of well-paid jobs and moved the investment away from London to the North.

During the first Boris Johnson Parliament almost 45,000 civil service jobs were moved to the North of England. The new House of Lords in York and the construction of the Northern Parliament in Leeds began to see a rebalancing from South to North, but this coincided with the foreign investors leaving London for Paris, Berlin and New York, London wilted and lost its shine.

The last four years had become an interminable routine. The country was on a full war footing with so many aspects of society closed. The entire south and east coast had been fortified, not against a mass military landing but against small vessels trying to bring refugees to the shores. There were two enemies the UK was fighting simultaneously, the Chinese and their allies, and the refugees from Africa. The Chinese were feared because they were a nuclear power, and according to the Government and the Ministry of Information, had long range ballistic missiles that could hit the UK. We were constantly told that our air defences were effective enough to take out any pre-emptive strike, but in the event of it happening, our nuclear submarines were continuously at sea ready to retaliate. This did not make anyone feel more comfortable. Most people did not anticipate a Chinese nuclear attack, but the Government kept reminding us about it to keep us in a constant state of fear.

When war was declared on February 24th, 2029, all Chinese Nationals who had lived in the UK less than ten years were given 14 days to leave. Their assets were put into a special fund to be managed by the Government for the national good with the possibility that they might be returned when the war ended. As the countries of the world decided which side they wanted to be on, the number of people looking to leave grew. Including the Russians and all the African nations, the number rose to almost 2 million people. It quickly became clear that two weeks would not be long enough. In the end it took almost six months to process and find transport for those that wanted to and could leave. Married couples were split, then the discussions began about whether children were British citizens. There were also many people who just could not leave, they had come to the UK as political refugees seeking asylum and to return would be suicide. In April 2029, the Isle of White was designated a holding camp for all of those who had been asked to leave the UK but could not or would not. Most of the 85,000 people who lived there were told to move and were given new housing on the mainland, much of which was being vacated by the non-British residents who had been asked to leave in the first place. Over 650,000 people were crammed onto the Isle of White. Temporary tented camps were set up for those that could not find accommodation. Of course, even during war money talks. Osborne House, Queen Victoria's home on the island was bought by a Russian Oligarch so he and his family could live out the war in luxury which caused a public outcry.

People were much more concerned by the other aspects of the war with China. There were always shortages. We relied much more on domestic production although we did still get imports from Europe, America, and Canada, but many of the things we had been used to for the last twenty years were no longer available. It did not take long after war broke out and all diplomatic relations with China were cut, to realise just how much of our industry we had shipped off to China, and just how many of our products we bought came from there. It had all seemed like a good idea at the time to close factories and move manufacturing to China where wages were lower, it had meant cheaper prices for consumers and better profits for shareholders, but it was always going to come back to bite us.

Gradually British companies started to make things to fill the gaps, but certainly a lot of everyday items that we had got used to were now either not available or were much more expensive. The

Government pushed the campaign to buy British extremely hard. As time went on, life became simpler as there was less to do. Car ownership declined, people lost interest in fashion, in fact it was frowned upon to be too colourful. The country took on a generally drab hue. Entertainment changed as well. Back in 2020, entertainment had become so politically correct after the Liberals seized the upper ground. The Woke brigade made life difficult for comedians, script writers and social commentators and that just continued. With the assault by the Government on freedom of speech and the liberal left pursuing their own agenda, entertainment and the arts became stultifying dull and indistinguishable.

This carried on and gradually we lost so much talent as writers and performers became fearful of speaking out or even saying the wrong thing as an ensuing social media campaign could ruin them. There were quite a few suicides of prominent writers who were harangued for views that were perfectly acceptable only a few years before. As the state surveillance increased, we all became fearful of everyone and everything around us, becoming very conscious of any utterance in case it fell foul of the political correctness that had swept the nation.

The War had accelerated the introduction of driverless vehicles. The Johnson Government of the early 2020s had announced a ban on petrol and diesel cars to come into force by 2035 with a move towards electric vehicles, which had been a shock to many people but the success of the autonomous trials by Oxbotica gave the Government the confidence they needed to bring the project forwards. After a year of successful trials in London, Oxford, and along the M6, the go ahead was given for autonomous vehicles to be launched by 2022. It was up to the ethicists and the lawyers to work out the finer details.

The logic for the Government was simple, even if the unintended consequences had not been thought through. Having announced the world's most ambitious carbon reduction programme 'leading from the front with another world beating project' as the Prime Minister put it at the time, cutting the UKs carbon emissions to zero by 2050, something radical had to be done. The technology was already there for driverless vehicles. The Government think tank believed that if driverless vehicles were available to be called up on an App, that car ownership would fall and eventually disappear especially with some carrot and stick encouragement. The challenge was always getting past the lobbyists for the car and petroleum industries not to mention all those car owners who loved their vehicles.

It was by far the most ambitious project the Government could have undertaken and without the 80-seat majority from the 2019 election it would have been impossible. They also knew that the opposition at that time was in disarray, there could hardly be a better moment to show that the UK was a leading proponent of Green policy which was perfect during the acrimonious Brexit negotiations with Europe.

The Government created legislation for a panel of ethicists and lawyers to discuss all the elements to bring forward the Autonomous Vehicle Act. All the opponents pointed to the moral dilemmas, would the car run over the child on the pedestrian crossing or the mother on the pavement. The same old arguments were rolled out but with the bit between their teeth the Government pressed on. Arguments backed up by fact were produced along with a national campaign, and it was pointed out that 27,000 people a year died or were seriously injured from road traffic accidents. It was acknowledged that some people would still die from road accidents but that the number would be markedly lower. The advert that really got the public behind it was saying that the engineers would not be programming the cars to drink and drive, drive whilst under the influence of drugs or make phone calls. Backed up with compelling statistics, the mood music started to change.

When the time was right and public opinion was building, the Government started to produce some figures that showed the costs of transport would drop for everyone and the system would be more egalitarian. There were concerns that people in the countryside would be left behind, but this was immediately dispelled by making companies who won licenses provide sufficient driverless vehicles at the same costs in rural areas.

The Government brought the ban on petrol and diesel vehicles forwards to 2030 which unexpectedly led to a crash in second-hand prices. The Government pushed through the legislation and offered the first autonomous licenses to commence in January 2022. The race was on to get 5G up and running and for manufacturers to start producing enough vehicles to meet demand. It became clear that there would not be enough driverless vehicles to meet demand even though so many people were by now working from home, so the Government introduced more legislation meaning that the first two million vehicles had to be supplied to operators in the cities for use by all and would not be available for private purchase.

The large technology companies had been developing their driverless vehicles for some time, but they were always going to struggle to ramp up production. This saw mergers between Google's Waymo and Mercedes who had the production capacity but by then Tesla's Giga factories were working at full pelt. They struck a deal with Uber who already had the interface and relationship with users. Against all the odds and the doomsayers, driverless cars came to the streets of the UK in significant numbers in late 2022. It was mainly driven by London.

It was considered one of the few positive unintended consequences of the CoronaVirus outbreak of 2020. Pollution in London fell dramatically as there were fewer vehicles on the roads. In 2019 Public Health England had issued some data concluding that 28-36,000 people were dying annually of diseases related to air pollution. The landmark case of Ella Kissi-Debrah, where the Coroner ruled that her death was caused by air pollution helped to speed up the changes. Driverless cars had already been tested on the roads in Stratford, Croydon, and Bromley. It had been done without much fanfare, but the tests had been successful. With the problems surrounding social distancing on Public Transport, Sadiq Khan, London Mayor at the time brought the introduction of driverless cars forward and within a year made them the only vehicles allowed within the congestion zone, which was enlarged to encompass everything within the M25, the transformation was sudden but effective. Pollution dropped 75% in the capital and once electric planes were introduced, pollution fell even further. As London reclaimed its streets and planted trees and gardens, the whole City became a much more pleasant place to live.

Of course, there were accidents, deaths and injuries and the press had a field day with headlines like 'Driverless Killing Machines', but very quickly the new technology was adopted. People who had used Uber for a taxi with a driver just got used to the vehicle arriving in the same way but without an operator. There were plenty who initially refused to get into the vehicles but after a few weeks of seeing others being driven around in driverless vehicles and then talking about it with their friends and colleagues, the reticence started to go away. The compelling financial argument also helped; the cost of journeys halved overnight. Without the cost of the driver and with all the vehicles being electric the running costs fell dramatically.

The unintended consequences were starting to happen, garages and petrol stations closing as demand fell away, Halfords and other car related business went bust, even insurance companies had to restructure as their businesses shrank. The AA and RAC merged initially and then had to shrink their operation. It was not long before people realised that in a rental Uber, if it broke down another would be along in minutes with barely any inconvenience. They no longer had issues about car parking, parking tickets, speeding tickets, MOTs, excise duty, they could call a vehicle up on their phone which would come directly to them and then charge a modest fare for taking them to exactly where they wanted to go as and when they needed it.

The old idea of tying thousands of pounds up in a car of your own that barely moved for 95% of the time became an anachronism, those who clung on to their old cars were being viewed as slightly stupid. It was expensive in comparison, and an environmental disaster, and was soon perceived as selfish and against the general interest.

The news switched to reporting accidents caused by drivers rather than by the driverless vehicles, which quickly came to be known as much more reliable and safer. As the technology improved, the vehicles were fully internet enabled allowing passengers to work or watch tv and movies. It helped boost the economy as it was much easier for people to go out and about without worrying about parking, drinking, or just affording to run a car. The money moved from the car and oil industry to the wider economy. The 15%-20% of household income that used to be spent on transport was now available for other things.

The impact it had on town centre planning and housing was extraordinary. Without the restrictions of car parking and planning to accommodate vehicles, architects developed extraordinary schemes, reclaiming the streets, and creating innovative housing solutions, turning multi storey town centre car parks into low-cost housing with public spaces on the top floor. This started to drive down the cost of housing as the supply went up, it was a massive boost for the Government, and society.

Of course, it was a disaster for many of the car manufacturers. Although the UK was ahead of the curve, its success was prompting other countries to introduce driverless vehicles too. There were always going to be winners and losers, but this was dramatic. Long established motor companies like Volkswagen, Fiat and Citroen got into difficulties. European rules about state aid were ignored as Germany, France and Italy tried to prop up such important National icons, but it was too late, they had fallen behind in technology. By 2026 China was now producing eighty per cent of the world's driverless cars, they were cheap and reliable, and the designs changed very quickly to suit the new form of transport. As the number of driverless cars increased and the number of accidents decreased, new vehicles became lighter, using less material as safety was no longer such a big issue.

Landowners saw the opportunity converting fields and brownfield sites to tarmac and installing solar panels and wind turbines. Quietly, hundreds of driverless cars pulled in and out around the clock, re-charging, getting cleaned initially by low paid workers and subsequently by purpose-built robots. Maintenance and repairs were also undertaken at some of these sites. The supply chain had been reduced to the four corners, the manufacturer, the interface, the charging and maintenance, and the financing. There was no longer any badge envy, transport had become utilitarian and egalitarian in one fell swoop.

The car you drove used to say something about you, and an entire industry had developed over a hundred and twenty years to exploit this. Society had bent to the will of the motor manufacturers and the oil producers. Cities were built to suit cars with roads and car parking dominating city and urban planning. The car and oil industry employed millions and represented 12% of the global economy and was immensely powerful, they were not going to go down without a fight.

These global behemoths threw everything they could to discredit driverless cars. It even came out that they caused accidents and deaths to try and derail the driverless revolution, but they were found out. An investigative journalist was contacted by a whistle-blower and broke the story. It was a sensation and only sped up the change. Both the whistle-blower and the journalist were killed on the same day in two different road accidents. Those responsible were never caught.

One of the upsides for Government was having millions upon millions of moving cameras at their disposal. With the improvement to 5G and then 6G, all the cameras used on the vehicles to monitor their proximity were seen by The Home Office as an opportunity to put more eyes on the street. Naturally, Liberty organisations protested that we would be living in a 24 hour surveillance society, but London was already the most surveilled city in the world outside of China so it wasn't a leap of faith for the Home Secretary to persuade that with nothing to hide, residents of London would be even more secure with the addition of cameras on driverless cars, they said it was like having more police on the beat and it did not take long to roll that idea out across the UK.

The UK Government was increasingly able to watch and control its citizens, but all via a Chinese supplied connectivity system. The impact of driverless cars to crime took everyone by surprise. Street crime, assault, gang crime, burglaries, drug related, all dropped dramatically. The authorities had eyes everywhere, they passed an Act of Parliament that allowed the police to sequester driverless cars if they were required to track suspects and even to go to the scene of a crime to act as the eyes for the police and authorities. In time, the authorities were able to use this technology to keep track of any person of interest, quite what determines a person of interest was always open to interpretation.

CHAPTER ONE

MONDAY 13TH FEBRUARY 2032

CHARLIE WILSON

As usual it was dull and damp, unpleasantly so, but at least it had stopped raining for the time being. Charlie Wilson was making his way through Waterloo and over London Bridge towards the cafe. Looking up, the sky was an oppressive steely grey with heavy clouds blocking out the sun and any chance of some vitamin D that might make him feel better. It had been this way for months.

As he crossed a surprisingly quiet London Bridge, he looked downriver towards Tower Bridge and the enormous torrent of water rushing underneath. There was no traffic on the river, the riverboats and water taxis had all been moved or taken out of the water. There had been almost 100 days of relentless rain across the British Isles and it felt that most of it had drained into London.

The emergency flood barriers along the embankment looked precarious and Charlie could not imagine them being of much use if they were called upon. The water was barely a foot from the top of the embankment and the forecast said there was no let-up in the weather due. The Thames barrier was doing its job and seemed to be controlling the tide, but he knew from a contact working there, that everyone was under stress and it would not take much for the system to fail.

Picking up a little speed Charlie had one eye on the door of the glass fronted cafe that he liked to call his church. The baristas were busy serving a short queue of customers but the pretty girl with the dark hair had seen him walking in as he put on his mask.

"Good morning Charlie, your usual?" she said cheerily, pleased to see him.

"Yes please Jasmin," he replied "And an almond croissant."

Charlie smiled, his favourite seat in the corner by the window was free. He had spent hours, sat at that window. As a journalist and a University Professor he tended to do most of his work and thinking here. He did not work well in solitude; he enjoyed the anonymous company of others. This was also a good place for occasional fortuitous information that came his way from the Houses of Parliament opposite. Sometimes it would just be seeing two members of Parliament together that could provide him with the spark for a new piece.

He unpacked his rucksack laying his iPad, telephone, notebook and pencil out in their familiar positions, removed a charger and cable from a side pocket and without even looking down, he had done it so many times before, plugged them in and started charging his iPad which was old and had lost much of its functionality. He preferred not to have a later model because of the all the spyware that was automatically fitted and notoriously difficult to remove. This old piece of kit suited him very well for writing and emails. He surfed the web using his phone to avoid corrupting his iPad.

As he settled into his usual position and routine, he remembered something else and took out an old book from his bag. He laid it down on top of the unopened iPad. It was a clean copy of George Orwell's 1984. It had arrived earlier by an Amazon drone copter only 23 minutes after ordering it on his Alexa speak. Twenty-three minutes had not broken the record of sixteen minutes for a delivery from point of order, but it was still pretty quick although it had become such a part of life, he hadn't thought about it too much. He was surprised for a book that was supposedly 85 years good the condition was, but it had probably been made on one of the last print runs of the 2020s.

He knew that his central file would be marked for ordering such a subversive book, but he felt he could justify it as his job as a freelance reporter and his other job as a University Professor. Charlie would be thirty-five years of age towards the end of the year, having left Bath University ten years ago with a master's in philosophy with such lofty ambitions. He had known things were changing whilst he was studying, the University loans scandal had broken and every ambulance chasing lawyer in the country got on the bandwagon. The press was full of it, "students sold a pup", "not enough jobs for the number of degrees". He had supported his own University Professor on the picket line, protesting about their diminishing pensions and working conditions. Several Professors around the country had lost their jobs over the issue of free speech. Being older they had been unable to control their views, still believing that Universities were meant to be places of open ideas and free thinking, but so much had changed.

As the Woke brigade and the #me too movement occupied the vacuum left by the neoconservatives, freedom of speech in the early 2020s was curbed, not by any political edict but just through fear. This was ably demonstrated during the COVID-19 Pandemic when any voices questioning Government policy over lockdowns and collapsing the economy were met with disdain. The National Health Service was deified as the media and Government made the whole crisis about protecting the NHS. Anyone who even suggested that the UK's disastrous performance might have been due to a centralised health service that was run inefficiently for the benefit of itself, was pilloried. Free open debate was a thing of the past and it happened seamlessly. They were exceedingly difficult times before the war.

Universities were no longer safe places of learning but had become hot beds for extreme liberal ideas and that did not sit comfortably with many of the older Professors, many of whom were hounded both physically and mentally. It was the social media that was however the most damaging, that could build to a frenzy, and was so difficult to combat. The dramatic rise in suicides amongst Professors should have sounded the warning bells but even the Deans were afraid to speak out.

It was the great trade war started by President Trump in 2019 that really changed everything. The mood swing against the Chinese was sudden and severe. Once Huawei had been awarded one third of the 5G network, social media went crazy about security. The first great CoronaVirus epidemic did not help matters and Chinese students were picked on. They were easy targets as they were never seen without their masks. With the new Immigration rules and the points system introduced by the Home Secretary it became much harder for Chinese students to come to the UK. With the dialogue of the Chinese stealing our Intellectual property and starting the COVID-19 outbreak, it was hardly surprising that they decided to stay away.

Nobody had quite realised the impact. The Chinese represented 20% of all University income as well as millions donated for research. Their reluctance to come to the UK along with collapsing numbers on the back of the student loan crisis led to 46 universities going bust by 2023. With so many degree students unable to find jobs, more and more became Professors until there was an oversupply. This, combined with rapidly falling student numbers, meant salaries for Professors halved between 2020 and 2026 just as Charlie was finishing his Phd.

Fortunately, Charlie knew somebody on the faculty at the London School of Economics and managed to secure a part time position, unfortunately with no contract, which meant no holiday pay or pension contributions. This just about covered his basic living costs in London which he had supplemented ever since with freelance journalism. Journalists had also had a tough time with so many newspapers going bust as increasingly people took their news online or through social media, often for free although of course nothing is really free.

Jasmin brought over a double espresso in a large round cup and a small jug of hot milk along with the almond croissant.
"Thank you" Charlie said cheerfully removing his mask as he was seated.

" Always my pleasure ", she replied with a beaming smile. "That's eighteen pounds fifty or Six Amazon units?"

"Eighteen fifty" he replied and waved his watch across her pouch. A quiet ping rang out to say the transaction was done.

"I will bring you another one at noon," she said.

"Thank you Jasmin, you always look after me" replied Charlie. Every Monday, Wednesday, and most Fridays the same thing would happen, Charlie would arrive about 9.30 and stay until 4 or 5 unless he was meeting contacts. He used the cafe as office, laboratory and inspiration. Tuesday and Thursdays, he lectured and spent time with his students at the Lincolns Inn Fields faculty buildings of the LSE.

His parents were shocked that he had to have two jobs just to make ends meet, but that was just the way it was. After the CoronaVirus Pandemic of 2020, the second peak after the mutations in 2021, and the ensuing global recession, everything changed for the worst. Perhaps if he had retrained as a plumber, data analyst or re-programmer, but it was what it was, as he told himself. He loved what he did, but it was getting harder by the day due to the restrictions brought about by the war both on freedom of speech and the ability to investigate without interference.

He knew he could have got a better deal by buying his coffee in Amazon units, but the University only paid him in digital pounds, they were still old school like that, perhaps their little rebellion against the changes. It could be quite painful having the two currencies running simultaneously, you had to keep your wits about you in case the exchange rate moved dramatically on the announcement of some good or bad news generally relating to the war. The introduction of the Amazon currency in 2024 seemed like a novelty at the time but it quickly grew in appeal just as the loss of faith in Government and the establishment gathered pace. Alternative currencies were springing up everywhere after Bitcoin went to $100,000 making some people extraordinarily rich. The war meant a dramatic drop in value of the pound which only led to more people using the Amazon currency as an alternative. It was originally designed just for transactions within the Amazon community but with the elimination of cash and everything going digital it just became an alternative medium of exchange. Amazon had become so embedded in society once it took over the procurement and distribution for the NHS, it was hard to remember a time without Amazon. The Amazon Bank became the largest bank in the UK within two years, and then the largest in the world, it was quite extraordinary.

He poured all the milk into his double espresso, stirred it, and looked out of the window. It was drizzling again. The pedestrians looked miserable as they passed by, some with umbrellas, others just accepting that they would get wet but nevertheless trying to dodge under overhangs. It was eerily quiet, the driverless vehicles passing silently by, the rain muffling all the other sounds. He remembered when driverless vehicles became mandatory in London, almost overnight the whole City went silent. Without the backdrop of the noise of traffic, people began talking more quietly, almost in whispers. Not all the time of course, the bars and restaurants could still be deafeningly loud, but general conversation became muted, probably in part to the surveillance and eavesdropping.

Taking a sip of his coffee, Charlie picked up the book that had arrived that morning and looked at the cover. He had read this in his second year at university, Professor McAdams had suggested it along with Aldous Huxley's "Brave New World. Both books were offering visions of the future, completely different ideas and yet somehow similar, essentially society being controlled through a higher body, the end of Democracy. Given when they were written in 1932 and 1948, they were both taking a swipe at Communism, but both seemed to portent events now. The first Coronavirus of 2020 enabled the Government to pass draconian laws that restricted freedom of movement and limited personal liberty that never returned.

What Charlie was really interested in was the main character Winston Smith. He wanted to remind himself how he had fought Big Brother and ultimately lost, was he the anti-hero? He could not quite remember as the book was quite nuanced, but the reason for his interest were recent events.

Just yesterday a fifth person had immolated themselves outside the House of Commons. He could see the police tent over the crime scene from where he was sitting, Pathologists passing in and out in their white overalls, with clipboards and digital devices.

Of the five people who had killed themselves in this way over the previous three months, four were men and one was a woman but the thing they all had in common was that they had changed their name to Winston Smith by deed poll just before they came to Parliament Square to set light to themselves.

For sure, there was a movement against The Party and the authorities in general, but what makes someone do such a thing? Committing suicide is one thing, it shows despair and a loss of faith and trust, but to do it in such a public and painful way? He had seen two of the immolations on YouTube. It is hard to imagine that anyone would record such a thing but apparently there were dozens of these types of videos. You could feel the pain as the bodies contorted and writhed in agony. In all five cases the victims had come to Parliament Square, stood in front of Parliament close to the statue of Winston Churchill and poured petrol over themselves and then struck a match. The police were on high alert, but all five victims just looked like ordinary people. They did not carry obvious petrol cans either. One had two containers secreted in a Harrods bag. These burnings were not the serene motionless death of the Vietnamese Buddhist monk Thich Quang Duc in 1963 during the Vietnam War. Charlie had been reading widely on the subject and had read an article written at the time by the journalist David Halberstam "As he burned, he never moved a muscle, never uttered a sound, his outward composure in sharp contrast to the people wailing around him". The people who killed themselves in Westminster did not die quite so serenely, they were horrifically contorted and screaming.

The Home Secretary quickly pushed through a law under the war footing that meant nobody could change their name by deed poll to Winston Smith anymore, and any attempts would result in arrest. She also introduced a law that said nobody could buy petrol in cans anymore. This was patently absurd as there were no longer any petrol stations and anyone who wanted to get hold of petrol could only do so on the black market, or from a Government mandated supplier, it was just her way of trying to assert some control.

An old University chum Daniel Harding had written as much in a freelance piece just a week ago for an online publication. He had been immediately denounced as a paedophile, which was a tactic commonly used by the Government to taint anyone who questioned their authority, and a story was constructed on social media about him. He was immediately pilloried and harried both online and in his real world. It did not take much to discredit somebody these days. Daniel left London and went to stay with his parents up in the Lake District whilst things blew over. It was not easy to embarrass the Government these days, which stopped many journalists even trying to do so.

Was there something in Orwell's book that would explain why these five people would do such a thing? Charlie finished his croissant, opened the book and started reading.

After an hour or so his mobile started to vibrate. Emma's name appeared.

"Hi Em, how's your day?" he muffled into the microphone.

"Pretty good. Sorry I didn't say goodbye this morning, you looked so peaceful asleep so I thought I would let you lie in". Emma and Charlie had been together for over three years. She had been a post graduate student in one of his classes. It had been a slow burn but once they started dating, they realised they were a good fit and on the same wavelength which was probably the most important thing in these unusual times. Emma moved into Charlie's one bedroom flat in Battersea and they had been together ever since.

"Thanks for that, I slept really well, think the red wine last night may have helped" said Charlie.

"It was a lovely evening and thanks for cooking. That was a real treat. I still don't know how you managed to get hold of lamb and red wine".

"I have my contacts, they come in handy sometimes."
"Did your book 1984 arrive?"

"Yes, purely for research. It was of no interest, I relisted it on Amazon, see if I can get my money back," he said.

"Oh ok. Will I see you later?"

"Yes, I should be back by 7, see you then."

"Are you stopping by The Borough? We are going there from work for drinks."

"Yes, I was planning to, might see you there then. Love you."

"Love you too," and Em was gone.

Charlie did love Emma, but these were uncertain times. Emma Harrison worked for the Department of Information, an offshoot of the War Department. She was in administration doing a low-key job for which she and the rest of the department were overqualified but that was the same for almost everyone. As much as he thought Emma loved him, he did not want to take any chances by saying he still had the book. He would not have told her about buying it, but she had seen him order it by chance at the flat. It was better she thought that he had just sold it on without reading it, in case she was ever interrogated about it. He also had to consider the possibility that she was keeping an eye on him for her employers, although he really hoped not.

Charlie returned to his book, 1984. It was more interesting now than when he had been an undergraduate. He was shocked at some of the similarities between Big Brother and today.

His second coffee came and then he had his sandwiches that he brought with him. Of course, he was not really allowed to bring in his own food, but there was no way he could afford to buy lunch every day, and the staff seemed to cast a blind eye. By 4.30 he had devoured the whole book and leant back in his chair and stretched.

He remembered as a twenty-year-old reading it and thinking it really was a dystopian view of the future and that nothing like that could ever happen. That was back in 2017 before everything seemed to go wrong. The main character Winston Smith had certainly tried to push back against the establishment but in the end after torture and retraining he had come to love Big Brother. Perhaps the story of individualism against collectivism was the inspiration for the poor souls who set themselves alight, or was there more to it? If they were really railing against the state, why hadn't they changed their names to Emmanuel Goldstein? He was Orwell's head of the dissident organisation 'The Brotherhood' fighting back against 'The Party'.

Perhaps I am reading too much into this, he thought to himself, but something was nagging at him. Did any of these people know each other? Was this an organised protest, did it represent something bigger? People were disillusioned, and for many, life had become hopeless with no future. Charlie knew that an article suggesting an organisation questioning The State was a risky thing to be publishing and would bring him lots of unwanted attention, but this is what he had gone into journalism for. He could construct the article so that it appeared purely objective but suggesting the reasons why someone would set light to themselves might get his message across, in the third party. It was risky but he had to do it.

He opened his iPad and started typing.

'The Brotherhood' Does the Government have an enemy within? He paused.

The words stared back at him. He knew they were not just innocent words, another article joining the countless other articles published daily, this would be picked up immediately by one of the many Government organisations and their algorithms searching out for anything that questioned the Government, that was subversive and 'a threat to society'. He wondered if this would come across Emma's desk and what she would do with it. He looked out across the road where the men and women in their chemical suits were still busy going in and out of the tent like bees returning to the hive. The rain had just started to ease so Charlie packed up his things into his rucksack and headed out.

"Bye Charlie, see you Wednesday," said Jasmin looking up from behind her counter with a broad smile.

"See you Wednesday, have a great evening," he replied.

The rain had stopped but the sky was still overcast, the pavements were wet, they were always wet, rain and damp were all he could remember. There was a time when protesters would march through London and camp in Parliament Square, protesting about climate change. The new powers under the War Act stopped gatherings of protest years ago. The changes in the weather became more extreme for a while until they settled down in the late 20s with increasing amounts of rainfall against a backdrop of warmer temperatures, almost equatorial. He made his way along the Embankment past the Pier looking across to the spot where the London Eye used to sit before it was removed. The river was fast flowing, lapping up against the barriers. He noticed that additional sandbags had been put out in the last couple of days to support the barriers and keep the water back. London looked particularly gloomy today, autonomous pods glided silently by.

As Charlie walked along the embankment passing Waterloo and Blackfriars bridges and crossing the river at Southwark Bridge towards The Borough, he could feel their eyes upon him. He was always a bit paranoid, but the purchasing of 1984 had him on edge. It was innocent enough in its own right, but there were departments on a war footing looking out for any kind of subversive behaviour or 5th columnists.

It was a good forty-minute walk from the café to Borough market but having sat for almost seven hours working, He always enjoyed the walk. He could have taken an Uber but he looked forward to clearing his head. He cut through into the market which was just getting busy ready for the evening crowd. Lots of people frequented Borough Market after work even on a Monday. Although there were some shortages, the traders there were pretty smart, and most things were available here if you knew who to talk to. He stopped at a small café bar and went up to order a drink.

"Hi Charlie, how's it going?". He offered his hand and gave a hug.

Charlie had been calling regularly at this bar on his way home for the last two years.

"The usual?" asked Edwin, the owner.

"For sure, thank you Edwin, how's it going, good weekend?" asked Charlie.

"Pretty good my friend, plenty of eating and drinking."

Edwin poured a 'Dark and Stormy', rum, ginger ale and lime, gave it a stir and passed it across to Charlie. He passed Edwin some cash, a rare sight these days.

"Any luck with the prawns Edwin?" he said.
"Sure have man, come and see me when you go, I have them wrapped up for you, something special."

Charlie sat with his back to the wall looking out over the hustle and bustle of the market. Lots of things had changed over the last fifteen years but somehow The Borough Market kept going and maintained its bohemian feel. He liked to stop here on the way home, not every time but once or twice a week. It was a chance to unwind, pick up some supplies from Edwin and some other traders and relax before heading home.

He had discovered the Dark & Stormy one Friday night when out with Emma and a couple of friends, it was very warming, comforting even, and a long drink. He sipped it and felt a chill run down his back as the ice-cold liquid entered his body. Because he did not eat that much it had an immediate hit which he liked. He relaxed into the bench seat that was softened by a variety of cushions. The café was outdoors like most of the stalls at the Borough market. He pulled his collar up and shuffled down into his overcoat and closed his eyes.

Sometimes he wished he could just drift away and think of nice things like sandy beaches or picnicking with Em, but his brain just did not work that way. Ever since school he had been inquisitive and interested in everything. He had lived every moment of the last fifteen years and constantly recalled them, he could not help it, whenever he closed his eyes they were just there.

Charlie started to think about the war, how it had started.

"Here you go Charlie, your prawns, I have to go now, things to do, you know."

"Cheers Edwin, what do I owe you?" said Charlie.

"Sixty pounds Charlie."

Charlie passed across three notes as subtly as he could and took the bag from Edwin.

"See you next time," said Edwin as he left.

Charlie was lost in his thoughts, thinking about how the war had started and the events of the last few years, his life at the University, his relationship with Emma. He found it difficult to switch off. He would often find his mind wandering onto all kinds of other subjects.

Twenty minutes later he finished his drink, put the bag of prawns into his satchel, and started walking through the market. There were crowds of people gathered enjoying drinks and food together. Borough Market was always buzzing despite the shortages and rationing. Charlie thought the stallholders were left alone a lot more because it was quite close to Parliament and a place where MPs and Government could still find the nicer things in life.

As he passed through the crowds, he saw Emma stood at one of the bars with a group of people. She had very distinct red hair and always stood out. He held back to see who she was with. He recognised a few of them as her work colleagues. He had been to a couple of work events as a plus one at the Ministry of Information. They were quite a young office and would go out after work once or twice a week. With driverless cars so available and so cheap, it was easy for her and her colleagues to get an Uber to Borough which was much more relaxed than the bars and pubs around Whitehall. Charlie watched how Emma interacted with the group, she was so confident, he loved that about her, always animated and engaging with everyone. As a couple, she was by far the more outgoing, he was quieter and reserved. He liked people and company but was comfortable enough in his own skin and never found the need to make a great effort. He was watching intently, catching every move she made, she was so beautiful.

He felt a strong hand on his shoulder and shuddered.

"Evening Charlie, I wondered if I might bump into you here?"

It was Karam, a fellow Professor from LSE. Karam lectured in International Relations. He had been kind to Charlie when he started, helping him out with the way the University worked, the geography of the campus, where the best dining areas were, and most importantly, where the best coffee was to be had nearby. Karam Shahid was a Syrian who had come to the UK in 2022 as a refugee of the Syrian Civil War. Charlie had learnt from him that he had been an outspoken critic of the Assad regime and so was given political asylum as his name appeared on the Mukhabarat list of dissidents. He had previously been lecturing at the University of Damascus for two years when he was forced to flee because his articles were considered subversive.

He was a tall man with distinctly Arabic features, olive skin and a perfectly coiffured beard. He looked rather good for someone of about 40 years of age.
"Salaam Alaikum Charlie."

"Wa-Alaikum-Salaam" Charlie replied.

"Did you have a good weekend? You were going to visit friends in Brighton, weren't you? Charlie asked.

"Yes, that's right, but it got cancelled, I couldn't get my travel documents authorised in time. I did think about driving down, but if I got stopped and jailed, the University would probably hear about it, so I didn't take the chance."

"You should have called me; Emma could have pulled some strings at The Ministry" Charlie replied.

"It was no big deal; it gave me the chance to catch up on the Paper I am writing. We also had that break in the rain on Saturday afternoon, so I took a long walk through Hyde Park and St James's, it was good to get the sun on my face, it's been getting hard to remember what the sun feels like," he laughed.

"I know what you mean, Emma and I did the same, but we headed out to Clapham Common and then just kept walking. We went to Crystal Palace and enjoyed the views out over London. Then the rain came again, and we had to get an Uber, but we enjoyed those few hours too. Are you here for your Hummus?"

"Yes, Hassan's wife was making some at the weekend. I don't know what she does, but her Hummus is the best in town. He has just baked some flatbreads, and made some falafel too, they are still warm, try some. "

Karam opened his bag, broke off some warm flatbread and opened the pot of Hummus for Charlie to dip into. He was right, it really was the best, sprinkled with pine nuts and paprika.

"That is so good" said Charlie laughing. "One good thing about all the shortages is that when we get to taste something good it really is something special."

"I know" said Karam, tucking in. The two of them leant against the supporting girder laughing and enjoying their food.

"Have some more Charlie, what is mine is yours."

"That is very kind of you, but I am actually going home to cook, although I think I may swing by Hassan and see if he has any left," said Charlie.

"He hasn't! All his regulars were there waiting, I only just managed to get some. Here take some of mine, share with Emma."

"I have a better idea, why don't you come back to ours for dinner now."

"That would be wonderful my friend" replied Karam putting his arm around Charlie, "If you think Emma wouldn't mind?"

"I am sure Emma would love it, but let's go and find out, she is just over there with work friends, let's tell her what we are up to, I have just acquired some lovely prawns too, we can make a party of it."

Charlie took Karam by the arm and starting walking towards Emma and the group.

Karam suddenly stopped, pulling back on Charlie's arm.

"Many apologies Charlie, what am I thinking, I am teaching an evening class this evening at UCL, I got carried away with the invite, really sorry, here you keep the Hummus, Hassan said he will have some more on Thursday, really sorry, see you tomorrow, coffee, usual place?" and he turned and walked away.

"Yeah, for sure Karam, see you 9.30, Ma'is Salama", he always liked to try and speak some Arabic when he was with Karam.

As he turned to wave him goodbye, Karam was gone, mingling with the bustling crowd.

Charlie walked over to Emma and put his arm around her waist.

"Evening gorgeous, fancy meeting you here."

She turned to him, her eyes widened, and she kissed him on the lips. "This is lovely, so pleased to see you, come and say hello to everyone."

Emma took him gently by the hand and started to introduce him to all her colleagues. Charlie had met them all before, so no introductions were necessary. He said hello and the usual chit chat. An attractive woman approached Charlie smiling.

"Hello Charlie, nice to see you. Where has your friend gone, I would have liked to have met him". The inquisitor was Sophie Hallam, Emma's direct boss, someone Charlie had never warmed to. She was always overly interested in everything, and Charlie just got the impression that she was quietly keeping an eye on him.

"Sorry Sophie, who do you mean, I am on my own" replied Charlie.

"The chap you were with over there by the column, the tall, good looking Arab gentleman, he looked really interesting, it would have been nice to meet him, what's his name?" Sophie enquired quite forcefully.

"Oh him, I think his name is Mohammed, he works at one of the food stalls, sometimes he gets me fresh falafel or hummus, here it is" as he held the bag up. "Fresh for us tonight darling, as he tugged at Emma's dress."

"Lovely"", she replied, "did you get some flatbread too?"

"I did, that's dinner sorted. I am sure you can find him at a stall near to the entrance on the right Sophie," said Charlie.

"Thanks, she replied, I might check that out, especially if the hummus is as good as you two think it is." Sophie looked at Charlie just a little longer than was necessary, and not for the first time send a slight chill through him. Charlie had always been a good judge of character, and he thought that Sophie Hallam was taking far too much interest in him, her good looks could not stop him feeling uncomfortable.

"Listen Em, I am going to go home, I managed to get some fresh prawns and thought I would get started on dinner. Did you want to come with me, or shall I see you a bit later?"

"We have only just arrived, and I have just got this drink, I will follow on. Be home for 8, is that ok? I will get an Uber, and I expect you will walk as usual so I shouldn't be that far behind you," she said.

"Absolutely fine, see you at 8. I will run you a bath and have dinner ready, just text if you want to stay out longer, I won't cook the prawns until you are in."

She put her arms around him and pulled him in for a kiss.

"Bye everyone, have a great evening", Charlie said waving as he left to a chorus of goodbyes.

He walked away and casually turned, expecting to see Sophie Hallam looking at him, but she was not, she was engaged in conversation on her phone. He carried on walking through the market which was packed. He stopped off at a stall that he knew had some chillies, another for some chocolate, put them in his rucksack and headed off home to Battersea. It was quite a walk, almost 4 miles, but Charlie was tall with a long stride and liked to walk fast, he could do the journey in 50 minutes. He did not play sport much anymore. It had become so difficult to organise anything with all the Covid restrictions and the waterlogged facilities, so he was happy to walk 8-10 miles a day to keep slim and in shape. He passed out of the market, past Southwark Cathedral and picked up the path along the river.

It was drizzling but his umbrella was keeping him dry. He did not need to think about the route, he had done it hundreds of times and was on autopilot. He was thinking about Sophie Hallam, and her interest in Karam, and why Karam suddenly disappeared. He thought about ringing him but knew he would be seeing him in the morning. He did not want to appear too obvious; his inquisitive journalistic mind was starting to whirr.

He passed The Golden Hind walking along the river, looking out across, marvelling at the power of the water rushing under the bridges. His mind started to wander as it often did.
The rain was coming down a little heavier now as Charlie passed The Red Anchor pub and dropped down to The Thames. The water seemed so close here, the river flowing so high and so fast. As he walked a little further, closer to the Millennium Bridge, he looked across at St Pauls Cathedral. It had survived the last World War, everything The Luftwaffe could throw at it, would it survive this one? Could London be obliterated in one attack?

Charlie felt uncomfortable and sensed that he was being watched. He looked up and saw a few drones carrying parcels. There was one a little higher that did not seem to be moving with any purpose, just hovering. He could only make it out by the flashing red lights. He moved on with a little more purpose and then dodged into a gap between two buildings and tucked himself into the shadows. He took out his phone and put the reverse camera in play and positioned the phone outwards to see what was happening. He could see the lights of the drone as it lowered to about 10 metres above where he had been standing. It was scanning the area. As he looked through the gap in the buildings, he could see a car that had stopped. It was motionless and driverless. The illuminated sign above was off indicating that it was occupied or travelling to a customer, but there was nobody inside and it was not moving. Charlie knew he was being watched. This was not that unusual, with the enormous amount of technology at the State's disposal it was so easy to track almost anyone. We were on a war footing so being watched happened to most people at some time, but Charlie thought it was too much of a coincidence after what Sophie Hallam had said back in the Market. This was probably the phone call she had been making, to instigate the surveillance.

Charlie slipped out of the shadow and made out he was adjusting his fly, as though he had been caught short, and carried along the footpath. He picked up speed as he felt he wanted to get home and indoors away from the cameras.

He was conscious of the drone overhead as he passed the Tate Modern and the Oxo Tower. He did not look up; he did not want his watchers to know that he was aware. He passed The National Theatre and the Southbank book market. He looked across the river towards Big Ben through where The London Eye used to stand, but really, he was looking to see where the drone was. It was still there a few hundred feet up. It was definitely tracking him, no doubt in his mind. He looked at The Houses of Parliament and where he had started his journey home. It was circuitous, and he could have picked up a driverless cab, but he liked to walk and think.

He had now walked along the Albert Embankment and just passed the New Covent Garden Market, walking along below the old Battersea Power Station that had been converted into flats. He remembered visiting a friend who was staying at his parents there in 2019 whilst he was at University. It was a lovely flat with great views but was a crazy amount of money. Most of them had been bought by foreign investors and remained empty for a long time. When the impact of the global recession took hold, the investors had tried to sell and the prices collapsed, as did so many other properties in London.

The City of London never really recovered after the Covid-19 outbreak and the majority of people worked from home, this led to a steady trickle of affluent people leaving London and moving to the suburbs or the countryside. Empty offices were converted into flats, initially, for the luxury market but when demand did not pick up, they became affordable housing. The Government crackdown on laundered money through unexplained wealth orders also led to an exodus of foreign money from London. As prices fell, top end properties came to the market as London was no longer considered a haven for hiding wealth.

The drone was still there. He wondered if this was anything to do with Karam. Sophie Hallam had seemed particularly interested in the man Charlie was stood with. Was Karam of interest to the Ministry of Information? He had been a Syrian refugee but that was years ago. He was just a Professor at the London School of Economics now, but why did Karam leave so quickly? Charlie had not really thought about his friend in any other way, he only knew him to be a diligent Professor at University who was always kind and friendly. He did not know much about him, he had been to his flat in the Elephant and Castle, well, outside his flat to be precise, he met him there before they went to The Imperial War Museum together. They played five a side football once or twice a week, he seemed a normal kind of guy.

Charlie walked on, and into Battersea Park. The rain had eased up, he shook his umbrella and put it down. He had been lucky enough to buy his flat in Warriner Gardens four years ago. He needed a lot of help from his parents as well as an inheritance. He could not borrow much money on his salary as a Professor and his freelance income as a journalist was not considered regular enough. Fortunately, prices were half of what they were only ten years before. He now had a small mortgage on a great flat but with an interest rate of ten percent it was still a challenge, however, Emma had helped turn it into a lovely home for the two of them. He always knew when he passed the bandstand and came up to the three standing figures, as they were known, that he was nearly home.

As he passed through the park and the sports ground, he emerged onto Prince of Wales Drive. Cars were passing silently up and down, but once again he saw one driverless pod stopped with its light on for no apparent reason. He crossed over and brushed passed the vehicle heading up Alexandra Avenue. Once again, he put his phone into reverse camera and saw the vehicle moving slowly behind him. He could hear the faint buzz of the drone above. There was silence, just the rustle of leaves that had fallen beneath him. He turned left into Warriner Gardens and approached a fine terraced house, waving his wrist over the lock, the door opened. He went in and pushed the door shut behind him. He could feel his heart racing. He breathed deeply and took a moment to compose himself then headed up two flights of stairs and waved his wrist against the lock of the door of the flat marked number two. He looked at his watch that told him the trip back was fifty-five minutes and 7000 steps, but he knew that, he had done the walk so many times. He dropped the bag on the table, went to the fridge and took out an opened bottle of wine, removing the stopper, pouring himself a glass and took a gulp. His heart was still racing. "Alexa on. Alexa I'm home" he said out loud and with that the table lamps came on. Charlie hung his coat up on a hook in the hall by the radiator, it was very damp from the walk home. He went to the window and looked out on the street below from behind the curtain. The driverless car was parked on the other side of the road and he could see the tell-tale sign of the red flashing lights of the drone above the house. There were other drones delivering parcels along the street but this one had no payload and was motionless apart from the whirring of its blades.

Charlie checked his phone. No calls. He text Emma to see what time she would be back. He took off his shoes and stacked them tidily on the plastic sheeting in the hallway, Emma was very tidy and meticulous, and it had rubbed off on him. He sat on the sofa, put his legs up and took another sip from his glass.

Why are they following me? He thought to himself. I have never been followed that far before and now they have eyes on me from outside. Could it have been his purchase of 1984? Emma had told him that there was a renewed vigour within the Ministry of Information. They believed there was a real and present threat from within the UK. Could he be considered part of that? It was just a book after all. Some of his recent articles could be construed to be challenging the Government, but he always chose his words carefully.

He sank further into the sofa and took another sip of his wine. His mind drifted back to the start of the war. It was hard to believe it was 5 years ago. The first six months had been frenetic, conscription, gearing up to a war footing, preparations for a nuclear attack, there was so much panic and most of it by the Government. People tried to go about their business, but the practice air raids were a constant reminder of the situation. It was all the media talked about and it was impossible to get away from it. The Government introduced immediate rationing and started to stockpile, and nothing happened, not here or anywhere else. The USA continued to build its defensive barrier which stretched all the way from Hawaii to the mid-Atlantic. It was mostly missile defence systems, minefields, and the navy patrolling. Apparently, defences were being dug in and created on both the east and west coasts at enormous expense but that was more a gesture to the people. This was never going to be a conventional war and was more likely to be fought where it could not be seen.

Charlie got up, went to the fridge, and topped up his wine. He checked his phone. Em was getting an Uber pod home and would be back in 20 minutes.

"Alexa, play midweek dinner playlist for Charlie," he said.

"Playing midweek dinner playlist for Charlie from Charlie's Playlists."

Rossini's Barber of Seville streamed through the speakers. Charlie started unpacking the bags, put the oven on and took out the prawns that Edwin had got for him at the market.

He chopped some shallots, garlic and ginger and put them in a pan with a little butter singing along to Rossini. Cooking relaxed him and stopped his mind from wandering. He threw in the prawns with their shells and started to toss them, after a few minutes he turned the heat down, removing the prawns and laid them out to cool.

He started to think about what he might say to Karam in the morning. Would Karam say anything first? Karam had never said or done anything to make Charlie suspicious, but he did think that although he had known him for six years, he did not really know that much about him.

Karam had told him that he had fled the Syrian Civil War in 2018 and was being actively pursued by the Syrian regime as an outspoken dissident. After spending some time in a camp in the Beqaa Valley in Lebanon, Karam had gone to a Turkish refugee camp on the border with Syria. Through contacts he had been promised an interview at Ankara University for a Professorship. After making a difficult journey from Lebanon to Turkey, he was detained at the border and incarcerated at the Reyhanli camp outdoors on semi-arid land and exposed to harsh weather conditions for three years.

He never got the job at Ankara but was offered asylum in Britain two years later. In 2024 he arrived in London and started work at The London School of Economics through contacts, where it appears, he had done a good job, integrating into London life and the University community. He joined a few societies but nothing inflammatory. He had never heard him speak out against anyone or anything apart from the Syrian Government. I asked him why he did not get involved in the anti-Assad groups that were in London. He had said that that part of his life was behind him and he would no longer be known as anyone important in Syria, that his new life was here in England. I had never pursued it further, I always felt he was a man of strong convictions, so it seemed odd that he had not wanted to continue his struggle, but he had been through a lot in the various refugee camps. He told me that once, because the Turkish/Kurdish border was very porous and there was so much corruption, that the Syrian Secret Police had found out where he was and came to kidnap him one day.

He was warned and hid, and then had to move camps. He said it never happened again, and he thought the regime finally thought he was not worth bothering about.

Charlie started peeling the prawns laying out the meat, tossing the shells back into the pan. Once they were all done, he turned the heat up and added some fish stock, bay leaves and seasoning. He measured out some rice ready to cook and left the mixture simmering. He washed his hands and returned to the sofa with his wine replenished.

The last four years but become an interminable routine.

Charlie started to think about 1984 that he had read earlier that day. There were so many comparisons between Orwell's vision and what was happening today fifty years later.

He heard the whirr of the lock and the door opened.

"Wow, something smells good" said Emma, hanging her coat.

"Glass of wine?" asked Charlie.

"Yes please" she replied. "Did you walk home?"

"Yes, I did, the river walk, it was great actually, my best time to date, 55 minutes."

"Well done. I got an Uber, managed to do a ride share, it was only three Amazon units."

"Nice one. Dinner in about ten minutes?"

"Great, gives me time for a quick shower," she replied.

"I have already run you a bath, take your wine, dinner on the table in fifteen minutes."
Charlie put the rice on to boil and strained the sauce which had

cooked nicely. He threw the prawns in and left on a very gentle heat. Once the rice was cooked, he turned it out in a small bowl shape and poured the sauce and prawns over the top. He would have finished with coriander but that was hard to find these days, for some strange reason herbs were always in short supply. He would save the falafel and flatbreads for tomorrow.

Emma came back in wearing a bath robe and glowing.

"I'm impressed" said Emma, "I think I have made a good choice in boyfriend."

They sat together and ate, enjoying the food and the wine and chatting. When they were finished, they washed up and sat on the sofa. The play list was still going, "quieter Alexa" said Charlie.

"Do you know if your department is on higher alert at the moment?" he asked.

"No more than usual, as far as I know. There's talk of another big cyber-attack coming, but that always seems to be the rumour. I have also heard that the Government wants to extend the anti-immigrant defences further along the coast. Why do you ask?"

"I just felt I was being watched on the way home tonight. I might have just imagined it. I did think that Sophie Hallam was taking a little extra interest in me as well." Charlie paused. Emma knew who Karam Shahid was. She had met him a couple of times at LSE events. He did not want to draw any additional attention to Karam.

"Oh, ignore me, it's my paranoia, I think it was ordering that book, got me all jittery. I read it today. It was a good read, better than I imagined. Orwell had a surprisingly clear insight into the future."

"It's not that bad really is it? After all we are in the middle of a World War and trying to stop another pandemic. Given everything that's going on, I think the Government has been doing a pretty good job just keeping everything going. Look, we have just had a lovely prawn supper, enjoyed some wine, life can't be that bad, can it?"

"Of course, you are right, I was just feeling a little melancholy today. I think it's the relentless rain getting me down a bit," said Charlie.
"I know what you mean, it does get a bit depressing. It is the price we are all paying for climate change. You have to take your hat off to all of those activists back in the day, they knew what they were talking about. Do you remember that Swedish kid who was on the news all the time?"

"Yeah, I do, Greta, Greta, Thun……"

"Thunberg, yes, Greta Thunberg, I wonder where she is now?" asked Emma.

"Do you think its global warming or climate change or perhaps the Chinese?"

"Don't be so silly! I know you have never believed in global warming and what homo sapiens have done to the planet, but how do you explain the weather we have been having the last few years, it's been raining for 100 days Charlie," she said.

"I know, but maybe it's just nature and the way the planet works. I'm not saying that man hasn't contributed to changes, I don't worry about it, mother nature will mend the planet when we are all gone. I think we get a bit carried away; we are just one species in a moment of time. If this war really takes off, we might not be here at all for much longer!"

"Don't say that Charlie, you know I hate it when you talk about that kind of stuff."

"I'm just being a realist. I think we worry too much about what we have done to the planet. We know that every time there is a lockdown, and we stop, the air clears, and pollution drops. Having said that, the end of the combustion engine has made a huge difference anyway. We have started to reclaim the streets, planting more trees, maybe it's all the extra trees causing the rain?"

"Don't be so silly. All I hope is that it stops raining soon, the flood defences are under pressure everywhere. They keep talking about it at the Ministry. I think they are very concerned."

Charlie and Emma spent the rest of the evening chatting and listening to music. They found each other's company very relaxing and could talk easily but could also sit in silence without it being awkward. Under different circumstances Charlie would have asked Emma to marry him, even though the number of people getting married in the UK had fallen dramatically over the previous decade, Charlie was a conservative sort of chap, and knew his Mum and Dad would like to see him married. He just felt with the war and the current situation that the timing was off. Neither of them had ever mentioned it, they did not talk about having children, somehow it did not seem right bringing children into this crazy world with so much uncertainty, he was also still concerned about Emma's position at the Ministry and if she was keeping an eye on him, but he thought that was just paranoia. At ten thirty, having just watched the news they headed for bed. They, like most people watched the news at ten o'clock. There was always a statement from the Government which rarely said very much at all. The news was very thin as quite frankly not much was happening and for whatever reason there was barely any reporting of events outside of the UK. They switched off the TV and went to bed.

CHAPTER TWO

KARAM SHAHID

Karam had spotted Sophie Hallam looking at him and quickly made his escape, apologising to Charlie. It would have been nice to have had dinner with Charlie, but Karam knew he was being watched. He handed Charlie the bag and slipped back behind the columns and made his way to the exit. He pulled a baseball cap over his head, then pulled the hood up on his jacket and stepped out into the rain whilst moving quite fast. He headed along Borough High Street to the tube without looking up at all. He stepped into the entrance and turned the camera in his phone round to scan the street behind him. He felt sure he had not been followed. He swapped caps with one he had in his rucksack and carried on without looking up, the road becoming Newington Causeway, he crossed over and walked up Avonmouth street into Tiverton Street, and into Bath Terrace through a gap in the low wall and on to Stephenson House.

Stephenson House was a red brick former council block. Most of the flats had been purchased from the Council and subsequently sold on at huge profits during the redevelopment of The Elephant and Castle fifteen years previously when property prices in London were going up relentlessly. Karam rented a one bedroom flat on the third floor. He took one final glance behind him and ran up the external stairway, along the walkway and up to a blue door, number 28. He rattled a key in the lock and went in. He stood in the hallway while he gathered himself. Although he had walked extremely fast and sprinted up the stairs he was barely out of breath. Karam looked after himself and was very fit. He walked into the lounge, threw his coat over the back of a chair, moved it against the radiator and sat down. He looked at his phone expecting to see a message from Charlie but there was not one. He went to the fridge and pulled out a beer which he poured into a tumbler. Karam had been a practising Muslim all his life and had never drunk alcohol but things had changed for him a few years ago. He had lost his faith and believed that his God had abandoned him. Charlie knew some things about Karam, but they were sketchy and there was lots missing. It was not surprising, Karam had tried to hide his past and had been diligent in doing so and with good reason.

Yes, he was Syrian, and had been a lecturer at The University of Damascus. He had been an outspoken critic of President Assad and the Syrian regime and had organised protest meetings and marches. He was also married to Jamal, his childhood sweetheart. They had been together since school as a couple and had married in their last year at University. Jamal had trained to be a doctor. In March 2011 in his second year at The University, the Syrian Civil War started. Karam had been closely following the Arab Spring and as a lecturer on International Relations was well placed to talk on the subject. He spoke freely at university about the Assad regime and as the war developed, Karam was forced to flee Damascus with his family. He joined the Free Syrian Army while Jamal helped as a doctor. The couple were forced to keep moving around the country as the war changed shape.

Karam found himself fighting Isil and Al Qaeda in his own country on one side and the Syrian State on the other, but during this time they did experience some joy, as they welcomed into the world a son and a daughter. Their happiness was short lived as the situation deteriorated and Karam became increasingly fearful for his family having witnessed some of the atrocities that Isil has perpetrated. He took his family and fled to the refugee camp in Lebanon in the Beqaa valley. There the family found some safety although the conditions were extremely basic. The family spent two years there whilst Karam appealed to all his academic contacts. Finally, he got an opportunity for work at Ankara University and the possibility of Turkish citizenship. He left Jamal and Amira his four-year-old little girl at the camp where by now Jamal was the head doctor and was well established whilst he and his son Nabil headed to Turkey. It was a long and arduous journey passing through the Kurdish held territories which carried its own dangers.

When Karam and Nabil arrived at the Turkish border, Karam showed the letter from Ankara University but instead of being allowed through he was taken to a detention centre at the Surac tent camp. There Karam was tortured. His name was on a list of dissidents and freedom fighters. It did not really matter what side he was on; his name was on the list and the Commander at that time was a brutal sadist. They kept him for nine days before they threw him back out. He had broken ribs, a broken arm, internal bleeding, and deep cuts. There were friendly people in the camp who had heard about his arrival. They knew he had been detained and taken inside and what would happen to him, they had seen it happen so many times before. Someone waited outside every day in case he was released, and they had also taken in Nabil and looked after him. As soon as he was released, he was picked up by the medical team at the camp who were all Syrians.

Karam could not walk. They stretchered him into their makeshift hospital and put him on the table. He cried for his son, but they said it was better Nabil did not see him like this until he was patched up and looking a little better. Two days later Nabil was brought to him and burst into tears. He would not let go of his father clutching his arm and wrapping himself around him.

Karam got better and stronger during the next two weeks. Although the resources at the camp were basic, they provided him with most things to help him recover including food. He told them who he was, and they corroborated his story. It was important to find out people were who they said they were. As Isis was being defeated, all sorts of people were coming to the camp fleeing the conflict, and The

Turkish Government and the Assad regime were known to have planted spies in the camp.

At last, Karam was strong enough to be able to walk out of the hospital on his own two feet. He was missing some teeth and now carried a heavy limp, but he was alive.

Karam and Nabil found a tent and were given some clothes and basics by other Syrians. He found that he had two cousins in the camp who helped him get established and vouched for him as well. He was able to get in touch with Jamal to let her know they had arrived in Turkey. He was economical with the truth as he did not want to worry her. He tried to contact the University, but it was difficult. When he eventually got through to his friend, he was told that the position was no longer available. The Commander who had tortured Karam had made sure that the University would not support him anymore. Clearly the officer did not want Karam to be in a position to complain about his treatment. The genteel academics at The University were frightened by the threats of the Turkish Officer Yuzbasi Demir and backed down.

Karam started writing frantically to all the Universities in Turkey and then further afield especially the UK as he had linked his courses in Damascus to a couple of Universities in England, but as time went by, he became more despondent and thought about returning to Lebanon. He and Nabil had been in the camp for almost two years and it was taking its toll especially being separated from his wife and daughter.

Then one day whilst Karam was teaching at one of the schools in the camp, three officers of the Mukhabarat came looking for him. They had been given a tip off by Yuzbasi Demir who had taken to supplementing his income by giving information to the Assad regime. Karam had been writing and supporting the resistance to Assad from the camp, publishing articles online denouncing the regime. He had become more vocal and had become of interest to the Mukhabarat.

The officers came to Karam's tent, but he was not there. Just as they were leaving Nabil walked in. He had returned from his school and met the three officers. They asked him if he knew who Karam Shahid was. He told them he was his father. Then they asked him if he knew where he was, so he told them. He was only eight and his father had always told him to tell the truth. They slit his throat and left him to bleed to death. The three men emerged from the tent and went in search of Karam. The neighbours who had been watching rushed in and found Nabil, he was already dead. They made some calls and got through to Karam and told him to hide. They did not say what had happened to Nabil. Karam left the school and hid in a building close from where he could see what was happening.

The three men walked into the school. He heard voices and saw them come out and look around and then they were gone. He ran as fast as he could back to his tent and found his neighbours crying. Inside, his beautiful son was lying on the ground in a pool of blood. Karam took him in his arms and cradled him sobbing uncontrollably. There was nothing he could do. Jamal and Amira were distraught when he told them about the murder of their precious son and brother, he had been such a gentle, loving child. They had not seen him for such a long time apart from on Skype and now he was gone, and they would never hold him again. The family were shattered.

As he sat in his flat in The Elephant and Castle tears started streaming down his face. It had been such a long time ago, but the memories were still there. He went to the fridge and got himself another beer.

Karam thought seriously about returning to Lebanon, to his wife and daughter, when he received an invitation from the London School of Economics. It was the brightest news, the chance for the family to be together somewhere safe and to start a new life. Karam started applying to the British Home Office to gain a visa. This proved to be exceedingly difficult. Although there were a number of places for political refugees, the situation had become much stricter after Brexit. The new points system had some advantages for Karam, he was educated and had a job offer, significantly higher than the fiscal threshold set by the British Government, but he failed on almost all the other criteria and he was coming from a war- torn area where the threat of Isis whilst diminished, still existed.

He continued to apply, spending almost a year writing and pleading. Finally, the London School of Economics whilst sympathetic to his situation said they could not keep the post open indefinitely. He had three months to present himself of they would have to give the job to someone else.

Karam had to make a huge decision. He could travel back to Lebanon to be with his family, but that still would not offer them a future, or he could make his way to England. He knew that if he could land on British soil, with the job offer in hand his position as a political refugee would be much stronger. He decided to try and get to Britain. He had held on to some family jewellery for just such a trip. He packed his things, what few there were, and said goodbye to his friends at the camp. They were sad to see him go. He was highly educated and cared for the people there, supporting and teaching. He was a kind man who had brought some rays of sunshine during a depressing time and would be missed.

He began his arduous journey. He could follow the well-trod routes that would involve using smugglers, or he could try to go it alone. He decided with his language skills, education, and appearance that he would try his luck travelling alone. He still had his Syrian passport and some old papers that he would try and use. He contacted friends he knew at Ankara University and headed there first. The hardest part was getting out of the camp and finding transport. Having spent two days walking and keeping out of sight, he made it to a main road where he knew there was a bus that would take him to Ankara. He had enough Turkish Lira that the people at the camp had gathered for him and paid the driver. It was a 12-hour journey. He had eaten all his food but had water. He slept most of the way, stirring occasionally when the vivid nightmare of his son's murder woke him with a start.

Just after midnight, the coach pulled into the central bus station in Ankara. It was only eight minutes from the University. Karam did not want to disturb his friend at home so decided to wait until the following day. He slept in an alleyway and the next morning found a food stall, had something to eat and then cleaned himself up in some public lavatories.

At 8 o'clock he set off and arrived at the University by ten past. He asked at reception where he would find professor Polat and was directed to his office on the first floor. He knocked and was greeted by a hug from Altan Polat, a man he had known only by email and skype.

"As - Salaam Alaikum," said Altan.

"Wa-Alaikum-Assalaam," replied Karam.

"What has happened to you my friend?" He sat Karam down and made some Turkish coffee and offered him some Baklava.

He told the Professor his story and started to tremble when he talked about the Mukhabarat and what had happened to Nabil. The Professor was clearly shocked that such an educated man should have gone through such trauma.

"I am so sorry my friend for the things you have been though. I will do everything I can to help. What can I do for you?"

"I am trying to get to England. I have been offered a post at The London School of Economics, but it has taken so long to get the papers in order that I am in danger of losing the position, I must get to England and apply for political asylum. I think with the job offer I will be able to stay."

"Can we apply for you from here?" asked Altan.

"We can try, but I have less than three months to be in England before the job offer is taken away, I don't think I have the luxury of sitting around in Ankara waiting to see what the British Government decide, I have already been trying for over a year."

"Yes, I see what you mean. Let us try again today to see what they say from here at the University, and then we can make alternative plans if there is no progress." Professor Polat arranged for another senior graduate to take his class for the day and then put in motion some calls to the Home Office in London. After eight frustrating hours he concluded with Karam that nothing was going to happen in the near future, if at all. There seemed to be an unwillingness to move his application along, that it was much easier to say no, rather than look at each case on its merits.

That evening, Altan took Karam back to his home in the suburbs of Ankara to have dinner with his family. Karam told his story again to the professor's wife and three grown up children who were all shocked and upset. Of course, they knew about the Syrian Civil War and the refugees but to hear it brought to life by such an educated man who had lost so much was truly shocking.

After dinner Altan showed Karam to his wardrobe and found some new clothes for him to wear. They were of a similar build and size, Karam a little taller. He insisted that Karam take two of his suits as he would appear more credible on his journey and in front of the British authorities. He also gave him some new shoes which Karam was so thankful for, getting shoes had been such a problem for so long.

That night Karam was given his own bedroom with clean sheets, the smell of Jasmin wafting in from the garden. He slept the whole night, for the first time in a long while.

The next morning at breakfast, Altan made a suggestion.

"Do you think it would be easier for you to drive across Europe? A smartly dressed man in a reasonable car might attract less suspicion. I can give you my Mercedes. It is old but reliable. I also have my passport. We can change the photo for one of you. We can take one here at home and photoshop it."

"But what would happen if I got caught, you would be in a lot of trouble?" asked Karam

"I googled the journey; it says it is a 33 hour drive. You would have to stop on the way, but if you could make the journey in 48 hours, I would report the theft of the car with my passport and wallet inside the glove compartment. You could use my credit card to buy fuel and food along the way. I will say the car had been locked in my garage and was stolen. I hadn't planned on using it for a few days so didn't realise it had been taken. I will say that I always leave the keys above the visor."

"What can I say Altan, but thank you, thank you so much. If I make it, it will be thanks to you, and I will repay you," said Karam.

"Brother, we must help one another, what has happened to you seemed an impossibility, but what we have learned is that it could happen to any of us. Turkey may seem stable right now, but who knows what may happen in the future. We have packed some food and things for you for the journey. There are also some medical masks that you will have to wear in many countries because of the CoronaVirus, you don't want to bring any additional suspicion on yourself, in fact it may help you as people in the West don't want to get too close to anyone at the moment because of the Coronavirus".

"I can't thank you enough. You have been so kind to me, you and your family."

"Good luck my friend, I hope the next time I hear from you it will be when you are safely in England. When you get settled, I will come over to visit you, who knows, I might drive the car back," Altan laughed.

"Ok, let us get started, I need to take your photo for the passport, stand against that blank wall." They spent the next hour taking the photo, adjusting it on the computer and replacing Altan's photo in the passport with the new one of Karam. Karam was younger than Altan but they were both hoping that the passport would only get a cursory glance at customs.

"I think it is time my friend." They embraced, then Altan led Karam to the garage, opened the door and handed him the keys. You have the passport, a couple of credit cards and this, He handed Karam some Turkish Lira notes and three hundred euros." Be careful and good luck.

Karam got into the car, plugged his phone in to charge and to get directions, and pulled out of the drive. He had not driven a car for some time, but it quickly came back to him. He could see Altan waving goodbye in the rear mirror. In the tragedy of war and flight, he thought about the kindness he had found from the fellow refugees at the camps and of the Polats, who had taken him in. He felt energised and determined to make the journey, get to Britain and to be reunited with his family.

Crossing the border from Turkey to Greece at Alexandroupoli was quite simple and they waved Karam through. He had been incredibly nervous about this and had not taken a break apart from refuelling, and some food since leaving Ankara. Once in Greece, he pulled over down a quiet road and got some sleep. A few hours later he drove on to Igoumenitsa and caught a ferry to Ancona in Italy. From there Karam drove north through Italy, Bologna, Milan and across the border into France and on to Nice. He thought if he took a more tourist trail it might draw less attention to him. He also knew Nice from having visited it as a student, he had been a rarity, studying French whilst at school in Damascus. He parked and sat on the pebbly beach at the Promenade des Anglais. He called Jamal who answered immediately.

"Where are you Karam?"

"I am in France, on the Riviera," he replied.

They talked about their future and Karam spoke to his daughter. He felt lightened. Everything was going very well. He continued his journey up through France and only forty hours after leaving Ankara, found himself in Calais. He bought a ticket for him and his car online, through his phone, paying with Altan's card, it all went through. He joined the queue for the ferry and passport control. He had a stolen Turkish passport, his own Syrian passport and was driving a stolen Turkish car. He hoped his fear did not give him away. He put on his mask as everyone else was wearing one. Unknown to him, a new variant of Covid had recently been discovered that was more transmissible, causing higher case numbers, and everyone was on edge and wary.

As he got nearer, the road split into two, one for EU and the other for non-EU citizens. He pulled across to the non-EU and pulled up behind one car with Rumanian plates and another with Polish. They edged forwards. His turn came and he pulled up to the window. He tried to pass across the Turkish passport but the inspector told him to hold it there and to open it up so he could see. He was five feet away.

"Why are you going to the UK" he asked.

"I have been invited by The London School of Economics to be a visiting Professor for a term" Karam said and held up a letter on LSE headed notepaper. The Customs officer lent forwards and cast an eye over the document.

"Length of stay" he asked abruptly.

"Three months" replied Karam.

He paused, the official peered over his mask and looked Karam up and down. Without a word he waved him on.

Karam's heart was racing. He went to pull away and stalled, quickly started the car again and drove on. He sat in the queue for the ferry for half an hour and composed himself. After everything that had happened, he could not believe how simple it had been. He just had to get across the Channel into the UK.

The incoming ferry docked, lowered its ramps and the cars started to drive off. Once unloaded, Karam and the other vehicles were waved on. Once onboard, he locked the car and went upstairs into the ship. He bought a coffee and a hot meal and went and sat on his own away from everyone else. It was a moment of relaxation. Although he knew he still had a hard part to come, he felt normal, dressed in a suit, eating a hot meal in safety. Sat there in the café, with other people around, he was part of humanity, doing ordinary things even if what he was about to do was quite extraordinary, he had not felt like this for years. The crossing felt like an eternity. He returned to his car, and in line with everyone else drove off the ferry. Approaching customs, he started to panic, he could feel himself sweating and trembling, what if he had come this far to be stopped at the last hurdle? The cars were all passing through, there was no one there, everyone was driving on, it could not be that simple, surely somebody would stop him. He carried on up to the customs area, and still there was no one appeared. He drove through and within minutes was out of the port and on the roads in Dover. He continued until he found a place where he could stop. He pulled over, turned the engine off and screamed. He text Jamal with the word 'Safe'. She replied with three kisses.

He had not really thought too much about what he would do next. Here he was in the UK, illegally. Yes, he had a letter of invitation and a job offer from a prestigious UK University, but he did not know what their reaction would be once they found out he had entered the country illegally. Should he go to them and plead for mercy or turn himself over to the authorities and take his chances? He sat for over an hour deliberating what to do next, trying to second guess from what little information he had what the British police might do. He knew it could not be as bad as dealing with the army in the refugee camp in Turkey, but always in his mind the most important thing was for all the family to be together somewhere safe.

Karam decided to stick to his original plan. He drove to London and met a cousin who had fled Syria seven years earlier when it was much easier to get asylum in the UK. He was thrilled to see him and gave him a bed and dinner. His house was in Muswell Hill, he had since carved out a successful career as a Neurosurgeon at St Thomas's Hospital. It was fantastic to be reunited with family and they spent the evening reminiscing about life in Syria before the struggles. He told them what had happened to Nabil and how he hoped that Jamal and Amira would be able to join him one day.

His cousin said he could stay for as long as he needed, and to use his home as his address for which he was most grateful. That night he telephoned Jamal to let her know he was safe and with family, then he called Altan Polat and told him about his journey and everything that had happened so that he could report the theft of his car and passport. Altan changed his mind. The story about the theft would have only come into play if Karam had been caught. Instead, he told him to put his credit cards and passport into an envelope and send them to him by DHL. He said not to worry about the car for now, they would sort something out later, but it might be best to get the car registered in the UK at some stage.

The following day he packaged up the items to send to Altan, looked up a DHL office and dropped them off. Then he went to Hatton Garden where he spent the whole day getting the best price for his family jewellery. He would have got a much better price if he had a bank account, but he had to take cash, even so, he got almost £13,000, enough to make a fresh start. He thanked his grandmother for the heirlooms that would give his family the opportunity of a future and safety. The following day he made calls to the University, the Home Office and started looking for accommodation.

His visit to The University went very well. He could not tell them the whole truth which he hated, regarding his status in the UK, but they seemed happy enough and asked him to start straight away as one other professor was about to leave on maternity leave. That afternoon he went to Croydon to The Home Office screening unit where he went through his first interview as an immigrant. It was a daunting prospect but as an educated man with perfect English and a letter from The London School of Economics, he was treated well. He did not require any accommodation; they were impressed when they substantiated his claim that he was staying with a highly respected neurosurgeon. He also did not require any financial assistance. They gave him a date for his Substantive Interview six weeks thereafter and issued him with temporary papers.

Karam returned to Muswell Hill feeling the most positive that he had done in years. if he could qualify for asylum, he would be able to ask if his family could join him, it all seemed to be going better than he hoped.

He settled in quickly at the LSE. His students were keen but perhaps not as attentive as those back in Damascus, and his colleagues were friendly although he could tell they were all tired and jaded from the changes in circumstance they were experiencing as University staff. He thought that the financial package was excellent, but then again, he had barely earned any money for years. The other University staff complained bitterly all the time that their wages were falling under the weight of inflation and that they were not getting any wage rises because of the austerity to try and bring the National debt down, that had been out of control for years.

Karam was happy to have some routine and normality in his life. He was keen to get a place of his own but thought it best to stay at the same address until he had passed his Home Office Interview. The six weeks passed quickly, he spoke to his family twice a day, joined the University five a side football league and explored London. He also got in touch with various Syrian Refugee groups in London. Some were still activists; others were just looking to recover after all the trauma they had been through and wanted to share their stories with other Syrians. He remained cautious amongst these groups, aware that they would be watched by the British Authorities and may contain plants put there by the Assad Secret Service.

His date for his Substantive Interview arrived, he wore his newly dry-cleaned suit, shirt, and tie. He had been offered an online interview but felt he would do better in person. He returned to the same offices in Croydon. He was interviewed by a panel of three, all wearing masks sat behind a large Perspex screen with each officer separated from one another by more Perspex. Karam arrived in plenty of time and declined any legal representation. The interview went very well, he was an extremely credible applicant. He showed them his injuries he had sustained at the refugee camp, explained about the threat from the Mukhabarat, and had pictures on his phone of his son Nabil. He had also kept articles and pieces of news he had seen online from the Assad regime about their desire to capture him. His case was very compelling. They said they would be in touch within four weeks but less than ten days later Karam received a visit from a Home Office official to tell him he was being granted political asylum subject to a twelve month probation. Of course, he was delighted at being allowed to stay but was also disappointed that he would not be able to submit a proposal for his family for at least a year. He called Jamal to let her know. He could hear the disappointment in her voice, but then she rationalised it and said that one more year would not be too much to bear if they could all be together.

Now the time seemed to drag. Karam tried to immerse himself in work and life in London, but he found it difficult, all he wanted to do was to be reunited with his family, but they just had to wait for the year to go by and his probation period to finish. He took to praying, wishing for Allah to intervene and show kindness on him and his family. A new Professor arrived at The University working on a part time basis whom Karam took under his wing. Charlie Wilson had only just completed his PhD and managed to secure a part time teaching job. Karam took to him immediately, he was a kind and considerate young man. They would have coffee or lunch together and talk about all kind of issues going on in the world. He was interested and therefore interesting, but Karam never gave much away. He remained intensely private and did not like to discuss what he had been through. He did not mention his family and kept information about himself to a minimum.

The probation period came to an end. It was March 2026. It felt as though it had taken an eternity. Karam immediately made an application for his wife and daughter to join him in London. He had by now secured his own flat in The Elephant and Castle and had been working at the LSE for almost 15 months. He had savings and had been offered a contract by his new employer, but still his application was turned down. Many more applications were also turned down and each one seemed to take so long in the system when disaster struck. On July 9th, 2027 war was declared with China and life changed forever. The removal of foreign citizens who were now declared as enemies of Great Britain was taking up all the resources of the Home Office. Existing approved applications for asylum or even just immigration were put on hold. In a very frank conversation with a lady at the Home Office that Karam had got to know very well over the years, she told him that the chances of getting his family into the UK were extremely slim, almost non-existent. The Government was trying to determine who its allies and who its enemies were. His family were listed as displaced people and whilst in ordinary times the British Government would look sympathetically upon family members, times had changed.

Karam pleaded that if the Home Office had not taken so long, they would be here by now, but it fell on deaf ears. There was a National Emergency and foreign citizens were at the bottom of a long list of things to do. This had been coming for some time. the Foreign Aid budget had been cut from £15bn in 2010 to £10 bn in 2021. By 2025 it had completely disappeared. The United Kingdom was not the global power it had once been and like America, was becoming more inward looking. Its attitude towards all refugees was getting tougher and less sympathetic.

It broke his heart when he called Jamal that afternoon. She tried to sound positive, but he could hear in her voice that she was broken. For fourteen years their lives had been disrupted, no place to call home, constantly on the move, living in camps, separated by circumstance, distance and the loss of their son Nabil.

Karam put his phone away and went straight into a pub. He had never had a drink as a Muslim, but now he felt abandoned and cast adrift. He had tried everything he could, to do the right thing, but his God was not helping him. It was at that point he realised that for him, God did not exist, there was no God anywhere, that it was all an elaborate story to give people hope, but now he had run out of hope, now, he knew it was down to him and him alone, no God was going to come and help. He drank, beer and vodka and wine until he was sick and staggered home to his flat.

Karam thought about what to do for the next couple of months considering all options including returning to his family in Lebanon. One Monday morning in his favourite coffee shop close to the University he picked up his newspaper and read the story about migrants who had landed on the Isle of White on a boat from Nigeria. It made him think.

His best friend from school was head of the mission at the Syrian Embassy in Abuja in Nigeria. If he could get Jamal and Amira to Nigeria, perhaps he could get them on a boat from Nigeria to the UK. He knew that the Nigerian Navy was being used for the journey to the UK. He felt sure that if he could get them on to British soil, the authorities would be only too pleased to get his family off their hands if he was there to take them.

Karam looked at the options for travel to get his family into Nigeria. He looked at boats, trains and even getting them a vehicle to drive there, but then he had an idea. He searched for the number of the Syrian Embassy in Nigeria and rang Ebrahim, his school friend and explained everything that had happened. It was risky for Ebrahim to even be speaking to Karam as he was on a list of interesting people to the Mukhabarat, but they went back such a long way and had been like brothers. They had hardly spoken since the Civil War started but like all great school friends, they were able to pick up straight away. Ebrahim was also a father of two girls and was very sympathetic to Karam. It had been high risk to even call him, he did not know if Ebrahim was the same person he knew all those years ago, but Ebrahim wanted to help. He offered to send a letter from the Embassy for Jamal and Amira to grant diplomatic passage into Nigeria. This meant that Karam could potentially get them on a direct flight from Beirut to Abuja.

Jamal was naturally apprehensive about this plan but trusted her husband. She wanted to wait a few months because Amira was now 12 years old and had friends and was studying, also, she did not have a passport. Ebrahim helped with this and after some clever forging by some teenagers in the camp, they were ready to go.

Jamal had to plan an exit from the camp and get to Beirut. Although after many years, people in the camp were able to come and go, nobody was just allowed to leave so they would have to plan their departure and keep it secret. Eventually the time came. Karam had sent through the airline tickets and some money. Jamal and Amira had a farewell dinner with their closest friends and some family members at the camp. Jamal had wanted to say goodbye to everyone at the field hospital she had help create over the years, but she knew she could not. She had told them she was having a few days off. That morning they both walked out of the refugee camp in the Beqaa valley as though they were going for a walk as they had done on a few occasions the previous few months so as not to attract suspicion. One mile down the road a pre-booked taxi pulled up and drove them the hour and 45 minutes into Beirut. Amira was astonished at the taxi, the landscape and then Beirut. Her only memories were of refugee camps and the small world she had inhabited. Beirut was like a fairy-tale to her, Jamal asked the driver to cruise around the centre of Beirut for half an hour for Amira to take it all in. Jamal asked the driver to stop and they bought some food, things that Amira had never tasted before. She was so happy and excited.

They drove on to the airport, Jamal's heart was pumping as they checked in. They only had two small suitcases that had been given to them at the camp. They had tried to repair them and make them look as smart as possible; friends had also given them clothes so that they looked like International travellers. As they approached the customs desk and passport control, Jamal felt her legs wobble. Amira held her hand tightly. She was questioned by the female officer.

"Syrians, "she said.

"Yes," replied Jamal, my daughter and I.

"Why are you going to Nigeria?"

"Work," she replied, at The Embassy, and passed across the letter that Ebrahim had sent to her.

"Well, good luck with the new job and enjoy your time in Nigeria, you too, little girl, look after Mummy," she said.

And with that they were through. Jamal's heart was still racing but she was euphoric. As sad as she was to leave her home, life had been hard for her and her daughter. This was just the first step but perhaps they would be reunited with Karam and be a family again soon.

The flight was with Turkish airlines and took five and a half hours. After the initial excitement, Amira slept almost the whole way. Jamal did wake her for some food, she was tired and needed the rest. Jamal wanted to sleep but could not, she was turning everything over in her mind and wondering what lay ahead for them and if they would see Karam again.

She was so relieved to be finally out of the camp, but it had become familiar, it was her home and the people there had become her family, but she missed Karam. It had been so long, sometimes she had to look at his photo to remind herself of what he looked like. They had spoken almost every day since he left the refugee camp, but it was not the same as having him there. She long to be hugged, she had missed that, and she longed to see Amira in his arms. As she thought about it, she could not help but cry, out of happiness as well as sadness for the wasted years. She hoped that this was the start of their new life together. Karam had told her so much about life in London, sometimes he would walk around London with his phone, showing her and Amira Big Ben, St Pauls and the shops in Oxford Street. His apartment was small, but it would be home to the three of them.

The plane landed in Abuja. It was nine o'clock at night and dark. They passed through customs and collected their bags. As they emerged, there stood a very smart man in a suit holding a sign saying, 'Jamal and Amira Shahid'. Jamal burst into tears.

Ebrahim hugged Jamal and greeted Amira. He took their small bags, led them out of the airport and towards his white Mercedes parked close by. He paid for a parking ticket, put the bags in the boot and they got inside. He gave them both a bottle of water and some fruit.

"Where are we going now?" asked Jamal.

"You are going to come home with me, you will meet my family, I have two daughters, both close to Amira's age." He replied.

They drove for thirty minutes and approached a house surrounded by a high wall with security gates. As Ebrahim pulled up, a guard came through the door to meet them. He pulled back the gates and they drove in. The car pulled up outside a single storey white building. There were gardens outside with a fountain, swings and a trampoline. Two women and the young girls came out of the house to meet them. Three of them looked middle eastern and one was African.

Jamal and her daughter were welcomed by Iman, Ebrahim's wife, and his two daughters Rima and Fatima. The African lady was their housekeeper who had a tray with some glasses on, with sweet tea and baklava. Amira was very shy, but Rima and Fatima took her by the hand, "Come on Amira, come and see your room."

Amira looked at her mother who nodded. "Go ahead Amira, have fun!"

She disappeared into the house with the other two girls.

"As Salaam Malaikum," said Iman and gave Jamal a hug.

"Wa Alaykum as-salam," she replied.

"You must be so tired, has it been a difficult journey," asked Iman.

"Do you mean today or since the war started?" replied Jamal. She immediately regretted saying it as soon as the words left her lips. Not only was it rude when these people were showing her and her daughter such incredible kindness but also because it would be dangerous to question anything to do with the war to an officer of the Assad regime.

"I meant today, but I know you have been through a lot. We had so wanted to leave Syria too, but it was impossible. Ebrahim had his career in Government service." Iman lowered her voice and turned to one side so the housekeeper could not see her speak.

"We didn't agree with what Assad was doing, but by then the secret police were watching everyone. We could have done what your family did, but we just did not have the courage. We stayed where we were. When the Syrian Day of Rage happened in March 2011, it was considered civil unrest, nobody thought it would become Civil War. Ebrahim was just doing his job. At one stage it looked as though we had made a terrible mistake as the war closed in on Damascus. We thought the Assad family was going to flee Syria, and we would have been left to face the rebels, being on the wrong side. Then the Russians got involved and turned the fortunes round for the Assad family.

In 2018 a position came up here in Nigeria. We didn't want the girls to leave Syria, but we heard that the Mukhabarat were looking into Ebrahim. He had already helped some Syrian refugees with documentation. He tried to do his best as a human being. Nothing is as simple as it looks. Ebrahim has taken a great risk helping you and your family, he always talks about Karam and would do whatever he can to help him. This is a big risk for us, you understand?"

"Yes, I understand" said Jamal, "we really appreciate what you are doing for us. It has been difficult for everyone."

"We have told all of our staff that you are my cousin visiting from Damascus and Amira must say the same and there must be no mention of the Civil War or refugee camps. Ebrahim is second in charge at the Embassy, he does not think his boss would be sympathetic to your cause so we must keep your visit as low profile as possible. Neither of you will be able to leave this compound while you are here, do you understand?" said Iman.

"Yes, I understand, we will not be any trouble."

Iman introduced Jamal to Maalika, the family housekeeper who showed her to her room. Amira was there with the other girls.

"Look Mummy," said Amira, "What a beautiful room, with beds and clean sheets, I am so happy."

"That's wonderful Amira. Girls would you let us both unpack please" said Jamal.

The girls turned around and left. Jamal closed the door. She sat Amira on the bed beside her and took her hands. She explained what Iman had said and explained the difficult situation with Ebrahim, the war, which sides the two families were on, his situation at the embassy and everything. She knew it was a lot for her daughter to take in, but Amira was much more worldly wise than most girls her age, she had already lived a full life and experienced so much more. Amira nodded, said she understood and would be careful what she said. She hugged her mother tightly; Jamal could feel the stress pouring out of her.

They both took a shower, with hot water, a novelty for them, with soap and shampoo, they dressed and joined the family for dinner.

Jamal had prepared a Syrian meal of hummus, babaghanouj, a salad and kibbeh. It was delicious and reminded Jamal of how good life had been in Syria before the War. They drank wine and talked about life in Damascus before the conflict and laughed, something Jamal could not remember doing for a long time.
Just before they went to bed, Iman said that she would find some clothes for both Jamal and Amira. Jamal had tried so hard to keep them both looking reasonable, but their clothes were old and threadbare, even the ones they had been given when they left the refugee camp. Ebrahim also said that they would talk in the morning about their journey to the UK.

That night Amira fell asleep in her mothers' arms in a bed with clean sheets and comfy pillows for the first time in her brief life. While she slept Jamal telephoned Karam and told him everything that had happened. There was only one hour's time difference so there was no problem ringing him at 11 o'clock at night. They spoke excitedly about being together again and told each other how much they had missed one another. It all seemed so real and possible after so much waiting.

The following morning Ebrahim explained to Jamal that he was working on getting passage for the two of them on board one of the many vessels that were regularly taking refugees, but it could take some time and would cost a lot of money, perhaps as much as $10,000, he was making enquiries but had to be careful, then left for work.

Amira spent the day playing with Rima and Fatima, Jamal talked with Iman and slept in the hammock in the garden. When Ebrahim returned home she was eager to find out what was happening.

Ebrahim told her that the demand for places was extremely high due to Coronavirus and the various wars that were breaking out all over Africa due to Chinese interventions and disruptions. He had a lot of insider political information. He said that he had considered trying to get them on a direct flight from Abuja to England, but since war had broken out, it was impossible to get any valid documents to enter the UK, and Nigeria was one of the countries that the UK had banned even though Nigeria had not signed any peace treaties or allegiances with China and her allies. The problem was that in the decade leading up to the outbreak of war China had invested heavily in Nigerian infrastructure as well as Nigerian manufacturing employing over one million Nigerians making consumer goods for the growing middle classes. This had been Chinese policy for the previous two decades, not giving foreign aid, instead Chinese businesses invested and created close ties with countries, a much more hands-on approach which was now paying dividends, and Nigeria also relied on China as a market for its natural resources.

He told her not to get her hopes up too high, that it could take some time, and it did. It was almost a year before Ebrahim was able to secure a place on a vessel. Karam had raised the money and wired it out to him who had converted it into dollars, which he drew out in small amounts over the coming weeks to avoid suspicion. In October 2028 he told Jamal and Amira to prepare themselves for the journey which might happen anytime in the next few weeks. Every evening when Ebrahim returned home Jamal would be waiting inside the gates only to hear that there was no news. Then on the 2nd of November he came home early and told them that they would be sailing on the tide that night. They packed their little cases and said goodbye to Iman and the girls. Iman gave Jamal a basket with food and a knife." Take care Jamal, Allah Ma'ak."

Ebrahim drove them both the two-hour drive to Lagos. He took the coast road to the port, and just outside, he pulled the car into a layby.

"Jamal, Amira, this is as far as I can go. I had not told you this because I didn't want you to worry, but my boss Mohammed Hussein has become very suspicious. He knew you were staying with us and kept asking why you had been there so long and what you were doing. I found out that he had made enquiries about Karam. As you know, Karam had been speaking out against the regime. I think he has been watching me, he knows about this vessel leaving tonight, he may be here trying to catch me. But do not worry, I have arranged for someone to meet you to get you on board. Follow this road for five hundred yards, you will see a sign for the naval stores. Turn left there and walk two hundred yards which will bring you to the edge of the port area. There will be a metal gate. Knock on it twice, pause and twice again. A man will meet you there. Give him this envelope. He will take you to the ship. Give the man on the gangway this piece of paper and this envelope which has the other half of the money for your passage. The journey will be 12 days. You have the food that Iman gave you. Assume that you will not be given any food during the journey and eek out what you have, it will be a bonus if you are given food. There should be plenty of water but take this money in case you have to bribe someone. Keep yourselves to yourselves. You don't have to worry about the other refugees although some of them may have the Covid-28, it is the smugglers you need to be wary of. Always keep your knife by your side, they will always target the easiest victim.

"Why would they attack us, we have nothing?" asked Jamal.

"You are still a young woman and so is Amira, just keep the knife with you and keep alert."

"Thank you for everything that you have done for us, I hope one day we can repay your kindness" said Jamal and she gave Ebrahim a long hug. Amira joined in and squeezed him tight, he had been so kind to them and shown love and affection.

Ebrahim was starting to cry. He got back in the car and watched them walk down the road with their little cases as he pulled away. He knew he had done all he could, and now they were in the hands of Allah.

Amira pointed to the sign that said 'Naval Stores'. It was written in English which was the prominent language in Nigeria. They followed the sign and came to the metal door in a wall and banged on it twice, then twice again. A young Nigerian man in jeans and T shirt opened the door. They handed him an envelope. He opened it, counted the money and beckoned them to follow him.

They walked one hundred yards to a pick-up truck and got in. He drove along the quayside past a container ship, a dredger and a couple of other large craft. At the end was a grey modern battleship, quite big with a lot of people queuing to get on board, there were two gangplanks going into the hull of the vessel.

"You see the man with the clipboard in the orange jacket? "he asked.

"Yes, I can see him," said Jamal.

"They call him Luke. See him, give him the money and your letter. Say nothing else to him and keep your daughter close. Do not look at him. Good luck to both of you."

They alighted, grabbed their bags and starting walking towards the ship, joining a queue of people, all races, a mixture of men and women, more men though and younger, seeking a better life and opportunities, some children with their mothers, only a few older people. They approached the top of the gangplank; Jamal could see the man they called Luke. It was their turn, they stepped forwards, Amira was holding on to her mother's arm tightly. She handed the envelope over to him along with the letter. He opened the envelope and passed it to another man who started counting. Luke read the letter and looked up at Jamal and then down to Amira. He smiled showing the most perfect set of teeth, very expensive shiny white teeth were what Jamal noticed. The man handed the envelope back and he waived them on. As they passed him, he said.
"I shall come and see you later to make sure you are settling in."

Jamal shivered. The way he said it frightened her. They boarded and took the stairs to the top deck. From this vantage point they could see down over the side to where more people were queuing to get on board. She heard raised voices and saw an argument ensuing between Luke and a young man. Luke's muscleman was waiving an envelope. Luke grabbed it and threw it in the air. Some notes flew out and started fluttering down to the quayside with some falling in the water. The young man was protesting and aimed a punch at Luke. The big man with Luke hit the younger man with a truncheon across the head. He toppled over the side and fell twenty feet; his head made a sickening thud as it hit a metal bollard and he bounced into the water between the ship and the quay. He did not resurface. Everyone on the gangplank, along the quayside and on the vessel looking over were shocked. They had all gasped together and started screaming. Luke shouted at everyone to shut up. He shouted out that anyone who tried to cheat him, or did not have enough money would get the same treatment, but that if you paid the money, were quiet and no trouble, then in two weeks you would be in England.

Two young men who had been waiting on the quayside slipped out of the back of the queue and headed off. Amira was sobbing holding on to Jamal who was herself trembling, but she tried to be strong for her daughter.

"Amira, in just a couple of weeks we will be in England with Daddy. We will have our own flat, you will be able to go to a school with English children, make new friends and have a new life. We only have a little more to get through. Let's go and find somewhere to sleep and make home for the next two weeks." Jamal took one more look at Luke and then headed inside with Amira. They made their way below and found a bulkhead where Jamal put their bags and unpacked two blankets. She gave Amira some water and a piece of cake, and they sat huddled together.

Ebrahim had been right, there was no offer of food in the first few days but there was a plentiful supply of fresh water. Jamal could not understand why they were on a naval warship being smuggled into the UK. She met a teacher from Angola called Kapano, who was trying to escape the Civil war and genocide there. He told her that the Chinese were pitting people against one another and de-stabilising his homeland and the surrounding countries, that Covid was getting worse, and was being transmitted in all sorts of ways. His parents had both been murdered and he feared for his life, so he fled, catching a ride up through Angola, Congo and Cameroon until he reached Nigeria. He had heard about ships heading to the UK. He knew from friends how difficult it was to get into Europe from Libya or Algeria, and the gangs on the coast there were brutal with many people enslaved. He thought he would get to Nigeria to see what his options were. He had found somewhere to stay and made lots of enquiries until he secured a place here today on this vessel. He had asked lots of questions and heard about the trips that Luke was organising. He told Jamal that the man liked to be called Luke because he had seen the film with Paul Newman as 'Cool Hand Luke' and fancied himself like that character. His real name was Adebeyi Salisu. He was married to the middle daughter of the President of Nigeria. He had been in the army and had the rank of Lieutenant Colonel. He was only a second Lieutenant when he met the President's daughter but was quickly promoted.

When war broke out and Africa descended into chaos, he and his father-in-law saw an opportunity to make some hard currency from people smuggling. The President ensured that all the right people were involved. Luke had already made two successful trips, one to Portugal and one to Spain. Each carried more than five hundred people and with an average of $10,000 per person, it was good business. This trip was going to England, to the south coast near Devon.

Jamal asked how they would get ashore as this was too big a craft to get close by and dock. Kapano said that they would board landing craft that would bring them in close to the beaches and that this would be done at night. Jamal could tell that Kapano was a good man and they spent time over the next couple of days talking. He was wonderful with Amira, giving her some lessons in mathematics, history and English.

On the seventh day Jamal was asleep when she felt a hand on her arm. She looked up to see Luke and one of his thugs next to him. She sat up and went to scream. Luke put his hand over her mouth and wagged his finger. Jamal tried to struggle free, but the other man was holding her legs. Amira woke up and started to scream. Luke went to put his hand over her mouth but freed Jamal just enough to bite him on the hand, he yelped, released Jamal who grabbed her knife and pushed it up to Luke's throat. Just as she did this, people started coming down the corridor to see what was happening. Luke stood up and backed away.

"Nothing happening here, he said, everyone back to bed, just a misunderstanding" he looked at Jamal and wagged his finger and left. Jamal sat trembling holding Amira. Kapano and another man also from Angola, sat beside the two trembling women, and that is how it remained for the rest of the journey, with various members of this flotsam of refugees taking it in turns to look after Jamal who had become popular on board as the only doctor, always willing to help anyone.

Jamal stayed on permanent alert and did not sleep well, but they were not troubled again. The journey was tough, but the refugees became quite resourceful, finding some line, and fishing over the side of the vessel. They cooked what they caught and shared it, supplementing their meals by things they were able to steal from the crew's mess and stores. Jamal was thankful for Ebrahim's foresight to provide them with enough food to last the journey. They were hungry but they were safe, and it was only a few days until they would be reunited after many years separated from Karam.

They were told by Luke that there was just one more day's full sailing, that they would approach British waters at night and then ferry them into shore. They were going to land in a place called Mousehole. They had chosen their sailing to coincide with the New Moon when the sky would be at its darkest. They were informed that the landing craft would get as close as possible to land, and when they were in shallow waters, the ramp would drop down and they should get out and wade onto the beach as fast as possible. Once there they should split up and make their own way inland.

Jamal sent a text to Karam. They had already agreed a code, and now he knew it was going to be a landing at night tomorrow. He had been waiting for days for the message. When it arrived he sprung into action. He hired a van, let the University know that he was not feeling very well and would take the rest of the week off and set off along the M4. It was a six-hour drive and he arrived in the middle of the afternoon, parked along the coast, went for a walk and waited.

Jamal and Amira were below deck when they heard shots coming from their ship firing at something. Everyone started panicking. More shots were fired, and they felt the ship change direction. They heard the clatter as men started running down the stairs. Luke was shouting at them, but Jamal could not hear what he was saying as more and more rounds were being fired off. There was complete panic as the vessel lurched from side to side picking up speed. Kapano came and found them and gave them both life jackets and told them to put them on.

"What's happening" Amira asked, absolutely petrified

"There's another warship close by, and the Captain has started firing on them," he said.

"Which ship, which navy?" asked Jamal, but before he could reply there was a tremendous explosion above them, which rocked the whole boat. The lights went out and the hold was filled with smoke and fire. They were below the waterline and water started rushing in. The boat began to list immediately. The firing was continuing, and they could hear screams. The sirens started wailing, the water was rising quickly.

"Quick, we have to get out of here, put these on, leave your things. Kapano pulled the orange life vest over Amira's head and tied it at the side. She looked down at the upside-down writing and could make out it said 'NNS Aradu'.

Everyone rushed for the stairs to get out, water was coming in very fast. As they got closer to the foot of the stairs, they could see the figure of Luke at the top who held a gun and shot the two refugees closest to the top. They fell back down the stairs on top of people trying to escape, they all fell to the bottom. He looked down through the door and then closed it. It was the last ray of light. They were now in pitch darkness. Two young men found their way to the top of the stairs and shouted down.

"It's locked, he's locked it from the other side". One of them shone the torch from his phone on the door and looked for any kind of way of opening it but to no avail.

"What shall we do Kapano? "asked Jamal, and just then they felt the explosion as another missile hit the vessel and exploded. It was very sudden and everybody in the hold was killed instantaneously. The ship was now ripped apart and sank within minutes taking almost all the refugees down with her.

The crew and a few of the refugees who had been on deck, some with lifejackets, others clinging on to debris were now in the water. HMS Dauntless closed in on the wreckage and started pulling the survivors out, they were given blankets, and sat together on deck, all under the watchful eye of the armed crew of The Dauntless. They spent five hours picking the survivors from the sea and scanning the area before steaming into Plymouth.

It was the 8 o'clock news that announced the attack on HMS Dauntless and the sinking of the NNS Aradu. Karam had been asleep in the van and had just awoken. He only just caught the headline but then had a news alert on his phone. His face was ashen, and he started to tremble. He dialled the number and waited. There was no answer from Jamal's phone. He heard that the Dauntless was sailing into Plymouth with survivors. He turned the van around and picked up speed joining the A30. He tried to keep to the speed limit not wanting to draw any unnecessary attention to himself, but it was difficult, he just had to get there to see if his wife and daughter were amongst the survivors. It was two hours before he pulled into the docks. He could not get inside as the port was now militarised and heavily guarded. There were civilians and press everywhere, news stations and media agencies. He parked and headed for the gatehouse.

"Excuse me, excuse me, is there a list of the survivors available yet?" he asked of the guard behind the glass

"No list yet, who are you?" he replied.

Karam slipped back in the throng of people and waited quietly at the back. He tried ringing Jamal's phone three more times in some forlorn hope that she would just answer to tell him that they were here and to come and get them. He longed to hold them both, to have them in his arms and to put the nightmare of all these years behind them, to start life afresh, with hope and a future as they had planned.

Karam crouched down against a wall and put his head in his hands. Time just stopped still. Two hours went by and no list was produced. Karam walked around the edge of the base and decided to find some higher ground or perhaps a building where he might be able to see something. There was an administration building on the other side of the road. He walked in through the front doors. There was nobody in the reception area so he took the stairs and walked as far as he could go. On the top floor he found his way onto the roof. Fortunately, the door was open. He walked to the edge of the building and looked across. Six floors up he had a much better view of the dock and could see HMS Dauntless moored. There were people sitting on the dockside being guarded, they were all in rows. He squinted and trained his eyes, as he did so he could just about make out men and women. He started to scan up and down the rows. They were predominantly the crew of the vessel, mostly wearing uniform. As his eyes got used to the floodlights and the distance, he could start to determine who were civilians, those who might have been the refugees. There were not too many of them and they were also mostly men. He could not see Jamal or Amira. There was only one young girl and it was not his daughter.

Lorries started to pull up and the prisoners were loaded into them, this gave him the opportunity to see them move and determine if any of them were his family. As the last lorry pulled out Karam slumped on the roof. Jamal and Amira were not there. It was possible that they had already been taken or were in a building, but he knew he was clinging on to some forlorn hope. The news had said that a lot of refugees had gone down with the vessel. He had not heard from Jamal, but her phone could have got soaked in the water. He knew that there would be no manifest handed over to the British, most of the people on board that boat were illegals trying to smuggle into the UK. Some of the bodies might wash up, but they would not be identified, at that moment Karam knew he would never see his family again, but he could not bring himself to leave. The ship he saw was the last place they had been, and he felt he wanted to stay close by, and even though he knew they had gone, he still held some flicker of hope that they would suddenly appear, and that they would all be together. Karam stayed in Plymouth, between his van and the roof for the next two days. Finally, on Sunday afternoon he resigned himself to the facts and drove back to London. He was numb and empty. Everything he had done, struggling against all the odds to get to England and start a life that he could share with his family, his son murdered by Assad's men, his wife and daughter murdered by the British Navy. He was consumed by grief and tormented by blame.

He arrived in London, dropped the van off and went back to his flat. He saw the flowers on the table, the family pictures, everything he had prepared for the homecoming and slumped into his chair. It was at that point that Karam knew he had no God; his faith was lost. He went out and bought some beers and drank them all. It was only the second time he had drunk alcohol in his life, but now he just wanted to blot everything out.

The following morning, he woke with a dreadful hangover. He rolled over in bed, crying and sobbing as he had been the night before. It was then that he realised he wanted revenge. Revenge for everything that had happened to him and his family. He wondered who to blame and then he realised he blamed everyone. He could just blame the agents of the Muhabbarat who slit his son's throat, and he could just blame the Captain of the ship that put his wife and daughter to the bottom of the ocean, but they were just symptoms of a culture that ran through every country, the leaderships that tossed aside their people, only interested in their own power and prestige. The decisions taken in bland rooms that had repercussions on families and ordinary people, wars and conflicts, fed by industrial corporations, greed and the desire to control. It became clear to him in that moment of lucidity driven by torment and grief, with everything stripped back just how divided and corrupt the world had become, those in control of power, capital, and resources, playing with the lives of everyone else, disposable pawns in a game where there was only ever one winner.

Those vapid speeches, the disingenuous addresses to the people via television, radio and social media, the blatant insincerity, it had all become part of everyday life. There was no moral leadership, of men and women looking out for their fellow man, incrementally it had morphed into a global cabal of those seeking to hold onto power at any cost, and the cost had become too high.

These leaders and politicians used everything at their disposal to hang on to power, the full use of the internet and social media to spread fear and hate and loathing, to subjugate the masses, and to eliminate dissent. Freedom of speech was being eroded under the pretext of war, but really it was just another form of suppression to maintain the status quo.

His family were lying at the bottom of the ocean, nameless, not even appearing on a list anywhere, just another casualty of what life had become, life that is run and dominated by a few people who themselves are being manipulated in the shadows. Nobody was accountable anymore. There were not even elections, they had been put to one side whilst the war raged. Even if there were elections, Karam would have no say. He was not allowed any citizenship, he was incredibly lucky to even be allowed to stay in the UK, he had only just scraped in because of his job at the LSE, but he knew that he was constantly under surveillance.

What he must do now is not let anyone know what had happened. He must go in to work and appear as normal as usual and bide his time. He must plan what to do next. To rush in would be foolhardy and of no benefit and he might give himself away. He must decide and plan and execute. His head was full of strange ideas, thrown around in a jumble, nothing was clear except for the fact that he must slip back into life as normal as possible and not let anyone know what had happened. He had never spoken about his family to anyone, he always thought it best to keep life simple and uncomplicated. He thought how he had planned to introduce his family to his colleagues and friends once they were here, he had imagined how they would be amazed at their stories of their extraordinary life and journey, and how everyone would rejoice at the re-union and help them build their new life together in London.

He returned to work that week, and although some of his colleagues asked him if he was ok, because he seemed quiet, he passed it off as feeling a little unwell. He had been able to contain the unimaginable grief inside. It tore at him, but at the same time it was the most personal thing he still had with his family, it was them against the world.

Karam knew the worst thing he could do was to rush into something driven by rage, he would take his time and pick his moment and his course of action. He did not want to waste his opportunity as the act of someone driven mad by grief but wanted to deliver the ultimate riposte to counter all the wrongs that he and his family had endured, to send out a message that would be heard. It did not have to be this year or the next, but it had to make the world sit up and gasp.

CHAPTER THREE

SOPHIE HALLAM

Sophie Hallam was not a career bureaucrat. She had served in the army for six years after leaving Cambridge. She was smart, in the true sense of the word. She had passed all her exams with top grades and was considered an academic, but beyond that she was observant, analytical, and questioning. At a time when it was not considered progressive to question what you were told; she swam against the current. Her University professors liked that and warmed to her. She spent many long evenings in the company of her tutor and a handful of likeminded students who would discuss difficult topics and challenge one another. At the start of the intense Woke movement University Professors had been terrified of their own shadows. The sacking of Will Knowland, the English master at Eton College had sent a ripple of fear throughout the educational establishment. When even Eton College was reigning back on free speech and critical thinking, we knew that dangerous times were coming.

Sophie left Cambridge with a first-class degree and in the absence of knowing what to do, took a commission with the army as an Intelligence Officer. She quickly rose through the ranks and found herself very suited to the role. When war broke out in 2027, she was promoted to the rank of Major unusually early. She had not thought of a life outside of the army, but had already made a name for herself, which had been mentioned in high circles.

Cabinet had been discussing new departments to be created for the state of emergency. This war would probably differ from previous wars, how it would be fought, and the role of intelligence would play an even greater part. Sophie Hallam was widely considered to be the finest Intelligence Officer in The British Army. She was approached directly by The Home Secretary to see if she would be interested in setting up a new department. The conversation widened to include other Whitehall mandarins and two other ministers. Sophie agreed to the task but asked for two things. Firstly, that it be called the Ministry of Information. She wanted it to operate like a funnel, that information would come in from every conceivable source and channel through to formulate Intelligence. They all agreed, it sounded appropriate and would hopefully encourage citizens to pass information. The other request was more unusual. Sophie said that she did not want anyone to know that she was in charge. She would take a mid-rank position, enabling her to work with everyone in the new Ministry. They could appoint a figurehead who would be the only person in The Ministry apart from them who actually knew that Sophie was in charge. She would like it to stay this way until the appropriate time, which she would decide. This was most unusual, and they began to discuss it until Sophie stood up and said "Ladies and Gentlemen, this is not open for discussion. If you want me to set this up and run it, these are my terms, and they are non-negotiable."

They had not been spoken to like this before, but they were aware that she was the woman for the job and agreed to her conditions. Sophie left the army with immediate effect and began pulling her team together. Notionally in charge of the Ministry was her Commanding Officer from the Intelligence Corps, Colonel Charles Bell. She had considered the ultimate head, Brigadier Finian Seymour-Cant, but she felt he was more of a career soldier than an Intelligence Officer and she knew he would never agree, he was a misogynist that no amount of sexual equality training would ever change. Colonel Bell could be relied upon, he was a first class organiser and motivator, would ably run the show whilst keeping privy to their secret, and she knew that he would not take umbrage about the arrangement.

Over the next six months Sophie and Charles targeted a few key personnel from the Army Intelligence Corps and ran adverts looking for the brightest and best. There were some specific skills that they sought, but most of the time it was for freethinkers who might see something that others might miss. Emma joined with a raft of graduates to fill various administrative posts of which there were many. Sophie positioned herself in the centre of the Ministry, geographically and managerially. The Ministry was afforded access to every type of surveillance and conduit of information enjoying hot lines to the Prime Minister and GCHQ. It was an exciting time for Sophie who thrived on the work and the opportunities it presented. At the age of twenty-nine it was the biggest challenge and very flattering to have been given the opportunity, but Sophie knew she was the person most likely to make all of this succeed. She was also aware of the difficulties an attractive young woman would encounter if she were seen to be running the whole show, it was better this way, for the time being.

There were the domestic issues of 5th columnists and keeping the general population sufficiently informed whilst also encouraging them to inform, then there was the global situation. China, Russia, and other enemies were becoming very adept at misinformation and disruption. In previous wars it was important to push back against propaganda, but the internet and social media meant that Britain's enemies were able to maintain a constant feed of misinformation to undermine the Government and the war effort. This had been going on for some time before war broke out but now it was supercharged. Any difficult event was immediately jumped upon by the UK's enemies who manipulated the news to sow doubt amongst the British population. The migrants fleeing Africa were a real and current threat, but the misinformation supporting it implied it was out of control and that the migrants were carrying a plague. This instilled in the British Public a constant feeling of terror. Sometimes the British Government used this to their advantage; keeping the public in a permanent state of fear was one of the best methods of control, the authorities had learned this in 2020/21 during the Covid-19 crisis when they were able to change public opinion and behaviour in a short space of time with hardly any dissenting voices. Covid-19 had turned around one hundred years of free speech and civic freedoms in only a few months. The Johnson Government had been surprised how compliant the British population had been, not like British behaviour at all. They saw a real opportunity to manipulate the population to suit their agenda. Laws introduced for the duration of the pandemic were not rescinded but built upon during the next Coronavirus outbreak and then the war. Freedoms that everyone had taken for granted were removed under the pretext of external threats and the safety of the population. Before anybody had realised, they were in essence living within a police state.

One of the worst social media attacks was in 2028 when the UK was flooded with posts and blogs saying that the new Coronavirus vaccine was dangerous, had been rushed through the tests and due diligence, and was now carrying terrible side effects including narcolepsy, liver failure and loss of sight. The campaign was so prevalent and successful that the NHS and Public Health England could only get an 18% uptake of the vaccine, leaving the UK in a permanent state of Coronavirus alert for almost two years severely hampering the war effort. Economic output fell 23%, temporarily impoverishing the country. This one event did the greatest damage to the UK without a shot being fired. It was this that prompted the Home Secretary to approach Sophie to create a Ministry to combat these types of attacks.

Sophie Hallam thought about things differently to most people. Initially the Government had put out denials and statements that none of this was true and that it was all Chinese propaganda. Sophie knew that the public's faith in Government, and its ability to tell the truth was so low after the myriad events that followed Covid-19 where misinformation had been taken to new levels, that simply denying would not make a difference.

Against the advice of almost everyone else, Sophie instigated a campaign that told of the improvements to the vaccine after some initial problems, that they had been ironed out, that the two examples of blindness were temporary, and the patients had made a full recovery. She developed the story to say that the latest virus strain was the most complex and therefore the scientists had some initial issues but now they were overcome. She arranged for The Prime Minister, the Chief Medical Officer and the Chief Virologist to have their vaccination jabs on tv. Within two months the mass inoculation programme had achieved 77% take up, better than both previous Covid immunisation programmes. Ministers were pleased with themselves, the appointment of Sophie Hallam had been inspirational, she had taken a disastrous situation and turned it around. Her Ministry was given even more funding and resources and quickly became the most important cog in a Government machine that was expanding constantly.

Sophie Hallam had the capacity to keep an inordinate number of balls up in the air. Her capacity for work and her memory were legendary in the Ministry, it was a wonder to many why she was working in her position and not running the whole show. She could move between departments, investigations and projects without notes and be as knowledgeable as any team leader on specifics. Many pieces of information came across Sophie Hallam's desk. The Ministry of Information was always on the lookout for anomalies, things that looked different, that did not follow a pattern or were plain different. Sophie Hallam had asked the personnel at the Ministry to go back ten years, long before the war had started to seek out any potential fifth columnists, or possible Trojan horses. This was one of the key remits of the new Ministry. It was a huge amount of work for the staff, but they had access to all the files, and almost everything was digitised.

From the huge amount of information available, thousands of files were created that might be of interest. These were then pored over by some of the finest inquisitive minds in England. One file made its way into what became known internally as 'The Cream File' reflecting the interesting information that had risen to the top. This file was then picked out by one of the top intelligence offices who brought it to the attention of Sophie Hallam. It was almost the oldest piece of information that they had, and only just made it into the ten-year time frame Hallam had asked about.

Back in December 2024, a note had arrived from the Immigration desk in Croydon about a refugee who had made his way here from war torn Syria. He had arrived in England undetected by driving through Europe from Turkey and crossing the Channel. He had already secured a job at the prestigious London School of Economics, had a place to stay, his own finances and yet he had been in refugee camps and fleeing from the Assad regime for the previous few years. He was in his thirties, good looking and presentable, but made no mention of family. He spoke perfect English and wore a tailored suit when he entered the immigration office. He had not been summoned, nobody knew of his existence in the UK, he had found out where to go and turned up. Karam Shahid was not like most refugees. His story did not sound like most stories and that intrigued Sophie Hallam. She did not do anything about it, but a couple of months later another note came through from the same office in Croydon to say that he had returned for his substantive interview and had passed with flying colours. There was absolutely nothing suspicious about his application at all which made Sophie Hallam suspicious. Who was this enigma Karam Shahid?

Sophie created a 'Low Importance General Enquiry' at the Ministry which meant that within 72 hours a file would be created and various desks within the ministry would be alerted. They would pull any documentation they could find as well as internet searches. Sophie would wait to see what they discovered before deciding what if anything she would do.

That Saturday she received a mail headed 'Karam Shahid Prelim Enquiries.' She poured herself some coffee in her apartment in Little Venice and opened the file. It was unusually small, only 4kb. There was a head and shoulders photo which had been taken in the Immigration offices.

There were a few personal details, age, place of birth, parents, employment, but beyond that nothing. No mention of family or contacts. After his education information and the start of the Civil war there was a 14-year gap before arriving in the UK. It listed a couple of refugee camps but there was no detail.

Hallam was intrigued. It wasn't unusual for refugees to have spasmodic details, gaps in their history, but Karam Shahid was like a ghost, a highly educated ghost, and not the sort of man not to have a family unless he was homosexual perhaps. That might account for the brevity of the information. Coming from a country where homosexuality can lead to three years of imprisonment as well as being beaten, it would not be surprising that he kept a low profile. His name had come up because he had been a vocal anti Assad protestor, linked to several Syrian refugee groups in London but almost overnight he had gone quiet.

Hallam took out her Montblanc ink pen, one of the few indulgences she allowed herself, and wrote at the foot of the file "further investigation required, including phone tap and surveillance, urgent", and signed it S.H. Most Ministries used acronyms and internal references, but Sophie Hallam had banned all of these from the Ministry of Information via Colonel Bell. She did not want any of her staff hiding behind corporate speak, she wanted everyone to put their name to anything they were doing, to carry responsibility.

She made a call and within fifteen minutes there was a knock at the door. She handed the sheaf of paper to a young man who was acting as runner at the weekend, who would return them to the Ministry for further detailed investigation. The Ministry never slept, the country was on a war footing and the Ministry of Information was at the centre of things, it was important to remain vigilant.

Once a case file had been activated, the apparatus of surveillance moved into overdrive and very quickly. Most laws about privacy had been overridden by The War Act of 2029. Surveillance could be instigated without warrants or court approval by a few Government bodies. The Ministry of Information had access to every part of a citizen's life, phone conversations, emails, bank details. The person being watched would not necessarily know what was happening unless they had some sophisticated personal tracking technology. Sophie Hallam would have some more information about Karam Shahid within a couple of days.

Sunday was a day of rest for Hallam. She lived alone, she liked it that way, relationships were casual, she did not like to over complicate life. Her time was valuable, she had a job to do and considered it the most important thing in her life. She treated Sundays as a time to re-boot. She would do a fifteen-mile run through the streets and parks of central London and have brunch at a cafe close to her flat. In the afternoon she would listen to music and read, she found both past times the best way for her to unwind. In the evening she would have dinner with friends or her parents. She did not socialise with anyone from work. She would use this day to de-clutter her mind, she found it helped with problem solving and lucidity. She could eliminate unnecessary thoughts and let insignificant issues go. Monday's often left co-workers disappointed that she had completely forgotten about their pressing issue of the previous week. They knew that she had not really forgotten but had relegated it to something less significant. This all helped to keep her staff on their toes, only prioritising what she considered to be important.

The early part of the week was filled with meetings and all the new crisis that constantly evolved. The Home Secretary had taken to using the Ministry of Information and Sophie in particular, as a private sounding board. On Tuesday morning Sophie Hallam put a call in to the Prime Minister who had a quiet word with the Home Secretary to desist, such was Sophie's importance to the Government.

Just as she was heading to her favourite cafe for lunch, a file was passed to her. Information this sensitive was never emailed but was always presented in paper format, another idiosyncrasy that Sophie Hallam had introduced to The Ministry of Information. She thought that documents that important carried more gravitas and would be examined more thoroughly if they were in printed form. She read the heading 'Karam Shahid' and put it under her arm.

Settling in with a panini and coffee at a seat at the rear of the cafe, Sophie opened the file. Once again it was relatively small, just a few pages and lots of photos. The photos had been taken by CCTV, driverless cars and drones and showed Karam Shahid walking to and from work, a couple from inside one of his lectures, one showing him playing five a side football, a few of him at different classes, karate, kick boxing, mixed martial arts, and another in a convenience store buying provisions. The report stated that he travelled to and from the London School of Economics and did not deviate. His internet traffic and mobile phone did not show any unusual activity, mostly news feeds and standard searches. He subscribed to Al Jazeera, which was banned under the War Act, but anybody interested in the news went to Al Jazeera, it was the most reliable and objective of all the news agencies. The Intelligence field team had gained access to his flat and found nothing to remark upon. It was sparsely furnished, a good library of books, no photos, comfortable and academic was how it was described. The only slightly unusual thing to report was that on the Tuesday morning he met with another University professor who worked part time called Charlie Wilson whom he also played football with that same evening. They went for a drink together after football and then shared an Uber home, Shahid dropped off first at the Elephant & Castle.

Hallam closed the file, ate her panini and started to think. There was absolutely nothing unusual at all about this man. That seemed very strange to her. She put a call through to the Intelligence field team

"Harry? Sophie Hallam here."

"Hello Ma'am." replied Harry Barnes, who ran the department for fieldwork. "What can I do for you?"

"The job you did for me, Karam Shahid, at a flat in The Elephant and Castle yesterday," said Sophie.

"Yes, I went on that job myself with a team, we didn't have much on and I wanted to see them perform for myself," said Harry, an ex-guardsman and very proficient operative, handpicked by Sophie herself.

"I have just read the report, and there was nothing much in it?"

"That's right, a very tidy flat, simple enough to enter, two locks. The flat did not have much in it at all to be honest. I thought the lack of personal effects was unusual, but it is a single guy living there so perhaps not that strange."

"There were no photos at all?" returned Sophie.

"Just one of a football team lifting a trophy. There was a poster of the Taj Majal, and a print of New York, but I think there were both from IKEA as wall fillers," said Harr.y

"Didn't that strike you as odd, that there was nothing, no family pictures, no photos of Shahid on holiday, family, friends?"

"I didn't really think about it, perhaps he keeps all of his photos on his phone, lots of people do, it's not our job to analyse what we find, just to report it."

"One thing that wasn't mentioned, did you find a prayer mat?"

"A prayer mat? No, we didn't. Should we have?"
"Not necessarily, it just crossed my mind. I want to look inside the flat, can we arrange that?" asked Hallam.

"Yes, of course we can. I will take the team back in there tomorrow once we have confirmed Shahid is at work and relay the images back to you."

"That's not quite what I meant Harry; I want to go into the flat myself."

"That's most irregular," said Harry." Usually, Field Operatives are the only ones cleared for house entry."

"Don't worry about that, I can arrange it, leave it with me. Will you be free tomorrow morning?"

"Yes, I can organise a team, call me when you have clearance and I will set it up," said Harry, and then he hung up.

Sophie Hallam opened the file again and looked at the picture of Karam Shahid. Unassuming, thoughtful, was there more to this man than meets the eye? There was nothing to suggest anything untoward and yet Sophie had a doubt, something was nagging at her, an itch that needed scratching.

The following morning a black car pulled up outside her flat. Sophie was ready, dressed casually to blend in as best as possible, and joined three others including Harry in the car. He pulled the file up on the screen. Sophie did not take much notice; she had read the file and her extraordinary memory had already committed everything. She wanted to see what others might have missed. It was only a ten-minute journey to Shahid's flat in the Elephant & Castle. Harry had been watching the screen which picked up a live feed of Shahid making his way to the LSE. It was raining hard, and he had called up an Uber which collected him outside his flat at 8.45am. The CCTV showed him walking into the faculty fifteen minutes later. They could now see him sat in the canteen at the University. He was talking to another University Professor recognised by the facial recognition software as Charlie Wilson. The surveillance allowed the team to know the exact whereabouts of Shahid so that they would not be disturbed. The footage of the front of his flat over the last 24 hours showed that nobody else had gone inside.

The Ministry vehicle pulled up around the corner and they all got out. They started walking around the back to the foot of the stairs leading up to Karam's flat. Sophie stopped and looked around. It was raining and there were no people to be seen. One door opened on the other side on the third floor as a drone lowered and delivered a small package. The recipient did not look down and had not seen them there, oblivious to what was going on outside of her small world.

They climbed the stairs to the second floor. Harry set about the lock with a special tool which opened it within seconds and entered. Sophie stood on the balcony and looked around again. As she scanned the area, her eye caught a small black box on top of a ledge on the brick pier at the end of the corridor. She turned away and entered the flat. She knew what she had seen.

The flat was clean and sparsely furnished. Like the images she had seen in the file the day before, there were no photos or personal belongings. As she walked through the hall, she saw a dozen different baseball caps on the shelf. Hanging up on the hooks were six different jackets and as many different coloured rucksacks. She scanned the lounge which also accommodated a small kitchen. She saw the posters on the wall, the Taj Majal and New York. Her keen eyes noticed that there was a very slight bulge behind one of the skyscrapers. As she looked closer, without being too obvious she saw a small tear in the picture and something behind.

She briefly looked around the rest of the flat.

"Come on everyone, this is not our man, mistaken identity, let's go."

Harry returned the locks to the position that Shahid would have left them that morning. They walked down the stairs. The vehicle had pulled up beside them and they got in.

"Did you find what you wanted," asked Harry.

"I did, thank you," replied Sophie.

"And what was that? I couldn't see anything."

"I wanted to know if this man was of interest to us or not."

"And he isn't?"

"I wouldn't say that," said Sophie.

"But I thought you said back in the flat that he wasn't a person of interest?"

"That was for his benefit, but I doubt he bought it."

"What do you mean for his benefit, we were the only ones there?"

"He was watching us, or at least he will later. The flat had cameras inside and out. At least now I know he is someone worth watching. I want to scale this up to a Level Red. Full 24-hour surveillance, I want to know what Mr Shahid does with himself every waking moment. Put a direct alert to me for anything we find out, however trivial, Mr Shahid has become very interesting indeed."

"Shall we bring him in for questioning?" asked Harry.

"No, most definitely not. This is a very clever guy. He will have all his tracks covered. We need to lure him out and get him to make a mistake. Double up on all the surveillance but put your best teams on it. Mr Shahid is very smart, he will be anticipating everything. I think he has another place that we do not know about, that needs to be our priority, we need to let him think he has given us the slip so he feels he can go there. Let us not rush it, in fact, let's not start for another week, let him believe we aren't interested at all."

"Of course, Ma'am, we will start on the 26th, I will rotate three teams."

"Take a look at his credit cards and payments, see if there has been anything unusual. Go back as far as you can. The Professor lives very frugally, if there is anything unusual it should stick out," said Hallam.

"Of course," replied Harry.

It was raining hard again as the car pulled away. The woman with them had left a little earlier and brought the car round. Most people were using driverless pods, but The Ministry of Information had its own fleet of vehicles of all shapes and sizes it used for reconnaissance and transport. Hallam preferred older vehicles with as little factory installed tech as possible to try and remain unobtrusive and off grid. They took the short journey back to the Ministry; Sophie Hallam was considering everything she had seen. The cameras told her that Shahid was tech savvy and concerned about visitors. The excess of caps, coats and rucksacks suggested to her that he was adept at disguise and wanted to be low profile. The flat was so sparsely furnished as to give nothing away, but the thing that intrigued her most was the lack of a prayer mat or any indication of Shahid's religion. It was rare that anyone born and bred in the Middle East would not be religious, it was the most natural part of growing up. Of course, growing up in Syria, 60% of the people are Sunni Muslims, but there is a sizeable group of Shias Muslims. There are also Christian groups and even some Jews. Hallam had an instinct about these things, she could tell if something was not right. If Shahid did not appear to practice a religion, why would that be? Knowing he might become a person of interest, Shahid might purposely be hiding his faith, but it would still be unlikely not to have a prayer mat, unless he carried it with him to work. The other possibility that really intrigued Sophie Hallam was that he might have forsaken his religion entirely. If that were true, why would he have done that? Her interest was piqued.

The car pulled into the Ministry, they alighted, and Hallam returned to her desk and continued with her day.

A couple of days later Harry knocked on Hallam's office. She beckoned him in through the glass wall.

"Morning Ma'am," said Harry.

"Morning Harry, what have you got for me?"

"We have been looking into Karam Shahid, he is like a ghost. He goes to work, plays some football, he goes home. Very few friends, no social life apart from the gym. He was involved with Syrian refugee groups when he arrived in London, he was also a very vocal and outspoken critic of Bashir Assad and then it all stopped. He did not publish anything after November 2028. We checked all his finances, he is solvent, hardly spends and has built up some savings.

His credit cards are mainly used for food shopping, nothing unusual showing up there."

"I feel you are coming to a crescendo Harry, out with it," said Hallam.

"Four years ago, Karam Shahid hired a van from a company in Ealing. He paid cash so it did not show up on his credit card transactions. We only found it because of his unusual name, we are linked into the databases at DVLC. They had the reference because of the license check, we asked the hire firm to pull their records. Shahid hired the van for two days but called to extend it to four. He travelled 586 miles, perhaps not that unusual, apart from paying by cash, except for the fact that it is unusual for Shahid, the man where nothing in his life ever happens," said Harry.

"Can you check to see if there were any major events that happened during those four days, we can cross reference to see if there is a link."
"We have already done that Ma'am," said Harry grinning. "It was at that time that HMS Dauntless sunk the Nigerian warship, the Aradu In the English Channel not far from the Cornish Coast at Mousehole. You may remember it, it made the news, they think four hundred or more may have drowned when she went down. I checked the distances, Ealing to Mousehole and back is 560 miles. If you include a detour to Plymouth where HMS Dauntless docked, it would have been a 585 mile journey."

"Now that is interesting. That is really good work Harry, excellent work. Can we get the manifest of the survivors from the tragedy? My feeling is that Shahid was hoping to meet someone from that boat, but they never arrived. If they had, they might have appeared in his life, but let's check the manifest anyway. There might be some names that we can link to Shahid, otherwise see if we can track any of the survivors in case they know anything about those that died when the boat went down." Hallam's brain was racing, analysing all the possibilities, she could run many permutations at once, seeing things that others might not.

"Leave it with me Ma'am," said Harry.

"Thank you, Mr Shahid is becoming more and more interesting by the minute."

The Ministry of information had such wide-reaching powers and access to so many records that within three days Harry's team had sifted through the manifest of survivors of The NNS Aradu. None of the survivors had the surname Shahid, most of the survivors were Nigerian sailors and some other Africans. Harry was able to interview some of the survivors who were being held in HMP Belmarsh. One of them was the son in law of the President of Nigeria who was desperately trying to get back home. He was more than willing to tell Harry everything he knew. He remembered that there was a Syrian woman aged mid-thirties, and her daughter who had been in refugee camps for years. She was trying to get to England to meet up with her husband. He did not know much more except that she was a doctor and very pretty. He had begged Harry to be released and was happy to part with as much information as Harry wanted if he could do something to help him. Being in a state of war there was nothing that Harry could do but he did not tell Luke that and was not inclined to help him anyway, he could tell what kind of a man he was and hoped he would spend a long time in prison.

Sophie Hallam did not like to jump to conclusions, but her instinct told her that Karam Shahid's family was trying to make their way to the UK to join him. He had driven to Mousehole to meet them as they arrived on the beach and to drive them back to London. He already knew his way around the immigration process and would have checked out their eligibility to stay. The more she thought about it, the more Sophie Hallam was starting to understand Karam Shahid and everything that he had gone through. If this was all true, why was Shahid worried about people watching him, hence the cameras at his flat? Why all the baseball caps, jackets and rucksacks? And why no sign of religion.

One thing that was really puzzling, it was over four years since

Shahid lost his family. If he were going to do something, why wouldn't he have done it by now? Usually if somebody is stricken with grief they lash out. If Karam Shahid had lost his family, and lost his faith, it was troubling that he had remained so low profile for so long, was he planning something? Hallam did not want to get ahead of herself. Although she had one of her gut feelings, she might be reading this all wrong. Shahid might just be running black market goods which would explain the cameras and the clothing, but Hallam knew that Shahid was not interested in money.

She would hopefully know more in a week or so once the surveillance teams did their job. That evening, a few of the staff were going to The Borough for drinks after work including Emma Harrison, who was going out with Charlie Wilson, who in turn worked with Karam Shahid at the London School of Economics. She did not think there was any nefarious connection between Charlie Wilson and her man Shahid, but Charlie might shed some light on what the man was like. She did not know Charlie well, but she hoped he might want to help The Ministry of Information.

CHAPTER FOUR

THE PLAN BEGINS

Karam had watched Sophie Hallam and her team enter his flat that morning. Both of his cameras had movement sensors that sent an alert to his phone. He was able to watch them on his mobile from his tutorial whilst he was with his students. The tutorial room at the University was private with no cameras to watch over him. He was able to continue with his students whilst he watched the stocky man pick the lock to his flat. He had no sound with the outdoor camera, but in the flat, there was a sound recorder running. He could tell immediately from the body language who was in charge. He had programmed the sound recorder and camera to stream in sync.

During the intervening years since losing his family, Karam had picked up many new skills including an excellent working knowledge of all kinds of technology, mainly through online tutorials that he had accessed through the Dark Web in order to remain anonymous. He had taught himself programming and was well versed with onion routing to keep himself anonymous, encapsulating his messages in layers of encryption, then transmitting data through network nodes, each one peeling away a single layer uncovering the data's next destination. Only when the final layer is decrypted does the message arrive at its destination.

He did all his learning and research on basic laptops that he would keep hidden and destroy completely every few months. He knew that it was almost impossible to avoid website fingerprinting, he could imagine the resources that The Ministry of Information would have at its disposal, and despite using the new Nemo protocols developed on the dark web by Spanish hackers to avoid detection, he knew the best way to remain anonymous was to not bring attention to himself in the first place.

Karam had been incredibly careful to stay under the radar, but he knew that the luxury of anonymity was over. He saw on his screen the momentary pause as the young woman looked at his picture of New York on the wall in his lounge. He could tell she had seen the camera hidden behind. He also knew that her remark 'Come on everyone, this is not our man, mistaken identity, let's go' was purely for show. He replayed their arrival and saw the woman glance up at his camera positioned to cover his front door. She was smart, very smart to have seen that, and the camera inside. What else did she notice? He did not keep anything in his flat that would give anyone an idea of his plans, but was there something that she had seen, something he had not thought about? And what had alerted them to him in the first place?

He knew about the Ministry of Information, he and Charlie would discuss it occasionally over coffee, he also knew that Charlie's girlfriend worked there. It has crossed his mind that Charlie might have been spying on him, but he quickly dismissed that. He knew that Charlie was genuine and was very scathing at the size and intrusion of the police state. He would often run his next journalistic piece past Karam for his advice on it falling foul of all the new guidelines of challenging the Government. He did not think it was anything to do with Charlie or Emma, but he would arrange to bump into them tomorrow evening, he knew that Charlie would be going to the Borough and he had mentioned that Emma's department were having drinks there too.

Karam knew he had been extremely careful in everything he did, especially in covering his tracks. How had he slipped up? Had the Ministry, if that is who they were, already discovered something about him? His tutorial finished and he said goodbye to his students and made his way downstairs below the faculty into the maintenance and storage rooms, along the corridor to the last door on the left marked:

Historic Files Storage.
Authorised Personnel Only

Karam switched off the corridor light and using the torch on his phone found the keyhole with his fingers. He took a key from his jacket pocket and unlocked the door, one more glance and then he was in. He locked the door behind him. He did not turn the light on so it would not shine under the door. He shone his torch around the room. There were bookshelves full of files covering every inch of wall. He checked the two cameras hidden carefully behind some of the files and then went over to the wall on the right and pulled out one of the boxes of files and placed it on the floor. He carried on taking boxes off the shelf, and once empty lifted the shelf out and stood it up against the boxes he had removed. He did the same with the next shelf and all the boxes on it. The boxes were all stacked neatly and methodically and within a couple of minutes he had created a hole in the bookcase a metre square. Through the gap was the outline of a door. Karam took another key from inside his jacket and found the escutcheon plate hiding the keyhole. He turned it and it opened inwards revealing a room behind. Karam climbed up onto the bookcase and slid through the gap into a room. He then leant back out and started re-stacking the files and the shelves as he had found them. Although quite tough to do, Karam had done this so many times that he made it look simple. The weights he lifted most days in the gym meant he had the strength of a much younger man, so lifting the boxes was no challenge for him. Once everything was in place and to his satisfaction, he closed the door. Using his torch, he pulled a rolled-up towel that was there across the bottom of the door. He then reached for the light switch that he knew was at shoulder height to the left and flicked it.

A strip light came on illuminating a room about three metres by two metres. On the walls were technical drawings and images of buildings and famous landmarks in and around London. Hanging up were various clothes and uniforms, police, fire brigade, ambulance, and on the back wall neatly hung were various weapons, pistols, machines guns and grenade launchers. They were all Chinese made and stacked neatly underneath were boxes of ammunition. On the desk were two inkjet printers and stacks of documentation. Stood up against the wall were various sheets of pre-printed metal with various names on them relating to ambulances, fire, police as well as general building works. They were all magnetised for fitting on to vehicles. On a separate small table were canisters, wires, detonators, most things required for bomb making as well as circuit boards and a large selection of mobile phones in various states of repair or cannibalism.

Karam had spent his time well building a small arsenal and an array of tools and useful items. Everything was found on the dark web except for the uniforms which he had mostly stolen when the opportunities arose. The weapons had been surprisingly easy to obtain. The PLA Unit 61398 also known as Byzantine Candor, the Chinese Army's computer hacking units, were all over the internet and had infiltrated The Dark Web. It had been high risk because The Ministry of Information also posed as enemies of Britain on the Dark Web to try and trap any fifth columnists or subversives.

Karam spent four years nurturing contacts he had made online and tested them first with some smaller requests of detonators, timers, and a small quantity of explosives. They all arrived in small packages in drones, completely undetected by the authorities. Karam could only imagine how far they might have travelled to get to him. He always had them dropped off somewhere remote where he could position cameras in advance. He then hid each delivery in an empty building and monitored it. Not once did he see an indication that it was a Ministry of Information trap. Even though he felt confident, he thought that The Ministry might be playing the long game. A year ago, he decided to declare himself to his dark web contacts and after a number of conversations was approached by Colonel Qiao Liang of Chinese Information Operations, the Chinese Army's equivalent of

British Intelligence. Colonel Liang was an officer in HUMINT, which oversees military human intelligence, housed in a twenty-two storey building off Datong Road in Pudong, a district of Shanghai.

He had famously written "Methods that are not characterised by the use of the force of arms, nor by the use of military power, nor even by the presence of casualties and bloodshed, are just as likely to facilitate the successful realisation of the war's goals, if not more so". How true this was.

Karam did not feel the need to tell Colonel Liang too much about himself or what he had planned. He talked about subverting the British Government from within, that he was a disgruntled citizen, always treated as second class, that his brother had been arrested and he wanted revenge. The Colonel appeared sympathetic but probably was not that interested. If he could wage war on British soil without committing Chinese troops, he would be happy.

Karam gave him a shopping list of things that he wanted. After a few mails it was agreed, the weights calculated and therefore the number of drops required. The Colonel didn't give away any information as to where the drones were coming from. Karam had no idea if there was already a cache of arms hidden somewhere in the UK or if they were being brought in from further afield. Because of the acceleration of technology during the war, drones had evolved, the largest ones carried payloads of more than two tonnes.

The problem for Karam was that his deliveries needed to blend in and arrive almost unnoticed, mixed in with the tens of thousands of drones that move silently around the sky daily. The latest polymer weapons were lightweight, but the ammunition was still mostly made of lead-antimony alloy in a brass and copper jacket which made it heavy.

Twenty-four separate deliveries were agreed over a three-week timeframe using twelve different drop off addresses. Karam was an excellent organiser and managed the logistics very well. His challenge was always smuggling the latest delivery into the basement at the University and secreting the firearms into his hidden room. He found out the maintenance staff rotas and watched them for the two weeks preceding to get an idea of when they might be down in the basement. He hoped he had enough information and that they would not change their routines. Should he ever be found in the corridor, he was not too worried as his sign on the door seem to deter them, they seemed to be slightly in awe of the Professor who would occasionally come down to look for some important files and documents. Quite frankly they were happy to stay clear and leave the academics to their own devices.

When the time came for the deliveries to be made, Karam set his cameras up seventy-two hours beforehand to monitor the situation. He did not see anything unusual, the deliveries arrived on time and precisely where they should. He had a variety of delivery uniforms that he rotated every time he collected a parcel, so that he looked quite commonplace walking along holding boxes. When he got close to the University, he would change in the toilets at The Honourable Society of Lincolns Inn, back into his normal clothes to go into the faculty. There was one camera between Holborn Tube and the toilets and another two between the toilets and the faculty. He knew that he would be taking a risk doing the same journey repeatedly over a short period, and constantly changing his clothes; he took great care to keep his face down, hidden under caps or hoodies. He used different delivery uniforms, varied the tube stops, and arrived on a number of occasions by UBER or bus. After the first week, he wore the delivery clothes over his University work clothes so that he could just strip off out of sight of the cameras.

Those weeks became increasingly nerve-wracking, he knew he could be caught at any time, picked up in the street, spotted going into the basement of the University, but it all went according to plan. Karam had become the master of being invisible, just blending in and not being seen which was not an easy thing given how much surveillance there was in London. By being open, looking like a delivery man and carrying a parcel, he was hiding in plain sight.

Karam looked around his room and everything he had gathered. He was approaching the last period of preparation, his plans were coming to fruition. He had been patient, but thought he might not have much more time, this lady at the Ministry of Information was smart and given enough time would find out what he was planning. He knew that even this place would not be safe, once you were on the radar of the Ministry it could only be a matter of time.

Karam took a small notebook from his pocket and put it on the desk. He took out two photographs, one of him and his son together just before he was killed and the other of his wife and daughter when they were in the camp in Lebanon. He put the two together, so they appeared as one. He paused for a moment, and as happened every time, he began to well up and tears streamed down his face. He wiped them away and placed the photographs to one side. He lifted a laptop from a bag on the floor, plugged it in and opened it up. After re-booting, he gained access to the Dark Web and started to type some messages. These would be the last ones he would be sending; he knew that the time was approaching. Karam needed help with his plans and had found some willing accomplices online. It was risky, he had never met them and if everything went according to plan, never would. They were ex-military, treated badly by the British authorities as so many had been, suffering from PTSD and not supported financially relying on Universal Credit and support from friends. Some had managed to find private work in security but still harboured resentment at having risked their lives for Queen and King and country only to be discarded. They had hoped that when war broke out, they would become useful again, but this was a different kind of war being fought in cyberspace. There was a need for a homeland security force, but they had not been considered psychologically stable enough to be eligible.

Karam had found two men and a woman he thought would be capable of the job. He did not know what their motivation might be, but during the email exchanges it quickly became clear that it was the usual, money, and to some extent, getting even. He mailed Colonel Liang, outlined his plan, and told him what he needed. Within a week, drones arrived delivering half a million pounds in cash and the equivalent of fifteen million pounds in diamonds. It would have been much easier to have done it all as a digital transfer, but that would leave a trail, especially now that he knew he was being watched. The half a million pounds of cash was to give his team some liquidity they might need, and the diamonds were easier for them to handle and transfer.

Once Karam knew that the diamonds coming from the Chinese were genuine, or at least appeared genuine, he had the drone deliveries re-directed to pre-arranged drop off locations for the three ex servicemen. He ran the risk that the soldiers would just take the diamonds and cash and disappear, but they were promised another ten million pounds each, transferred to anywhere in the world once the job was done and critically an exit strategy and a new life far away from Britain. He had asked Colonel Liang for this and was confident that if the job went as planned that the Colonel would be happy to fund it when he saw the disruption it was causing his enemy.

Once the three soldiers had their money, Karam arranged for them to get some weapons training, with the Chinese equipment. If they were who they said they were, ex SAS, then the training should be short. Karam arranged for the weapons to be delivered to them.

He asked them to hide the cache until they were ready to proceed, but also sent them some additional ammunition so that they were fully prepared at a moment's notice.

The three soldiers who now had the operational names of Simon, Tom and Alex reported that the firearms were excellent, that they had all been training and were ready to go. Karam had not shared the plans or the target with them. All they knew was that it would be within the next two weeks and was based in the South East. In a perfect scenario they could have created a practice area and trained specifically for the task, but the surveillance surrounding them, that would have been almost impossible. Karam was formulating a plan that if followed to the letter should work. He would give them the details forty-eight hours before the date to prepare themselves.

He looked around the room knowing that the time was getting close and that he would not be returning many more times. He switched off the light, removed the towel from the door and checked the cameras in the corridor and adjacent room on his phone. It was all clear. Using the torch on his mobile he unlocked the door, removed enough boxes, and slipped through the gap, returning everything as it was, relocking as he left.

Double checking the corridor again, he opened the door and walked out returning to his office three floors up. He made himself a coffee and sat down thinking about what he was about to do and the people who had been to his flat. Could they be aware of what his plans were? He thought it unlikely but knew he had to be even more vigilant. He looked out of the window at the world beyond. He had made London his home, but everything was about to change. He could stop what he was doing and just carry-on living, but what kind of a life was this? He could not forget his family and found that he could not move on. He had met and dated some women, but Jamal was always there, preventing him from moving on. He recognised that he was damaged, and as much as he tried to rationalise and adjust, he found that he just could not. There was one fellow lecturer he saw quite a few times, they had even slept together, but he was wracked with guilt and broke it off. He always had trouble sleeping so he exercised ferociously, the gym and martial arts, not just to fill the time and prepare himself for his tasks ahead, but also to make himself tired so he would not have to rely on sleeping tablets to help him sleep just so he could function. His life had become a struggle for normality. On the outside looking in, Karam Shahid looked like a well-balanced, intellectual who was fighting fit, a key part of life at The London School of Economics, but the truth was that he was a broken man torn apart by grief with a burning desire for revenge.

He had one more class in the afternoon and then headed home calling into The Borough Market to pick up some hummus, falafel, and flatbread. That was where he bumped into Charlie as he had hoped and saw Sophie Hallam. He recognised her immediately from her striking looks, he also knew that she had seen him. He made his excuses with Charlie and slipped off heading back to his flat as quickly and surreptitiously as possible.

CHAPTER FIVE

TUESDAY 14TH FEBRUARY 2032

Charlie Wilson headed off for work at the University leaving home at eight thirty. He had given Emma a Valentines card and made her a special breakfast. He and Emma shared an Uber, dropping her off at The Ministry of Information en-route. He had noticed that the empty Uber was still parked opposite although the drone had now gone. Charlie would have preferred to walk but it was raining even heavier that morning. The Thames looked particularly fierce as they crossed over Westminster Bridge. The army were reinforcing the temporary barriers all the way along the embankment and lorry loads of sand were tipping out into large piles. All sorts of hydraulic equipment were being delivered. Charlie thought things were looking a bit desperate, he wondered if it might be worth investigating for a piece of freelance, although he imagined plenty of other journalists were already covering it, and infrastructure was not his speciality.

The driverless pod pulled up outside the Ministry and Emma got out and raised her umbrella. She leaned in and kissed Charlie.

"Have a great day."

"You too, see you tonight at home, special Valentine's dinner," replied Charlie. The pod pulled away and headed up Whitehall, Trafalgar Square and Charing Cross Road. The speaker in the Pod told Charlie that they were diverting due to the flood risk and roadworks on The Embankment. The Pod silently passed along The Strand, turned left towards Lincolns Inn Field, and dropped Charlie off by the doors of the faculty. He had been watching the news on the holographic screen, but as usual there was nothing new, just a constant stream of propaganda. His watch pinged and flashed a message that the journey cost three Amazon units, unbelievably a quarter of what a Black Cab used to cost ten years previously. The cabs had all disappeared by 2030 along with so many other jobs replaced by technology. The door opened automatically, and he ran in dodging the rain. As he stood in the lobby, Karam came in, his Uber Pod had just dropped him off too.

"Good morning Charlie, how are you?" he asked

"Bit wet."

"I know what you mean. Will it ever stop?" replied Karam.

"How did your class go last night, such a pity you couldn't join us, we didn't have the hummus, but the prawns I got from Edwin were spectacular."

"Sorry about that, I had completely forgotten, it was a new class. It was fine thanks, the usual group of people, more bored than anything else, looking for something to do in the evening rather than being interested in the subject, but the money helps. I would rather have joined you for dinner."

"Coffee, usual place?" asked Charlie.

"Perfect," replied Karam. "Let me put my bag in my office." A minute later Karam was coming back down the stairs holding his umbrella.

"Let's go," he said, raising his umbrella whilst leaving the building. They walked a couple of blocks to The Fleet Street Press, their preferred café. Karam had come across this espresso bar when he first started at The LSE and had walked the entire area between lectures usually thinking about his family. Charlie enjoyed it as much as Karam, so it had become their regular haunt for coffee on a Tuesday and Thursday morning, and occasionally for lunch too.

As they walked along Karam casually asked,

"Who was that attractive lady in your group last night at The Borough? She was stood close to Emma when you went over."
"You mean the girl with the red coat?" replied Charlie.

"Yes, that's her."

"Why? Did you like the look of her? I am not sure she would be a girl for you Karam."

"Oh, why's that? I thought she was very striking. Does she work with Emma?" he asked.

"She's her boss, a very smart and sharp cookie. I have to be honest, I am not that keen on her, she is very inquisitive about everything, I always get the feeling she is watching me, well, watching everyone really."

"I suppose that's just her job, didn't you say you feel that way about Emma sometimes?"

"Yes, I did, it's probably just my paranoia," replied Charlie.

"I think I would like to meet her; do you think Emma could introduce us?" asked Karam.

"I don't see why not but I don't know what her reaction would be, I will ask Emma for you."

"What's her name by the way, this interesting lady?"

"Sophie Hallam, she used to be in Army Intelligence and now she works at The Ministry of Information. Emma says she is her boss and kind of middle management, but Emma thinks she is much higher up than that really."

"That's intriguing, she sounds like a clever lady, it would be interesting to meet her."

"Well, I have to tell you that she showed some interest in you too. She asked me who the tall good looking Arab gentleman was that I was talking to, I did wonder who she meant," Charlie laughed.

"Are you sure you two haven't met before?"

"No, but let's change that," said Karam.
They arrived at the café and took their usual seats in the window. The Barista waved to them, they did not need to go up and order, they had been in hundreds of times. A few minutes later a young man brought a tray with two coffees and two apricot danish pastries.

"My turn," said Karam who passed his wrist across the young man's pouch. His device pinged and showed thirty-eight pounds.

"Thanks," said Charlie.

"Karam, I had the strangest thing happen last night, although I am not sure if I am imagining it. I was pretty sure I was being followed home last night after I left the Borough."

"Who by? Did you get a good look at them?" said Karam.

"Not by a person, by surveillance, an Uber Pod and a drone. They stopped outside the flat when I got home and were watching me."

"Are you sure? Did they follow you all the way from The Borough?"

"Almost, I think they picked me up whilst I was walking back along the river."

"So, you don't think they had been following you earlier, just after you left the Market?"

"Yes, I think so unless I just hadn't noticed them earlier."

"They wanted you to know you were being watched."

"Really? what makes you think that?" asked Charlie leaning in to Karam.

"With the surveillance the authorities have at their disposal, they could have easily followed you without you knowing. They wanted you to know, probably to frighten you. What have you been up to? Teaching subversive behaviour in your lectures again?"

"No, I haven't, and I don't do that these days as you well know, none of us can anymore, and the warning I got was enough to make me stop doing that. But yesterday, I had a copy of George Orwell's 1984 delivered, I was reading it for a piece I am writing about the immolations and people pushing back against the state," said Charlie. "That sounds subversive to me, good for you Charlie. How had you ordered the book? I presume it is on one of the banned lists?"

"Funnily enough it isn't, it's still considered fiction but of course the themes are pretty relevant to society today. Do you think The Ministry would know I had ordered it? I returned it straightaway," said Charlie.

"Of course they know! The algorithms The Ministry use are so advanced. There would have been trip words which would have alerted them to your purchase. I wouldn't worry, in a couple of days they will realise they are tracking a very dull man and will leave you alone."

Charlie punched him on the arm "Well thank you!" said Charlie jokingly.

Karam rubbed his arm feigning pain but laughed out loud.

They chatted a bit about two of the other Professors, news of the war and their next league football match. At nine forty they got up and started walking back to the University faculty around the corner.

"See you later Karam," said Charlie and watched him ascend the stairs. All of this had been watched back at The Ministry of Information.

Karam returned to his office and checked the apps on his phone to see if anyone had disturbed the cameras he had set up, all seemed quiet. So now he knew who the team were that had come to his flat and forced entry. A team from The Ministry of Information led by Sophie Hallam. He pulled up his laptop and Googled 'Sophie Hallam Ministry of Information'.

The search brought up the usual bio, education, army, current employment, 'Management level Ministry of Information, Whitehall'. It was all quite impressive, but Karam knew there was a lot more to Sophie Hallam than the Google search was telling him. It had not come as any surprise, that as soon as Sophie had seen Charlie talking to him in The Borough, that she started to have Charlie watched. To get it done that quickly, demonstrated ed that she had some serious influence in The Ministry.

Karam knew that he was now under time pressure. It would not take long before Sophie Hallam found out enough to piece things together. He wondered if he could turn this to his advantage. He got through his day, a lecture in the morning, lunch with colleagues in the University canteen and then back-to-back tutorials. He did not want to be seen to be changing his routine at all as he knew he was being watched by Sophie Hallam's team.

At just after four, once he had said goodbye to his students, he returned to his office. He made a phone call to say he was setting off now and would be at football in forty-five minutes and made his way down to the basement, checking he was not being followed. He knew where all the cameras in the faculty building were and picked a route that took him off the CCTV trail for the longest time. Anyone watching the feeds would not know which direction he had gone in. He needed to be quick so as not to raise too much suspicion. He hoped the spurious phone call might buy him some time, it might if the ordinary surveillance staff were on duty, he just hoped that Sophie Hallam was not watching any of the feeds. He had assumed that by now they had bugged his office and were listening to all his conversations.

In the basement he made a final scan of the area to make sure he was alone and opened the door marked 'Historic File Storage'. He closed it behind him and followed the same procedure as before. Having cleared the files from the shelves he slid through into his hidden room, restacked the shelves and turned the light on.

He switched the laptop on and through the encryption sent three emails that had been pre-prepared. He had headed them all "Time to Play". Each mail contained the instructions for Simon, Tom and Alex. The date of the operation was set for the following day, Wednesday the 15th of February 2032.

Karam pulled a sports bag out from under the desk and took from within it three other bags, the type you use for mailing parcels. He took the uniforms off their hangers and folded them up into the large jiffy bags, each one pre-labelled and carefully placed them back in the sports bag. He took most of the notes, pictures and plans off the wall and put them in the metal waste bin, pouring lighter fuel, and setting light to them burning them all, turning them carefully to make sure there was little left. He knew that forensics would be able to sift through and even from ashen remains they would piece together some information, but it would take at least a few days and by then it would be over. Whilst the documents were burning, he changed out of his clothes into his football kit and put on a track suit top. He packed his clothes into the sports bag with one of the uniforms.

With the bag packed and zipped up, Karam looked around the room at what was left. Weapons hanging on the wall, a few boxes of ammunition, some photos and plans still displayed. He took a box which contained an incendiary device that he had constructed, from under the desk and put it on top, taking some fishing wire, he carefully set a trip that connected to the device. He hoped the fishing wire was discreet enough not to be seen. He checked his apps on the phone for the hidden cameras making sure everywhere was clear, opened the door, cleared the shelves, passed the sports bag through, then carefully closed the door behind him whilst at the same time pulling the trip wire closer so that it would be triggered the next time the door was opened.

He locked the door and replaced all the boxes of files, checked the corridor via his phone and then emerged into the semi darkness, locking the door behind him.

It had been twelve minutes since he left his office, twelve minutes that could not be explained, all he could do was hope he was not being watched by the cleverest people at The Ministry. Karam walked to the administrator's office and saw Margot sat behind the desk.

"Hi Karam, I haven't seen you for a while, everything ok?" said the overweight lady.

Karam was pleased it was Margot working today. The office was run on a job share, and today was one of Margot's two days a week. Margot liked Karam, and Karam knew that.

"Hi Margot, I have been around, I just think our paths haven't crossed, all good with you?"

"Much better now I have seen you Karam," she said naughtily.

"Could you do me a favour please," he asked. "I would like these parcels to be collected and delivered immediately." He took them from his bag and placed them on her desk. "They have already been booked in; the barcodes are pre-printed on them. They are football kits for my team, and they are playing in a couple of hours, so they need to get them straightaway. The Amazon drone service is the quickest and most reliable. Would you mind calling them up and having them ready? I am already late and need to get going, it would be great if you could," said Karam.

"Of course I can, I will do it straightaway, they should have them within half an hour, I can see the addresses are all in London." said Margot

"Margot, you are always brilliant, thanks," and with that Karam was already heading out of the door.

Karam waked out of the faculty just before four twenty. He was now in full sight of the greatest surveillance machine the world had ever seen with every vehicle watching him as well as the second densest CCTV coverage on the planet. He looked just like a guy heading off to play sport after work and that is how he would like it to appear.

In the Ministry of Information, the surveillance team given the task of tracking Karam Shahid was going through footage of his movements and creating a file to pass to Harry Barnes. The two analysts looking at the data were quite new to the Ministry, bright youngsters but relatively inexperienced. They noted everything they had seen, created the timelines and started generating a file. When a department was on a Red Alert, protocol dictated that a report should be filed every twenty-four hours unless something unusual was of interest. They were watching the live feeds coming through. Karam Shahid's facial recognition and body movement profile had both been entered into the system, enabling him to be tracked constantly. The huge bank of screens in front of the analysts were showing images of Karam leaving the LSE faculty building, turning right onto Kingsway and walking along towards Holborn. A combination of CCTV, driverless Pod cameras as well as drones gave the analysts nine different views of him as he made his way towards Holborn Tube. The screens would change as one camera lost sight, and another picked up. As he entered the tube, all the screens changed and were replaced by images from the cameras belonging to 'Transport for London'. They saw him descend the escalators, in his football kit, holding his sports bag, headphones in, and waiting on the platform. Nothing seemed out of the ordinary and certainly nothing to report as exceptional.

Karam knew that his every movement was being watched. He checked his phone. No movement in the basement, nothing happening around his flat. He had checked to see if he was being followed but knew that was unlikely, there was little need to follow anyone in 2032 when your every movement was being watched through technology. If Sophie Hallam wanted to pull him in, it would happen suddenly and without warning.

Back at the faculty, Margot carried the three packages and opened a door onto a small courtyard in the middle of the building. She could see the flashing lights of the drones approaching. All three arrived at the same time and hovered in front of her like giant flying bugs. The three of them almost simultaneously lowered baskets from within. The first drone asked "Margot Elsworth, LSE administration?"

"Yes," she replied.

"Package for Keynsham Court, Ealing?"

"Yes," she replied.

"Please place barcode under scanner."

The drone emitted a red laser from below. Margot waved the barcode underneath.

"Registered. Please place parcel in tray," said the drone.

Margot placed the package in the basket which retracted. The drone powered up and pulled away rising into the night sky and disappeared. The other two drones did the same thing and within a couple of minutes they were on their way. Margot was a lady in her late fifties, only fifteen years ago, what had just passed would have seem like the stuff of science fiction, but even for her this was commonplace, such was the speed of technological change throughout the twenty twenties. Margo returned to her desk and carried on with her work, Karam's parcels were on their way and she had been only too happy to help.

The tube pulled in and Karam took a seat. He was imagining the drones airborne and delivering his packages. He knew that everything was now in motion, he just hoped that he could keep Sophie Hallam at bay long enough to see through his plan, he must appear to be acting as normal throughout to try and avoid raising suspicion. He took the Central Line for three stops to Bank and then changed and walked through to pick up the DLR to take him to Shadwell Station in Wapping. When he alighted and started walking to the John Orwell Sports Centre, he noticed the whirr of a drone overhead and two driverless pods with no passengers close by. Karam immersed himself in the music coming through his headphones and tried to act normally. It was a ten-minute walk to the sports centre, and he knew he had been watched every moment.

As he arrived, he saw Charlie and a few others from the team warming up and kicking a few balls around. The balls were skidding over the AstroTurf which was very wet just like all the players soaked from the relentless rain of which there was no sign of easing up at all. This would be a good chance to switch off and think about something else for a while. Karam put his bag at the back of the goal and joined the others, the same as he had done many times before, this might be the last time he ever played football with these guys. He saw that a second drone had arrived, probably because there were not many cameras if any on the football pitches.

In Tottenham, a drone was lowering itself to a dreary block of flats. The Broadwater Farm was a large housing estate with a chequered history. After the riots in the 1980s, it had received a makeover and was completely rejuvenated, but the post Covid depression of the early twenty twenties saw it fall back to become a crime ridden estate again. By the time war had broken out, The Government was not interested in social problems in the United Kingdom and had resigned itself to a policy of containment rather than improvement, and it was here that 'Tom' was able to rent a one bedroom flat. After leaving the army, the first few years out of uniform were fine, he had joined several agencies and had a steady supply of work as an armed security officer or providing protection for high profile private clients. He had a six-month spell at a private clinic in Zurich, and another nine months looking after an Arab Prince but that was his last well-paid job. The PTSD was kept at bay when he was busy, but his dependence on alcohol and drugs was getting worse. Once the war started, he had hoped to get a job with the Ministry of Defence in some capacity but found that so many things had changed, he discovered he could not tick enough boxes, the computer always said no. His security work completely dried up when travel became restricted due to Covid. He found various part time jobs but nothing steady which led to more drinking and substance abuse.

His interest had been piqued one day whilst surfing the dark web. He was always looking there for work and opportunities. He knew he could have got work for criminals, they were always easy to spot, but no matter how desperate things had become he had not wanted to work for anyone involved in crime. Two years ago, he had seen a cryptic message appear on one of the message boards.

'Highly trained ex-military looking for a challenge and an opportunity to set things right?'

He had thought it unusual but intriguing and had replied. Every week he would have a conversation with 'Anton' who told him that a very lucrative mission would be coming up in the next two or three years that would mean he would not have to worry about money again and would help him get some revenge on the Government and system that had let him down after he had left the army. Anton would ask him questions about his experience and skills, and from time to time there would be some psychometric testing and personality profiling. Anton also set him a few challenges, endurance, and orienteering. He was happy to do them, he did not have very much else going on in his life, and it encouraged him to maintain his fitness. Then two weeks ago he received delivery of some Chinese weapons and ammunition and was told it was all part of the forthcoming operation.

To be able to practice with the weapons without being heard, he had to make a suppressor. For someone as highly trained as Tom this was easy. He went to a DIY store and bought some one inch and two inch plastic pipe, which he cut to length and drilled holes in. He made some end caps from scraps of wood and glued them together, filling the gap between the two pipes with mattress foam. He fitted it over the gun barrel and secured with a jubilee clip. It had taken less than an hour.

He took the tube to Loughton and then walked to Epping Forest. He had dismantled the three weapons and packed them in a rucksack. With his walking boots and all-weather jacket, he looked just like someone going for a walk in the forest. He made his way into the most remote part and hid down, camouflaging himself, hidden amongst the foliage. He waited an hour, and nobody came by. There were no well-trodden paths used by ramblers or dog walkers, he felt comfortable that this was as remote as he would find. He set up some targets at ten, twenty and thirty metres and proceeded to test the weapons. They were all perfectly adequate tools, and he was impressed how effective his homemade suppressor was in reducing the noise. He had been used to using a Heckler and Koch HKG36, and a C8 Carbine in the SAS, but they had been trained on many weapons, in case they ever had to improvise during battle. The transition to the Chinese arms was not a difficult one. Once he had adjusted the sights and was happy, he dismantled them and packed them away again in his rucksack.

He collected all the spent cartridges and cleared away any signs that he had been there and then waited for a further hour making sure nobody had been around, this would also fit well with any CCTV footage of him as his trip implied a three-to-four-hour trek around the forest which sounded plausible.

He felt back in his comfortable place, utilising all his training. He felt the most alive he had done for ages. Later that evening he reported back to Anton that his tests had gone well and that he was happy with the delivery. In all the time he had been conversing with Anton he had found out truly little. Anton would rarely answer his questions, just enough to keep him onside and not to appear rude. Anton offered the occasional thing, Tom believed him to be in his thirties and from Eastern Europe, possible Belarus. He seemed knowledgeable and thought he might be ex Spetsnaz, Russian Special Forces, possibly even from the Alpha Group, Russia's equivalent of the SAS.

Tom was happy to keep talking to him, he did not have many people to converse with and it was someone who could discuss things he was interested in. When the weapons arrived and the money, he was really pleased that he had carried on. Now he was intrigued to find out about the mission.

He accepted the package from the drone, took it inside and opened it. It was a uniform for a Counter Terrorist Specialist Firearms Officer. Anton had asked him for his height, weight and sizes a couple of months earlier. He tried it on, a good fit including the helmet and goggles. He packed it tightly away, pulled back the rug in the lounge, lifted a floorboard and pushed it into the gap next to the rucksack containing the weapons.

At the same time in Ealing, Simon was receiving his drone package. He had also received the weapons, and like Tom had been out to practice, taking great care to remain under the radar, whilst in Tooting Bec, Alex received her delivery, inside was her uniform, that of a paramedic. The week before she had also received a package containing bright yellow vehicle wrap and magnetic ambulance signage.

Within a few minutes of all of them receiving their packages, they got a notification ping on their mobile phones alerting them that they had messages in their inboxes.

Simon, Tom, and Alex with no knowledge of one another went to their computers and laptops and accessed the Dark Web. Putting in their unique codes and registering, they were able to download the mail that Karam had sent them on a delay just forty minutes earlier, detailing their mission and target. Each of them was prepared and even though the target was surprising, they were all ready.

Karam had given them all a task to do before they could start. Tom and Simon had to steal a medium sized van each that they could drive. It should not be too difficult, tradesmen still had their own vans and were not using driverless pods for work because of the issue of storing tools. Alex had to find an estate car and use the vehicle wrap and signage to make it look like an ambulance. She had access to a garage so was able to do the necessary work out of the view of surveillance cameras. They had to either steal the vehicle as close to the mission timetable as possible or swap the number plates in case it was reported missing. Karam knew he could leave this to them, they were all resourceful. They digested the details of the plan and then left to find the vehicles that they needed.

An hour later having showered and changed, at The Turners Old Star, the nearest pub to the John Orwell Sports Centre, Charlie and Karam were sat at the bar.

"That was a good game tonight," said Charlie, "you played well, seemed like you were really up for it."

"Thanks Charlie, I was, I fancied a good run around, full on day at work today."

"Did you see the drone and Pods following us here? I can't believe they are still following me, haven't they got anything better to do?" said Charlie.

"Well, it doesn't cost them anything and they have that building full of people all looking for something to do. Don't get so hung up about it, you haven't got anything to hide, have you? Is there something you want to tell me Charlie? Are you a fifth columnist disguising yourself as a mild University Professor? You are, aren't you? The Scarlett Pimpernel of our day! Agent ZigZig! I knew it!"

"Very funny, hilarious. You shouldn't joke about these things; you know the power The Ministry of Information has. If anyone falls foul of them there is no guarantee what might happen."

"But you haven't done anything and have got nothing to hide. They aren't going to arrest you over buying a book, things aren't that bad, at least not yet," said Karam.

"I hope not, so why do you think they are following me?"

"It might just be a surveillance exercise, the new recruits practising, they just pulled a name out of the hat, or maybe one of them fancies Emma and wants to frame you and get you out of the picture. Ha! That's it, it's a love rival, your card is marked Charlie boy!" Karam laughed out loud. He knew that their conversation was being listened to. The Ministry had sensitive speakers everywhere and could eavesdrop conversations. Karam just needed another eighteen hours without interference.

They both had a second pint and went for a curry at the Laksha Bay, something they regularly did on a Tuesday. Despite all the shortages due to the war, there never seemed to be a shortage of curry in the same way there was never a shortage of fish and chips during the Second World War.

They chatted, had another pint then shared an Uber Pod, dropping Karam off first and then Charlie.

As Charlie scanned his door lock, he glanced up to see a drone hovering and a Pod sat silently opposite.

"Hi Em, how was your day?" he asked as he hung his coat up.

"Pretty good thanks, busy as always," she replied.

Charlie unpacked his bag and threw his football things in the washing machine. They were soaked from playing in the rain, so he put his AstroTurf boots in as well. "Did you want to put anything in with the wash?"

"Not with your smelly things thanks!"

"Emma," he said.

Emma immediately knew something was up, Charlie always called her Em, on the very few occasions he called her Emma, he always had something important to ask her

"I don't want to sound paranoid, but I am certain I am being watched. Since last night when I left The Borough, there have been drones and Pods following me around everywhere and not so subtly. Do you know anything about it?"

"No, I don't. Have you got anything to hide?"

"Don't you start, I have just had that from Karam," he replied.

"Charlie, I shouldn't tell you this really, but Karam has been raised as a person of interest. I don't think I was meant to find out, but I had to take a file to Colonel Bell and passed through surveillance. I saw Karam on all the screens. He was being watched this afternoon. He was in his football kit presumably going to meet you to play. I thought it might have been a coincidence so after dropping off the file and talking to The Colonel I went back past the desk, and there was Karam sat on the tube. I made some idle chit chat with the two analysts at the screens who were new, I hadn't seen them before. I wondered if it was just an exercise. They saw my name badge with my security clearance and told me that this was a red alert person of interest on twenty-four-hour surveillance. I don't think anyone is following you, its Karam they are following," said Emma.

"That's bonkers! Why would they be following Karam? I did think it was strange the way he shot off last night and then Sophie Hallam was asking me about him, but I didn't think anything of it. But that doesn't explain why there are drones sat outside our flat right now," said Charlie.

"Charlie, you work with Karam, you play football with Karam, I presume you have just been to the pub and had a curry with Karam, that's why you are being watched. You are probably the closest person to him."

"I need to speak to him and find out what's going on," he said.

"You can't, at least you can't call him."

"Why not?"

"If you are being watched, your phone has probably been tapped, there may even be a listening device in this flat right now," she said lowering her voice.

"What do you mean? We are indoors," he replied.

"They may have sent a team in and bugged the flat or there are some very powerful listening devices that can work through walls," she said.

Charlie slumped into the chair and put his head in his hands. It was starting to make sense now, it was nothing to do with him ordering a copy of 1984, it was all a coincidence, they were really interested in Karam Shahid, the quiet and private Professor of International Relations at The London School of Economics who was granted political asylum here in the UK ten years ago, who had worked and never put a foot out of place, a model citizen. How can this be right? Surely there has been a mistake.

Charlie started thinking about Karam and the time he had known him, he started applying his forensic journalistic mind to the question. He had known Karam for over seven years, he was his first friend when he joined the London School of Economics. He had coffee with him twice a week, they played football together. They had not socialised much after work apart from after sport but that was not that unusual, there was an age gap and Karam had a busy life with all of his evening classes in martial arts, and the gym. Charlie had not thought about it before, but Karam was a good-looking guy and was in great shape but had not shown any real interest in dating. It had crossed his mind that he might be gay, not something either had ever broached, it was none of his business. Karam had never mentioned family or even friends, but Charlie had not wanted to ask, because Karam had been very private about his life before he came to the UK, he had once said that it had been very difficult, and he preferred not to talk about it. Charlie had respected his privacy and not mentioned it.

Thinking about it, he realised he did not really know too much about Karam at all. He knew where he lived but had never been inside even though Karam had been to their flat a few times. Charlie still could not think of a single reason why Karam would be of interest to The Ministry of Information. He had never said or done anything to give him any suspicion.

"What are you thinking about Charlie," asked Emma.

"I have just been thinking about everything I have known about Karam and realised it isn't very much. He is a very private man who liked to keep himself to himself. I have spent more time with him than any other person in the last seven years apart from you, I just can't believe that the Ministry would be interested in him. What could he have done or be doing?"

"What do you want to do then?" asked Emma. "You know that if you warn him you could be in trouble with The Ministry."

"What about you?" said Charlie, "I don't want to compromise you and get you into trouble."

Emma put her finger to her mouth and motioned shhh. She moved over to Charlie, cupped her hand and put her mouth to his ear. Whispering she said "if we are being bugged, I am already in trouble for telling you about Karam being watched, we need to make them think we want to help The Ministry if they are listening." She moved away from him.

"I should never have mentioned to you about Karam, it was wrong, I will have to tell Hallam that I let it slip, in the meantime, you must keep silent, not speak to Karam. I expect that once I have told Hallam that she will want you to come in for questioning to find out what you know. You can explain what you have just told me, that you are shocked and know nothing about Karam." And then she pointed at Charlie, indicating for him to speak.

"Yes, you are quite right, we need to let the Ministry know. It needs to be face to face so we will have to wait until the morning," Charlie said.

Charlie moved towards Em and whispered in her ear "How are we going to get a message to Karam? They will be watching our every move?"

"We can't go over, they will see us, we can't ring his mobile, it will be tapped, can we chance sending a note in a drone?" she said.

"Can we send an email?" he asked.

"No, she said, everyone's emails have been tracked since 2028 under The War Act. We have triggers for key words that bring them to our attention. Anyone who is a person of interest will have all emails read within minutes of sending or receiving them," whispered Emma.

"What, everyone? "said Charlie incredulously.

"Yes, it was one of the first sweeping powers that the Ministry were given. It means we have so much dirt on people that it allows the Ministry to lean on them if they need to. We know about every dodgy deal, every affair, every nefarious activity. We have so much information at the Ministry it's hard to imagine," she said.

"I can't believe it, is there no privacy anymore?"

"Sadly, Charlie there isn't, but we are at war and its information that keeps us safe," she said.

They both looked at each other thinking how they could get a message to Karam

"But you can't warn him, said Em, having considered the situation, what if he is a 5th columnist working for the Russians or the Chinese? You can't let him know he is being watched."
"I hadn't thought of that, I just wanted to let him know because he is a friend." Charlie paused before putting his mouth to Emma's ear, "let's speak to Sophie Hallam in the morning and decide what to do then."

They tried to carry on normally for the rest of the evening, had dinner, listened to music, and relaxed. Charlie had been thinking about Karam all the time and their friendship. He felt he had to do something.

At ten o'clock he said "Em, have we got any cards, I completely forgot it's my Dad's birthday tomorrow, I need to send him one, a blank will do."

"Yes, there are a few in the drawer in the kitchen, we always have some blank ones from The National Trust," she said.

Charlie went in, found the cards, there were five of them. He flicked through whilst walking back into the lounge. "What about this one?" he said holding up a winter scene from Bodiam Castle in East Sussex.

"Looks fine to me, pity you didn't get him an actual birthday card, I thought his birthday was in September?" she said.

"Thanks, this will be great" he replied avoiding the question.

Charlie went back into the kitchen, took two plain envelopes from the drawer and a couple of pieces of paper. He quickly addressed the envelope to his father's house in North Finchley. In the card he wrote, Happy Birthday Dad, 'Alea Iacta Est'. Inside that card he put a folded envelope addressed to his brother Harry, the note inside also read 'Alea Iacta Est', and inside that envelope he put a third envelope addressed to Karam in The Elephant and Castle'. The note inside read 'Can't make football Thursday, have to go and see Mr Charrington, know you will understand, Charlie.'

Charlie knew that this was very cryptic, but it had to be if he was to avoid suspicion in case 'The Ministry' picked it up and read it. Mr Charrington was a key character in George Orwell's 1984 who helped the antihero. The Latin phrase he sent to his father and brother; 'Alea Iacta Est' was something his father had come up with a few years earlier when the family were together one Christmas. They had all been discussing the erosion of Civil Liberties that had started back in 2020. His Dad came up with the idea that if any of them were in trouble and needed help, that their coded phrase would be this, that translated 'The die has been cast.' At the time they all thought it a little melodramatic, but now Charlie was pleased that his Dad had suggested it. None of them had used it yet, but he was sure that they would both understand. He hoped that they would call up another drone and forward the letter inside the one they had received.

Charlie sealed them all down and called a drone up on his app. Six minutes later he received an alert and headed downstairs. "Just sending this off to Dad so he has it for the morning" he shouted out to Emma as he opened the door and went downstairs. The drone was hovering outside the door. It asked

"Charlie Wilson?"

"Yes, he replied."

"Delivery to N12?"

"Yes, he replied," and the basket lowered from the body of the drone. Charlie dropped the envelope into the basket and watched it rise and disappear into the rainy night sky. It would have debited his account automatically.

He returned upstairs with butterflies in his stomach, knowing he was taking a great risk, but felt he had to do something.

"Did it go ok?" asked Emma.

"Yes, glad I did that, Dad always likes getting a card."

Charlie was relieved he had not told Emma what he was doing, he did not want her to be compromised, and he still had a fear that she might report back to the Ministry.

Ten minutes later the drone was diverted by the Ministry of Transport to one of their bland buildings in Vauxhall. The Ministry had the authority to take over any flight patterns of any drones in the UK under The War Act, all it took was a phone call. The drone descended and was met by a young Ministry surveillance officer. It offered up its contents and she examined the envelope. It was just a regular A5 card sized brown envelope, perhaps a little thicker than normal addressed to Martin Wilson, 64, Nether Street, Finchley N12 4AC. She made a call. "Reference Charlie Wilson code-file X31D. We have the package. It looks like a card; do you want me to open it?"

There was a pause at the other end. "Does it look normal enough?"

"Yes, looks like a normal card, but of course I don't know what's written inside," There was another pause.

"No, send it on its way, thank you," and the line went dead.
The Officer put the envelope back in the basket which retracted, and the drone rose and set off again into the rain and darkness. Twenty minutes later it arrived at Charlies' parent's house in Finchley. His mother came to the door and took the envelope passing it to her husband who opened it.

"It's from Charlie," he said. He opened the envelope and read it. "There's something up, I think Charlie may be in trouble." He went to his phone, brought up an app and typed in some details. He and his wife chatted, she knew the significance of 'Alea Iacta Est', although Martin had been the one who taught Classics, they had travelled together and in better times had visited Italy and stood on the banks of the Rubicon where Martin had explained about Julius Caesar's crossing and how the saying had come about and the translation to 'The Die has been Cast'.

A few minutes later he received an alert on his phone. He stepped outside and after the usual questions, another drone set off with the inner envelope heading towards his younger son Harry who lived in Belsize Park. Harry was at home, opened the envelope, and knew that something was happening. He did the same as his father, ordered another drone and sent the final envelope on its way to Karam Shahid whom he had never heard of.

It was eleven thirty when Karam's phone pinged. He saw the message, that he was receiving a drone delivery in two minutes. He opened his door and looked out. There was a drone, hovering on the other side of the flats that had been there since he got home, then another came into sight, descended to be in front of Karam, and lowered its basket. It was a simple white envelope which he hid from sight immediately and returned indoors.

He opened it and read 'Can't make football Thursday, have to go and see Mr Charrington, know you will understand, Charlie'.

Karam knew immediately that it was a warning from Charlie. Thursday night football was an ad hoc affair so there was no need to say anything two days before, quite often they did not even know if they had a game until Thursday lunchtime. Karam could not immediately think who Mr Charrington was, someone from the University perhaps. He googled on his phone and the first search that came up was 'Mr Charrington Character Analysis in 1984'. He understood what Charlie was saying, that somebody was watching him. He knew that Charlie had taken a great risk sending this note to him, even though he was already very aware of the interest he had triggered at The Ministry of Information.

Karam set light to the note, the less evidence the better, and watched it burn in the sink. He was thinking about his family and the events about to take place. He opened a beer, sat in his chair, and closed his eyes.

CHAPTER SIX

WEDNESDAY 15TH FEBRUARY 2032

Sophie Hallam arrived at her desk at eight thirty in the morning with a coffee and saw the files that had already been placed there ready for her perusal. She started to look through them and came across the 24-hour surveillance file for Karam Shahid. This would not normally have come straight to her, some other operations officers would have looked at the file first and only spoken to her if they thought it necessary, but Hallam had specifically asked for all information relating to Karam Shahid to come directly to her desk.

She started to read through the twenty-four-hour report. There was nothing unusual until yesterday afternoon. Shahid left his office at two minutes past four and emerged from the faculty building at four twenty. What had happened during those eighteen minutes? Every other minute of his day was accounted for. She opened a second file from the external surveillance team, once again nothing much to show, he left the faculty building, travelled to Shad Thames, played football, went to the pub, had a curry, all with Charlie Wilson which may or may not mean anything, then went home. The only unusual thing was that he received a delivery at eleven thirty that night, a small package, an envelope perhaps.

Hallam left her office and ran up the two flights of stairs to surveillance. She saw Harry Barnes and asked to see last night's digital recordings relating to Karam Shahid. The team who filed the report had been working through the night and were now off. She and Harry sat down and fast forwarded through the recordings, she knew what she was looking for. She forwarded to two minutes past four and saw Karam leave the office, walk down the corridor, and turn left to a stairwell. There were no cameras there. He did not re-appear until he went into the administrator's office at eighteen minutes past four. Hallam could also see him passing three parcels over to a lady who was in the office, which were then collected by three drones a few minutes later.

"Look Harry, where did he go for those sixteen minutes? What was in those packages and who were they sent to? See what you can find out and fast and tell me where Shahid is right now."

Sophie went back down the stairs and as she walked along the corridor her phone rang. It was Emma.

"Good morning Ma'am, sorry to be disturbing you at the start of the day but there is something that Charlie and I need to talk to you about urgently."

"Ok Harrison, take Charlie to the King Charles meeting room, I will be there in a few minutes."

She had been expecting the call that morning, it would not take people as bright as Charlie and Emma to be putting two and two together. She took the stairs down to the ground floor and walked into the meeting room.

"Well, what can I do for you both?" she asked.

"Ma'am, I made a mistake last night and said something confidential to Charlie that I shouldn't have done."

"Go on," said Hallam.

"I told Charlie that Karam Shahid was currently a person of interest to The Ministry. Charlie had realised he was being tracked, he had seen drones and Pods, he was worried and wondered why. I just told him about Shahid because I could see how worried he was. I only found out by chance. As you must know from the files, Charlie and Karam Shahid work together and are friends, I am sure that is why Charlie was being tracked, Ma'am," Emma looked down, embarrassed.

Sophie Hallam was not big in stature, but her presence was overwhelming, even Charlie felt quite daunted by her.
"Don't worry Harrison, I don't think there is any harm done although you know you have broken regulations, but I would like to ask Charlie some questions about Karam Shahid. You are quite right, it is Shahid who is the person of interest not Charlie. You see Mr Wilson, when somebody becomes a person of interest to The Ministry of Information, everyone they are in contact with also becomes to a lesser degree, how shall I put it, interesting. We are not interested in you, per se, it is your interaction with Mr Shahid that we want to know about. Mr Shahid seems to be a closed book, there is little that we know about him, perhaps you can help us build a better picture of our friend Karam? You work together, take coffee together, lunch together and play football together. You go to the pub and out for dinner afterwards, that is a lot of time to be talking about things. What do you know about Mr Shahid, perhaps some things that we don't know?" asked Hallam.

"I am not sure I know any more than you do," replied Charlie. "Karam is a very private individual. He does his work, his students like him, he is immensely popular in the staff common room and with the support staff. He does not talk about family or what happened before he came to the UK. Is this something to do with his time in Syria and the Civil War? Did he do something then?" asked Charlie.

"We have no interest in what Mr Shahid did before he came to the UK. We want to know what he does with his time when he isn't at work, who his friends and acquaintances might be, that sort of thing."

"Outside of work, he does karate and other martial arts, goes to the gym a lot, and I mean a lot. We play football, he is one of the fittest on the pitch, we have the occasional beer, that kind of thing. I don't know any of his friends outside of work and football," replied Charlie.

"Do you not think it strange that he has no family and has never mentioned anyone, nor that he appears to have no religion, unusual for somebody from that region?"

"I never asked, but perhaps he lost his family during the Civil War and doesn't want to talk about it. As for religion, he is well educated, perhaps he has worked all that out for himself?" said Charlie.

"Perhaps," said Hallam. "It doesn't sound as though there is anything else you can tell us or want to tell us." She looked straight at Charlie with a piercing gaze. He felt particularly uncomfortable, as though he was back at school in front of the headmaster.
"There is nothing else I can tell you, I swear it," he replied.

"Karam Shahid received a note delivered by drone last night at eleven thirty pm. You summoned a drone to take a note away at ten thirty, coincidence?" she asked.

Charlie's heart sank. Had the Ministry intercepted the envelope and opened it finding the note that was ultimately destined for Shahid? Was there anything they did not know about? He would call her bluff.

"It doesn't take a drone an hour to go from Battersea to The Elephant & Castle. I was sending a birthday card to my father for today," said Charlie.

There was a pause as Sophie Hallam looked at Charlie. She knew he was lying, and her stare told him that she knew.

"Ok, we will leave it there. Thank you very much for coming to see me and thank you Emma for your honesty. These things happen. I do not need to tell you the importance of keeping all of this to yourselves. We are in the middle of a surveillance operation that must be kept secret, I am sure you can appreciate the work that we do here Charlie, and the consequences of noncompliance, Emma understands the importance, don't you Emma?" and Sophie gave her a long stare.

"Yes, of course ma'am," she replied.

Sophie strode out for the room and took the stairs taking two at a time back to her office.

Emma walked Charlie out of the building. They stood out in the street. It had stopped raining that morning and they were able to stand out without umbrellas. Charlie took a deep breath in.

"Wow, she is harsh," said Charlie.

"She was just doing her job, it's what makes her the best," said Emma. "Was that true about the card Charlie?"

"Yes, of course it was," he replied. "I need to get going, have a good day and see you later. Thanks for sorting this out.". He kissed her on the cheek and headed off. Emma went inside, took the lift and made her way back to the office.

When Sophie arrived back at her desk, Harry Barnes was stood there waiting for her. "Ma'am, I think we have something. We have traced all the cameras in the faculty building. There are three places Shahid could have gone, some teaching rooms, a staff room or the basement."

"There must be a camera in the staff room surely?" she said.

"Yes, there is the security camera, but it was broken yesterday and hadn't been repaired," replied Harry.

"Are there any other devices in that room with cameras? Laptops,

TVs?" she asked.

"We are looking now; we would need to know who they were registered to."

"I'm not sure we have that kind of time. Karam Shahid knows we are on to him. If he is planning something, he may well have brought it forwards. Anything else, what about the parcels?"

"We know that they went to addresses in Tooting Bec, Tottenham and Ealing, and we know that they weighed between two and three kilos. We have requested visual ID from the drone companies, the recipients would have been filmed from the onboard cameras, we are waiting for these to come through. We have run a search on who lives at the addresses, one is a private landlord, one a housing association and the one in Ealing is a house owned by a Susan Walker who died two years ago. We are working on getting more information right now, who the tenants are, who else lives there, I have got our most experienced team on it," said Harry.

"Put another team on, maximum urgency, go on Harry go, I need all the information now!" Harry had never seen his boss this animated before.
Harry left the office and ran downstairs to his team, urging everyone to get the information as quickly as possible

Sophie Hallam pulled out a piece of A4 paper and a pen, she wrote Karam Shahid at the top, underlined it and started making notes on the sheet, adding lines, Elephant & Castle, Syria, refugee, family, Nigeria, LSE. As the sheet filled up, she took another page and carried on. She laid the two pages out in front of her and started circling key phrases, trying to picture Karam Shahid. She could see him looking at her in The Borough. He knew exactly who she was.

Twenty minutes passed. "Harry, where's that information?" she barked down the phone "What have you got for me?"

"We are getting there, you know what it's like trying to speak to anybody at the Council and Land Registry, nobody ever wants to make a decision or put their name to anything, and not all of the information is digitised, unbelievably the Housing Association still have manual files. I will call you as soon as we have anything, we are on it."

"Have you put surveillance on the three addresses?" she asked.
"Yes, drones, Pods and officers heading there now."

"Make sure they aren't seen; I don't want anyone alerted," she said.

"Understood," the phone rang off.

Sophie Hallam looked at her pages and underlined HMS Dauntless, Nigeria, Family, Van Hire. Is that what it could be about? Some kind of revenge or retribution? But against whom? She picked up her phone and rang Emma.

"Harrison, find out who the Captain of HMS Dauntless was in 2028 when it sank the Nigerian boat off the coast of Cornwall. Send me any media information from the time as well, straightaway if you don't mind."

"Yes, immediately Ma'am," replied Emma.

Charlie was walking from The Ministry to his regular café on Westminster Bridge Road. He was thinking about everything that had happened and Hallam's questions. He needed to speak to Karam, but how? He knew he was still being watched; the drone was following him overhead. He went into the café, was greeted by Jasmin and took his seat by the window. When his coffee arrived, he was deep in thought.

Should he go to The University and speak to Karam knowing that he would be tracked? Karam would be under surveillance as well and the likelihood is that their conversation would be listed to. Where could he arrange to meet him, where they might be able to talk privately? That was difficult these days, almost everywhere was covered by cameras and listening devices.

In Brentford, Simon was easing a metal strip down the window of a long wheelbase Ford Transit van. The van was parked outside some railway arches and there did not seem to be any cameras. There was no-one in sight and no Pods going by. Once inside, he quickly stripped back the ignition housing and started the van. It was an old one, much easier to break into and start. The engine revved and he pulled out, a large bag on the seat next to him.

At the same time, Alex had found an estate car in Tooting Bec, just around the corner from her flat. Most cars that remained on the streets were older, people getting the last few years of use from them. By now ninety percent of owned cars had disappeared from the streets as people moved across to hiring a Pod as and when they needed them. The cars that remained tended to be ten years old and easier to break into. Alex got the car started and drove to the lock up she had access to. Once inside and out of sight of the cameras, she took out the car wrap that Anton has sent her and started applying it, adding the fluorescent chequered green and white stripes and finally the Paramedic stickers. She took the paramedics uniform out of the bag and changed into it. Sitting in the car she opened the instructions sent by Anton she had printed out, and read over them again, visualising everything in her mind.

In Tottenham, Tom left his flat early before the sun was up and made his way to Wood Green, carrying a large holdall. He had scanned the area the night before and seen a van. He had watched two builders return, unload their tools and hang the keys up in the shed inside their yard. He had watched all of this from the other side of the road. In the cover of early morning darkness, he pulled himself over the wall, picked the lock, found the keys, and climbed back over to the van parked on the street. Just as he thought, the keys fitted. He opened the van, threw his bag in, and drove off. Just in case they reported the van stolen when they arrived, he parked under a railway bridge away from any cameras. He was quite sure that with the war effort, a stolen van would not really catch the imagination of the police. Just to be sure though, he had removed the number plates from a similar vehicle earlier and changed them over. He did not want to take any chances. These days, a person driving a van stood out a lot more amongst the driverless pods that moved silently around.

Like the other two, he sat composing himself and looking through the notes he had made about the operation ahead. He unzipped the sports bag next to him and looked at the uniform in the bag and checked the weapons. He closed his eyes and thought about what would happen later that day.

Karam had barely been able to sleep that night. His mind was buzzing, thinking through every detail of the events that would unfold later that day, also worrying about his friend Charlie and his efforts to try and warn him, but most of all about Sophie Hallam and the Ministry of Information. He thought he had covered his tracks as best as he could, but he knew that Sophie Hallam was closing in on him.

He wanted to give the impression that nothing unusual was going on. He got up and prepared for work as he normally would, although this morning he did spend a little more time in the bathroom. For the first time since he became a man, he shaved off his beard. He also shaved his hair very short. He fitted a false beard he had bought in a shop weeks before, that looked like the one he had just shaved off. He put on a wig from the same shop that looked just like the hair he had cut back. He looked at himself in the mirror and when he was satisfied, he flushed all the hair that he had removed down the toilet, leaving no trace of what he had been doing. He put on a baseball cap and left his flat at 8.30 with his holdall, the same as any other morning. The rain had eased off for once which suited him as he wanted to walk to work. It was a forty-minute journey which he had done many times. He put on his headphones and set off, aware of the drone overhead. He knew that every camera on every pod that passed by would be sending images back to The Ministry of Information. He picked up a coffee and croissant on the way and arrived at the University just before 9.30. His first lecture was at 10am. He spent twenty minutes in his study and headed for the lecture hall.

All of this was being watched by the surveillance team at the Ministry. Karam's whereabouts and movements were now being reported in real time to Harry Barnes, who was waiting for the information requested on the recipients of the parcels that Shahid had sent the previous afternoon, and the possibilities for the sixteen minutes that were unaccounted for.

Karam checked all the cameras on his phone. He could see that some people were once again entering his flat and looking round. Two of them had been on the previous visit, he knew exactly who they were. He could tell there was more urgency in their movements, the noose was tightening.

As he entered the lecture hall, Karam was conscious that he needed to get his timing right. He must appear as relaxed and normal as possible until the very last minute. He had fitted two cameras at the front and rear exits of the faculty building some time ago. He had not switched them on apart from occasionally testing them to save the batteries. He now turned them on to be warned if the Ministry were coming for him.
Back at Whitehall, Harry Barnes rushed into Sophie Hallam's office.

"Ma'am, he almost certainly went into the basement, we managed to find a camera on a laptop in the common room, he didn't go in there, nor the teaching room, there was a class being held there yesterday between three thirty and five."

"We need to find out what's going on down there. I don't think we can avoid alerting Shahid. Take your two best teams and find out what he's doing in the basement. I think you ought to take a team from bomb disposal with you. What time does his lecture finish? The file says he always goes out for lunch." Hallam's brain was going into overdrive.

"Yes, that's right, on Wednesdays he always goes to an Italian café half a mile away, he usually leaves at twelve forty-five, a real creature of habit," said Harry.

"Ok, get everyone in position, but don't enter the building until you have seen him leave. We might be able to do this without him knowing. Get a call in to the Vice Chancellor and make him aware of what we are doing, but tell him it is of the highest national importance, and discretion is a must, to only let the fewest number of people know. This isn't a blazing gun operation Harry, subtle and quiet if we can," said Sophie Hallam pacing around her desk, considering all of the permutations.

Harry left and started making calls on his mobile. By midday he had two SCO19 specialist firearms units and a bomb disposal team assembled in the parking area underneath The Ministry. He came down with two of his officers and briefed everyone. They were assembled in six vehicles, splitting up into three groups of eight, and made the short journey from Whitehall to Lincolns Inn Fields. They parked up three streets away and waited.

At twelve forty-five, Karam Shahid walked out of the faculty building, turned right as had been anticipated and started making his way to Bar Italia. Harry had a live feed from the surveillance team at the Ministry patched through to his device. He could see Shahid walking down the road.

"Let's go," he shouted down his radio, and all six vehicles pulled out, and drove to the front of the faculty building. The doors opened and twenty men and women in black and grey uniforms got out, secured the entrance, and entered. They were immediately followed by Harry and another man and a woman in suits. The Vice Chancellor, a lady called Karen Fielding met them inside the lobby and offered her help, asking what this was all about. Harry was very polite and asked where and what he would find in the basement. The Vice Chancellor called for the building maintenance man, who was called on his phone by Margot in reception, who was overly excited by all the commotion. A couple of minutes later an Eastern European man in his forties came down the stairs and up to the University Chancellor.

"This is Jacob, he looks after all our maintenance and knows everything that's down in the basement," said Fielding.

"Hi Jacob, my name is Harry Barnes, I am with the Ministry of Information. What is it like in the basement? Is it one large room, several rooms?"

"It is a corridor with five rooms that come off it, heating, laundry, electricity, a small workshop and some storage," said Jacob.

"Have you seen anything unusual recently down there, something out of place?" said Harry.

"No nothing, I am the only person who goes down there apart from specialist engineers for the service contracts, and access to the archive storage."

"What archive storage?" asked the Vice Chancellor.

"There's a room at the end used for storing academic files, I think it is looked after by the Syrian Professor, I helped him clear it out a year ago. It said restricted personnel on the door, I assumed the files were sensitive, it was only ever an empty room full of rubbish, I have been in there a couple of times just keeping an eye out for mice, there is nothing unusual," said Jacob.

"You have a key?" asked Harry.

"Yes, it's here" said Jacob as he took a large bunch of keys out of his pocket and jangled them until he had one in his hand that he held up.

"Thank you, Jacob," as he leant forwards and took the bunch from him.

Jacob protested mildly but Karen Fielding shook her head to say it was ok.

Harry gave the keys to one of the firearms officers and they headed off in tactical formation. The team made their way downstairs, leaving one officer at each junction for security. The bomb disposal team following closely, one of whom was wearing a heavy anti blast suit. They used cameras on flexible arms to look around corners and look down the empty corridor moving stealthily as a unit until they were in front of a door marked:

Historic Files Storage
Authorised Personnel Only

Five hundred yards away walking along the A40, passing The Shaftsbury Theatre, Karam was following all of this on his phone, his hidden camera picking up everything that was going on. He did not have a microphone in the corridor, but he had installed one in the file room. He could hear the key turn and the sound of boots as he watched them enter the room. He split his screen to watch what was happening from both cameras.

A similar image was now being watched by Sophie Hallam back at the Ministry of information via the headcams of the Firearm Officers.

"Room Clear," shouted the officer who now stood in the file room with his helmet torch.

"Harry, where are you?" shouted Hallam,

"Just coming in now," he said. Harry entered and switched on the light.

He stood in the room and looked around, shelves lined the walls stacked with boxes of files.

"Get the officer to scan the room with his headcam," demanded Hallam.

"Go round with your camera, slowly," Harry told the officers. The two men moved around the room sending back real time images to the surveillance team and their boss in the Ministry.

"There, what's that, behind those files, there's something behind them," said Hallam.

Harry went over and carefully pulled out one of the boxes. Behind them there was a perpendicular line running down the wall with a small gap.

"It might be a door, help me move some more of these boxes," he said. He started pulling them from the shelves, passing them down to the officers. When they were all removed, they dragged the shelving unit out of the way. A metal door was now exposed.
"Camera," Harry barked.

The Officer put his very thin camera, the size of a pipe cleaner into the empty keyhole and looked inside. The images relayed back to Hallam's office and to Harry's device showed the firearms on the wall and some pictures and files. There were a couple of boxes on the floor and a laptop.

"We need that laptop," said Hallam, "but be careful Harry."

Harry tried the key, but it did not fit. He looked at the huge bunch of keys in his hand and shouted

"Get Jacob down here, fast."

Moments later the Polish man entered the room.

"Jacob, did you know about this room?"

"Yes, it was open when we cleared the room out a year ago, just another empty storage room."

"Do you have a key for it?"

"Yes, the Professor borrowed it to get one cut, it's this one," he said grabbing a key amongst the big bunch. "I remember it because it has this red fob," said Jacob.

"Thank you," said Harry.

He inserted it into the keyhole and tuned it very slowly. They heard the click as it unlocked. Harry very gently pushed the door open and then walked in. He was so amazed at the guns on the wall, he did not notice the fishing wire pulling at a switch in a box. He was looking at the boxes of ammunition, some grenades and small bombs, and as he scanned the room, he saw the pictures on the wall, half a dozen of them of the Thames Barrier, from different angles, with arrows and lines drawn across them.
"It's the Thames Barrier he shouted into his microphone; the target is The Thames Barrier."

Just then he heard the fizzing of a fuse.

"Get out, get out, it's a bomb!" he screamed and dived back out through the door onto the floor.

There was a tremendous bang, a white flash and searing heat. The file room and basement were immediately filled with dense smoke. Harry was not wearing any breathing apparatus but some of the firearms officers were, they grabbed him and pulled him out, dragging him up the stairs and out on to the street. Their medical team doused his eyes with water and bandaged them. He had some burns on his hands and face. Karam was watching all of this on his phone. He had learnt how to make a phosphorous bomb from the internet. The materials were widely available, it was not a difficult task for a man with some intelligence and plenty of determination.

The Thames Barrier had protected London from high tides and storm surges since 1982. When required it is closed during high tide and opened during low tide to restore the rivers flow to the sea. In the 1980s it was only used 2-3 times a year, but by the 2030s it was being used 100-150 times a year. With the excessive rain of the last few years, the Barrier was critical to prevent London from flooding.

Sophie Hallam knew this, as a student she had visited the barrier and understood what it did, and the danger presented if it was attacked.

She picked up her phone to ask one of her team

"Find out when the next high tide is in The North Sea. And tell me where Shahid is right now."

A moment later a live feed on a screen in her office showed him entering Bar Italia on Frith Street.

"Where is he, get me eyes on him," she shouted. She left her office and ran up to the surveillance floor. She looked up at the banks of screens that were replaying Karam Shahid going into the Italian café.

"There are no cameras inside Ma'am. We can't find a device to log into."

"Have we got anyone on the ground nearby?"

"Three minutes away."

"Is he going to look too obvious?" she asked.

"She won't, she is a field operative in ordinary clothing."

"Can we get a Pod to sweep by?" asked Hallam.

"Happening right now," said the officer, and a picture came up of the entrance to the café. The Pod slowed down, and the camera came into sharp focus, but it could not see any of the tables as it looked in. Shahid was temporarily out of sight.

"Are you ok Harry?" asked Sophie into her microphone.

"Yes Ma'am, a bit sore, I am being treated. We need to know who those three were receiving the parcels, the Thames barrier isn't a target one person could handle on their own."

"I know," said his boss.

Sophie looked up and addressed the room full of personnel.

"What have you found out about the three targets who received packages last night? Who are they and where are they? Come on everyone I want this information, and I need it now."

This message was relayed to everyone in Operations as the whole department went into collective overdrive. Screens were changing between scenes as they looked for footage to give them the whereabouts of the three recipients of the parcels.
Hallam's phone rang. "Ma'am, the high tide is every twelve hours, its storm tides that are the problem. There are none predicted in the foreseeable future," said the man's voice.

"You are sure about that? There isn't one predicted the next few days?" she asked.

"No Ma'am, I spoke to the head of The Maritime and Coastguard agency in the TNBC control room," he said.

"What's the TNBC?" you know I hate to use acronyms here.

"Sorry Ma'am it's The Thames Barrier Navigation Centre," he replied.

"Ok, thank you," and she hung up.

Hallam was deep in thought. Someone as detailed as Shahid would surely plan something like this for maximum effect. Perhaps knowing he was being watched he was forced to bring the plan forwards, but there was a doubt in her mind.

Colonel Charles Bell entered the room

"At ease everyone. I have been following the operation, what else do you have?" he asked.

"We are following Karam Shahid, he is in a café in the West End, in the meantime we have discovered his secret room, like a military bunker, hidden in the basement of the London School of Economics. It looks like he is planning something at The Thames Barrier. We think it might be imminent, he contacted three people last night, we are trying to find out who they are and tracking them now, we haven't located them yet, but must be getting close," said Sophie.

"What have we done about protecting The Barrier?" he asked.

"Nothing yet Sir, this is all happening as we speak."

The Colonel took Sophie by the arm and pulled her to one side, speaking very quietly.

"Don't you think we should get an alert out to the Barrier and the Army to defend it. You have seen the height of the river, if the Barrier were to be blown up, the City of London would be under ten feet of water, the biggest financial centre in the world would stop functioning," he said.

"I am well aware of that, I am hoping to stop it before anything happens, but there is something that just isn't right about this," she said.

"This may not be the time for following a hunch, the stakes are extremely high. Shall I put out an alert?"

"Yes," she said.

The Colonel turned to leave the room; he already had his phone to his ear. He would have to get Ministerial backing to call the army. He spoke to The Home Secretary who gave approval and then he put everything in motion. Being on a war footing, it only took a single call to alert the Army. He called the chief at The Thames Barrier and informed him what might be happening. He had his own protocols with the local police and put those in place. This moment had been planned for since the day the Barrier was opened, a terrorist attack to disable or destroy it, they had run drills and worked through every scenario, but this was the first time they had a real and present danger. There had been several cyberattacks by the Chinese and Russians, but the depth of security was so great that their firewalls had never been breached.

A young woman with a file in her hand approached Hallam.

"Ma'am, we have identified the first recipient of the parcel. The address in Ealing, is a house belonging to Susan Walker. She died two years ago. The information is a bit scrappy, but it appears her son Anthony Walker has been living there alone since. He signed for the package last night, this is the image taken by the drone," she said passing across a piece of paper with a photo printed on it.

"As you can see, it's a bit grainy, not too clear, but we have also been cross referencing and think we have a match with an Oliver Anthony Walker who was with the Special Forces Support Group. He was part of the counter terrorism unit, rose to the rank of Captain, went to Sandhurst. He was awarded the Military Cross for his role in Libya in 2023 and then had it merited with a silver bar in 2026 for gallantry in the Galwan River Campaign against the Chinese. He left the army in 2028 suffering from PTSD. Did some private security and consultancy work, nursed his mother the last couple of years. She had dementia, fell foul of the National Savings Support Act, so she was not eligible for any Government help. Looks like she had to mortgage the house for her care. The rising inflation and falling property prices meant her money ran out and her son had to stop work to look after her. It appears the Council have been trying to re-possess the house for the last year, but he would not move out. There is a County Court eviction notice and there has been a visit by Bailiffs. These are photos from the MOD for his military ID, a regiment photo and one of him during the Libyan campaign. This last photo was taken just before he left the army, from his medical files."

"It looks like the same man," said Hallam. "He sounds as though he might be motivated as well. This is a serious character, well trained. Where is he now?" she asked.

"We aren't sure. We have a team at his house now. We should have it on camera." She tapped her device and on two of the screens in front of them, different angles of a three bedroom semi detached house in a quiet street came into view.

"That's our man going up to the front door now," she said.

The man in the picture was holding a folder for papers and was dressed in a suit and looked very authoritative. He pressed the bell, tried the doorknocker, peered through the letterplate and then started moving across the house looking in through the windows. After a while they heard him speak.

"Doesn't look like there is anyone here."

"Get inside, find out what's happening," said Hallam.

The man waved and the doors of two vans opened. A stream of people in combat uniforms ran up to the house. One was carrying a ram and positioned himself by the front door. He was aiming at where the locks sat. The man in the suit made sure everyone was in position. The ram was pulled back and thrust at the door with force. The door flew open and as it did a huge explosion was triggered in the hallway blowing everyone backwards. Another explosion went off just behind, blowing the side windows out showering glass over all the men and women in combats who were also flattened by the explosion. Three more explosions in sequence saw all the windows blown out and the roof start to cave in, the side wall started to collapse from the top, and the guttering and slates fell into the driveway that ran along the side of the building.

There was a sense of shock back in the Ministry as they saw the building collapsing and officers being dragged away from the falling debris. The dust meant that they could not clearly see what was happening, but they could hear the voices through the speakers. Although it was an awful situation, they were all professionals, there was no panic. After a few minutes, everyone was accounted for, there were no fatalities, a few broken bones, some cuts and bruises. Within ten minutes ambulances were arriving. The house had stopped collapsing and the dust was settling, it was a mess.

The officer in the suit working for the Ministry was Adam Green, an ex-Guards Officer. He was probably the worst injured and was concussed. Sophie Hallam asked to speak to the next in charge.
"Detective Amhurst Ma'am, Counter Terrorism," came the voice. She could see who she was talking to in one of the screens although he was wearing combats with a helmet, but the visor was up.

"Hello Amhurst. Can you get in the building is there anything left?"
"I will take a look, it looks precarious, give me a moment."

"What do we know about the other two? Have we found anything out yet? Clearly this Oliver Anthony Walker was expecting us, or somebody else to call. Quite an impressive greeting card I would say. We have these images, get them into the facial recognition software and find him," she said addressing the whole room, "Now if you don't mind!"

A voice came back down the line,

"Ma'am, there's nothing left, the whole building has collapsed, we might find something, but it will take hours if not days," said Amhurst.

"Set it up, I want the whole site cordoned off and excavated as a matter of urgency. Re-group your team, you have a couple more addresses to attend to, we will have to be more careful next time, get bomb disposal ready to join you, we should have an address shortly."

"Yes Ma'am," he replied.

"Where are we with the other two addresses, and what's happening with Shahid?" Hallam was remaining calm, she knew from her time in the army that it does not help a situation to appear to be panicked.

"Our officer is one minute away from Bar Italia, information just coming through now on the flat in Tottenham," said one of the officers fixed on the screen in front of him.

"The flat in Tottenham has had a tenant for the last three years, Sam Harding, a tenant of Haringey Borough Council. No rent arrears, never missed a payment. Police records say nothing Ma'am, a clean slate. Cross referencing with the MOD now, just a moment, here we are, Sam Harding, joined the army, basic training, promoted to Lance Corporal and then Corporal. Joined the 3 Commando Brigade Royal Marines and then went on to the SAS. Highly decorated, tours in Afghanistan, Libya, The Yemen and the Saudi Arabian Revolution. He left the army in 2027, some periods of unemployment, it's a bit sketchy. Worked for G4S on homeland security, but nothing for the last couple of years."

"Officer arriving at Bar Italia, awaiting instructions," said a young female officer sat in front of a bank of screens.

"Tell her to go in, order something and see if she can see Shahid," said Hallam.

Back at Frith Street a young woman dressed smart but casual, entered 'Bar Italia'. She had a look around as though looking for a friend and went up to the bar. She ordered a takeaway Cappuccino and waited, playing with her phone. She was able to casually spin round and keep looking. A couple of bench seats and a table were occupied but not by anyone fitting the description of Karam Shahid. She brought the image sent by The Ministry up on her phone. He was not there.

"Do you have a toilet? She asked.

"Yes, down the stairs."

"Thank you," she replied.

She went down into the basement area and saw two doors, one marked Signor, the other Signora. She gently pushed the door marked Signor, it opened and was empty, the same with the other door.

She called The Ministry. "He's gone, he's not here," she said.

Hallam leant into the microphone, "Check out the back, how did he get out?". She turned to the room.

"Have we got eyes on the back of the restaurant? Is there a drone there?"

"I don't think so Ma'am, checking all footage now, pulling up all live feeds within fifty metres of Bar Italia."

Karam Shahid was already two streets away and heading along Charing Cross Road to Leicester Square Tube. He had checked out the rear rooms of Bar Italia on previous visits to be able to use it as an escape route. At the rear there were the store-rooms, close to the kitchen, but not too close that he would be seen, and a rear door onto a courtyard. He had seen that the staff left the key for this door hanging up on a piece of string. One lunchtime he had taken it and had a copy cut at a hardware shop just a few doors along, and replaced the original without anyone noticing.
He had tested the door to make sure it opened and was not alarmed and worked out where it led. He had been able to go through a door from the courtyard and into what used to be The Prince Edward Theatre which had never re-opened after the 2022 Covid outbreak when most theatres closed and made his way through the building onto Greek Street. He had planned this route months before. In the theatre hidden inside a cupboard, he had left a change of clothes. It only took a few minutes before he was dressed as a community police officer. He had removed his false beard, and replaced his dark wig for a blond one, and added a pair of spectacles. He had swapped the contents of his sports bag and put them into a large satchel that he had over his shoulder. He looked like a completely different person

as he opened a side door that he had previously forced and secured with his own padlock. By the time the officer from the Ministry had reported that he had gone, he was moments away from the tube.

The team back at The Ministry were scanning the dozens of screens in front of them, the majority were fed by drones, Pods and CCTV cameras around the 'Bar Italia' in Soho. The others were from the drones hovering in front of the flat on the Broadwater Farm estate in Tottenham.

"Let's look at all local footage from the buildings at the rear of Bar Italia in the last ten minutes," said Sophie Hallam.

Screens flickered and changed, showing different viewpoints and angles. The streets were quiet without too many people around. They showed deliveries being made, others being collected, a few tradesmen, people going about their business and a couple of community police officers.

"Where is he?" she asked.

"Have we got the facial recognition loaded?"

"Yes Ma'am," someone replied.

"The firearms team are eight minutes away from the Tottenham flat," said an officer.

Sat in the café in Westminster, Charlie Wilson was considering what to do. He was torn and finding it difficult to decide. He decided to ring Emma to see if she knew what was happening. It went to voicemail; he left a message asking her to call him. He knew that she would have seen his call and not answered it because she was too busy or could not speak. He had spent the morning searching on the internet for anything he could find out about Karam but there was very little and nothing new. Jasmin brought over his second coffee of the day which Charlie nursed. He did not touch his sandwiches as he felt too nauseas. Should he ring Karam? What good would it do?

What was his friend involved in?

"We are here and in position Ma'am," said Amhurst the firearms officer. They had made the journey across London in extraordinary time. The advent of driverless vehicles with most vehicles now being run by computers that talked to one another constantly, meant that in emergencies vehicles could travel very fast across the City. There was also a fraction of the vehicles on the roads now that car ownership had collapsed making journey times much faster.

"Let's take more care this time, these are very dangerous people we are dealing with, no casualties please," said Hallam.

Amhurst and his team climbed the stairs of the block to the third floor. It was pretty grim, dense graffiti all over the walls, rubbish lying around, and the stench of decay. They edged along the corridor receiving constant feed from the drone hovering outside. They approached the door and pushed a camera through the letter plate. There was no movement inside, there did not appear to be any wires or any sign of a booby trap.

Amhurst noticed that the door was ever so slightly ajar. He gently pushed it and pulled away behind the wall. The door swung open and nothing happened. He pushed the door further so that it was completely open and looked beyond the hallway into the lounge.

Beckoning him, an armed officer pushed past with his gun at shoulder height, another officer followed him.

"Clear, Clear," they called as they moved through the flat. Two more armed officers followed them in. Within thirty seconds they gave the sign that the flat was empty. Through his earphone, Amhurst heard the first officer say "You had better come and see this Sir."

Amhurst walked through into the lounge which was empty apart from one chair and a tv on a box. There were two floorboards lifted exposing a gap below that was empty. On the wall was written in black paint in capital letters:

'HAVE YOU FOUND WHAT YOU WERE LOOKING FOR?'

The image was relayed back to The Ministry

"He left the door open and this message on the wall," said Amhurst into his microphone. "He knew we were coming."

"He certainly did, they both did, and I expect we will find the same when we get to the other flat," said Hallam.

"Have the police come in and search the whole flat, but I doubt we will find anything there. Head off to the third address in Tooting Bec, we don't have the detailed information yet, but we should have by the time you get there," she said.

"Have we got pictures yet of this Sam Harding?"
"Yes, we have, ex-military photos, a couple we pulled off an old Facebook profile and of course the recent one from the drone delivery but he was wearing a cap and had his face down, not sure we can get enough off it for the facial software."

Find out if he rented a garage or any kind of lockup. Get the facial recognition into the system, let's see if we can trace his movements over the last few hours. How are they getting on at The Thames Barrier? Has the whole site been searched, these guys have demolition expertise, distribute the photos to see if anyone recognised them there over the last few months."

"Yes Ma'am," replied the junior officer.

"There's something that still doesn't feel right about this," she said. "Pull up the recording of when we entered the file room and found the secret store, I want to have another look."

Images flashed across a screen then stopped. She could see the officers entering the room, the cameras panning around, the files being removed, the caretaker coming in, the camera going into the room, seeing the weapons and the images, Harry opening the lock, going in, looking around and then the explosion. What wasn't right about this? Hallam was thinking it through second by second. She just knew something wasn't right, but what was it?

Karam Shahid knew that he was being watched and yet he had left these things in the room despite having emptied everything else. Did he want them to find it?

"Harry, are you still at the University?" she asked into her microphone.

"Yes, still here," replied Harry Barnes.

"Can you get somebody to check in the file room and along the corridor, also on the entrance to the building, inside and out," she said.

"What are we looking for?" he replied.
"Cameras," she said. "Karam Shahid is always one step ahead of us. Did he know we were coming?"

"Do you think he has somebody inside the Ministry feeding him information?" asked Harry.

"It has crossed my mind," replied Hallam. She looked across at Emma Harrison who was busy at her screen and on her phone at the same time.

Hallam ended the call and beckoned an older officer across.

"Peters, I want you to pull the phone calls and texts made on Emma Harrison's phone in the last seven days, most recent ones first and bring them to me and nobody else. Nobody is to know about this."

"Yes Ma'am, understood." William Peters had been a Lieutenant Colonel in the signals but had been well known to Colonel Charles Bell. Sophie had interviewed him personally and liked him immediately, a no-nonsense sort of chap. She knew she could rely on him to be discreet.

Karam was already on the tube having taken the Piccadilly line and was heading to Cockfosters. His peaked Community Police cap shielded his face from the camera that was in the carriage and he held a book close to obscure the view further. Once at Cockfosters he alighted and walked a few hundred yards to a cul de sac with three lock up garages at the bottom. He put a key into the lock and lifted the door. Inside was a small plain white van. He pulled the door down behind him, switched on a battery powered light hanging on the wall and put his bag in the van. He checked his watch, it was just after two o'clock. His three contacts would be getting into position. He wondered if Sophie Hallam had fallen for his plan.

"Ma'am, we have the information on the third person. Gemma Laxton, 27a Tooting High Road. Ex paratrooper, Captain, three tours, decorated, left the army in 2026, had a protracted legal battle for compensation for an injury at work due to faulty equipment, and sexual assault, both thrown out. We have a drone in position now."

The screens switched to a scene of a flat ablaze above some shops. The fire brigade was already there dousing the flames. There was a crowd of people watching

"Amhurst, stand your team down for the moment, no requirement to go to Tooting Bec, our suspect has already left, stand by for further instructions," said Hallam.

"Yes Ma'am," he replied.

"I think we can safely say that our three targets aren't planning on going back home after all of this. Let's switch our focus into finding these three and Karam Shahid. Any news from The Thames Barrier?"

"The Army have arrived and are deploying. Bomb disposal are on site, the area is being searched," said an officer.

Sophie's earpiece beeped; it was Harry Barnes. "Your hunch was right, we found cameras in the file room, looking down the corridor and outside the entrance to the faculty. He was probably watching us the whole time, it's probably what alerted him while he was at the café," he said.

"I don't think we alerted him, and I don't think any of this came as a surprise to him. He has been onto us for a while. For someone who is so smart and plans so far in advance don't you think it strange that he let us find those images in his hideaway?"

"What do you mean? He wasn't to know that we would discover it?"

"I think he has a good idea of the depth of our surveillance. I think he used those missing sixteen minutes to lead us down to the room. The device that blew up, why was there a time lag? If he had wanted to destroy the evidence why didn't he do it before or why didn't the device explode straightaway?" she said.

"Perhaps he hadn't expected to be found, it was just a guarantee in case he was," replied Harry.
"Perhaps, but the timing is all too coincidental, the three accomplices all disappearing today, he knew this was about to happen, he could have cleared the room out before now, he wanted us to find it, to see the guns and the pictures. I don't think The Thames Barrier is the target at all. It seems like such an obvious target with the rain and river flooded, but I think he has something else in mind," said Hallam.

"Thank you, Harry," get yourself off to hospital and get looked at, I need you back and operational" and she was gone.

"Listen everyone, we need to find these people. They won't be using public transport or Pods, too many cameras and ways to track them, I think they are in their own vehicles. Check with DVLA, find out if any of them own a vehicle, also check with local police for any vehicles that have been reported stolen in the last week in and around Ealing, Tooting Bec and Tottenham. If that draws a blank extend it to anywhere inside the M25, I think there is a new target and it's not The Thames Barrier," she said.

"What do we tell them at the Barrier," said William Peters who had just walked back into the surveillance room.

"Nothing, I expect Shahid has cameras hidden there as well. Let's try to keep him thinking that his plan is working."

Hallam moved to one side of the room and spoke quietly to Peters. "What have you found?"

"Nothing, no indication that Harrison knows anything about Shahid. She missed a call from a Charlie Wilson an hour ago but hasn't replied to him yet," he said.

"Thanks for this, I don't think we have a mole, I think Shahid is very smart and very capable with technology, but if you can just keep an eye on Harrison's phone for me to see if there is any more activity especially if she speaks to Charlie Wilson."
"Yes, of course," replied Peters.

In Essex, two white vans were parked in separate locations with no knowledge of one another. One was on an industrial estate, outside the Admirals Park Business Centre, where an older commercial vehicle did not look out of place there. The other was just a few miles away near The Longreach Sewage Treatment Works, once again, looking perfectly natural, a driver sat in his van at lunchtime taking a break. Anyone looking in would have seen a driver with a black jacket reading and might have assumed it was a newspaper. In fact, they were both looking over the plan for the last time before it was put into action. Sam Harding was to enter the tunnel specifically at two twenty-eight and drive at 30 miles an hour exactly until he could see daylight at the other end. He then had to brake and pull the van across the road blocking it. Oliver Walker reading his file understood that he had to enter the tunnel at exactly two twenty-nine and drive at fifty miles an hour for one minute and forty seconds exactly. At that point he was to brake hard and swing his vehicle across the tunnel also blocking it.

He would find the traffic in front of him had now been stopped with several vehicles trapped between the two vans. He was to get out of the van and fire his weapon at the vehicles behind. They would quickly back away. He was to then start walking towards the other end of the tunnel wearing his SO19 uniform firing his weapons and causing as much panic and fear as possible. He was not to aim his weapons at anyone, and injuries were to be avoided at all costs. Sam Harding in the front vehicle was told that he should walk back into the tunnel until he met with his accomplice doing the same, firing his weapon and causing panic, he was not to fire at anyone unless attacked and even then, only to wound. Once they had met, they were to walk towards the end of the tunnel still firing.

On the other side of the river parked up in the Lakeside shopping centre carpark was a Paramedic's estate car. There, the driver was also busy reading, double checking everything. Gemma Laxton was dressed in a faux medical uniform. Hopefully, her role in this operation would not involve her having to fire a weapon if everything went according to plan. She had cleaned and double checked her weapons as a matter of course before setting off from her flat in Tooting Bec. As she left, she set light to her furniture that she had piled up in the lounge, she knew that once she embarked on this operation there was no going back, she would either end up on a beach, in jail or in the morgue.

"We have pictures of Gemma Laxton, in her army days, but we didn't get one from the drone delivery, she kept her hand over her face. None of them have vehicles registered to their names. We are waiting to hear about any vehicles reported stolen," said an officer.

"Thank you," replied Hallam. "Where are they? Have we not been able to pick anything up yet? How far have we thrown the search?" she asked.

Another young officer came striding into the surveillance room. "Ma'am, this has just arrived for you, it came by courier bike and was dropped off at reception."

Sophie took the manilla envelope addressed specifically to her. Inside was a piece of paper with the message:

THIS IS A TEN MINUTE WARNING.
THE THAMES BARRIER IS A BOMB

She passed the note around.

"What does it mean, the Thames Barrier is a bomb?" asked one of the officers.

"I don't know," said Hallam, but it's telling us to evacuate everyone from the Barrier. Why would he want us to do that?" she said. "Call them, tell them we have been informed there is a bomb, evacuate but seal the perimeter."

"Yes Ma'am." There was an immediate flurry as calls were made. Sophie Hallam was looking at images of The Thames Barrier on the screen. She knew it was not the target, but the damage it would cause to London and her career if she ignored it and she happened to be wrong was too great a risk.
"Have we had any divers look below the waterline?" she asked.

"Not that we know of Ma'am unless the team at the Barrier have done it. I will find out," said Hastings, the officer closest to her.

He made a call and moments later said "No, no divers have been down."

"We may be short of time but get a team of divers down there now, Shahid has been planning this for months, he has had plenty of time to plant explosives, use any underwater drones as well," she said.

Hallam was looking at all the screens showing the Thames Barrier in real time, and previous footage of the area around the back of 'Bar Italia.' She leant forwards "There, stop there, go back," the screen was showing an image from a CCTV camera in Greek Street.

"That Community Police Officer, can we zoom in on him?" she asked.

The screen moved and showed a grainy picture of someone walking down the street with a fluorescent jacket.
"Does that bag look right to you?" she turned her head to look at it sideways.

"It looks like he might be going home after a shift," said Hastings.

"Yes, it could be, but we are looking for anything out of the ordinary in this location in this time frame. Can we enhance this image?"

The cameras zoomed in on the figure walking along the road, then another camera came into play from a Pod driving by. It gave a better image until the subject raised an arm.

"Go back and freeze that," she said.

The image went into reverse and then was stopped at the best point.

"Zoom in," she said.
On the screen was a grainy image of a clean-shaven man with a mop of blond hair under his hat

"That's not him," said the officer sat looking at the screens.

"Are you sure?" said Hallam?

"Yes Ma'am, Shahid walked into 'Bar Italia' with a full beard and dark hair, how could he have changed so quick?" he said.

"Let us not underestimate Mr Shahid. He has been planning this for a long time. Run the facial recognition checks for him against this image."

An officer was tapping the data into her computer, screens showed some matching software that was timing down. The dial was whirring round and showing percentages. The room went quiet as it hit 80, then 90%, and the last few seconds. 100% match appeared on the screen.

"It's him!" said the younger officer surprised.

"Things aren't always what they seem," said Sophie. "Let's get tracking everyone, I want to know exactly where Karam Shahid went from here. Have we located any of the other three yet?"

"No, not yet," said Hastings, but there was a report of a stolen van from outside a builder's yard in Wood Green. It happened last night and was reported ten o'clock this morning."

"Ok, let's get the number plate and see if we can find it, see if there were any distinguishing marks in case they have changed plates," she said.

"Yes Ma'am."

Karam was checking his watch, it was two twenty-five. He looked at the app on his phone. He had two cameras on The Thames Barrier, and had seen all the troops and staff move away a few minutes ago. It meant that Sophie Hallam had opened the envelope, seen the bomb threat, and warned everyone to evacuate. He hoped that this would be her focus, but he knew he could not take any chances. The best thing he could do was stick to his plan, one carved out meticulously over the previous four years. He raised the garage door and pulled out in his van. He closed the door behind him and set off.

At the Thames Barrier the senior officer Major Brady was looking at his watch and then at the divers preparing to go down and inspect the Barrier below water level. It was two twenty-five. He shouted over to tell the divers to stay out of the water. There was nothing to say that an attack might start on the hour or half hour but waiting two minutes would not save the Barrier but might mean losing two men.

Sam Harding, Gemma Laxton and Oliver Walker were all checking their watches. It was two twenty-five. Each of them was approaching their allocated targets. Sam Harding was pulling on to the Dartford crossing approach, he knew he had to get the timing exact. He stayed in the slow lane and crawled along. It was quite easy to judge the timing as the traffic was free flowing. He kept an eye on his watch, the speedometer and his phone that was measuring the distance. He passed underneath the gantry and entered the tunnel at exactly two twenty-eight. He steadied his foot and kept the van travelling at thirty miles an hour.

A minute behind him Oliver Walker was coming down the same tunnel approach and entered at exactly two twenty-nine. He put his foot down accelerating to fifty miles an hour and set the timer on his watch. He glanced across at his weapons on the passenger seat and the helmet. He watched the seconds tick by, twenty, thirty, forty.

Karam was heading towards the M25, he had his phone mounted on the dashboard, he was watching the Thames Barrier, the traffic cameras at the Dartford tunnel, and another camera he had positioned weeks ago overlooking a unit not far from the Dartford Tunnel.

As the clock ticked towards two thirty, Major Brady paced around casting his eye up and down the length of the Barrier from his viewpoint. The second hand passed, and nothing happened. Everyone
was still expecting an explosion.

"Nothing happened Ma'am," said an officer back at The Ministry.

Hallam was unsurprised, she was not expecting anything to happen.

"What's the latest on Shahid, have we able to track him from surveillance?"

"We have traced him all the way along Greek Street, over Shaftsbury Avenue onto Charing Cross Road. We lost him around Leicester

Square, just picking up all the cameras there," said the officer.

"Tell me when you have found him," said Hallam.

Oliver Walker was checking his watch, thirty seven, thirty eight, thirty nine, forty. He braked hard and swung the long wheelbase van round at right angles to the tunnel blocking it. He checked his watch, exactly two thirty and forty seconds. He calmly put on his helmet and picked up his weapons, a submachine gun, an assault rifle, two pistols and ammunition clips.

He got out and saw the vehicles stopped behind him, a mixture of Pods and cars with their owners. Some of the doors were opening and people were starting to get out to see what was happening. He fired the machine gun overhead, bullets ricocheted off the walls of the tunnel, shooting out some of the lights of the vehicles nearest. He watched as people got back in their cars or started running away, then calmly walked around the other side of the van and headed towards the other end of the tunnel, firing as he went, mostly above the vehicles, occasionally into the bodywork, aiming for the lights as the shattering glass and darkness made it even more frightening. He could now hear gunfire from the end of the tunnel. He was not concerned; he knew that this would be someone else involved in the plan.

He had four hundred metres to cover and needed to do it within four minutes. He set off at a brisk pace, still walking but fast, firing as he went, changing ammunition clips. By now everyone was cowering in the vehicles, keeping down and out of sight. There was always the risk that there might be a have a go hero, but he knew from experience that when there is live fire, even the most trained soldiers take cover. The greatest risk was that a Pod might be taken control of by The Ministry of Information and used as a weapon against him. The cameras in the Pods could quickly be utilised by The Ministry who would then take control of the Pod and weaponise it. He knew that this happened all the time in the fight against crime and terrorism.

In Anton's plan, he thought it would take five minutes for the Ministry to be able to do that by which time if the plan worked, they would be out of there. 'Tom' continued shooting and could tell by the noise that he was getting closer to his operational partner with the call name 'Simon'. He was certain everything was going to plan as he could only hear the fire from one automatic weapon. He could see the muzzle flash in the near distance and thirty seconds later they met up, turned and without words headed back to the end of the tunnel. With the two of them firing simultaneously and the natural echo of the tunnel, the noise was deafening and terrifying at the same time, the vehicles were all still, and as they walked, glass crunched underfoot.

Karam was now on the M25 and heading rapidly towards the A12 turnoff. He could see the divers waiting at the Thames Barrier, and the soldiers bustling around. Just then he saw the camera wobble and a face come into view. The camera was pulled down and was clearly being taken somewhere. He knew that his cameras had been found at the University and that the services were now looking for them, but he hoped his plan was far enough along that it could not be stopped.

At the Ministry Hallam had given the instruction for a search to be made to look for cameras resulting in one being found at the Barrier. At two thirty-two news came through of a disruption in traffic at The Dartford Tunnel which was not traffic related. Traffic jams did not happen anymore now that eighty five percent of all vehicles were computer controlled. The only time the traffic stopped was by human intervention usually poor driving, the computers were constantly talking to one another so there was rarely a need for a sudden manoeuvre, accidents were no longer heard of.
"What's going on at Dartford, can we get eyes on it?" she said.

Images came up of traffic backing up going northbound through one of the two tunnels. The traffic on the bridge and the other tunnel was still running smoothly. It was clear there was an incident in just one of the tunnels.

"Can we get images from inside the tunnel," she said "the Dartford crossing cameras, Pods, anything."

"We are trying Ma'am, there seems to be something blocking the signals, we can't get connected," replied an officer.

In the tunnel, three Chinese made devices were pulsing a red light, hidden high above some maintenance cupboards mounted on the access path. Months before, Karam had made his way into the tunnel, dressed as one of the maintenance engineers. He had watched how they operate and where they went for breaks. He had bought similar trousers and boots online and headed there one Sunday when traffic and staffing levels were at their quietest, made his way to one of the staff portacabins and borrowed a jacket and helmet. It took an hour to walk through the tunnel and place the three small boxes out of sight, tucked away at the back of the cupboards. They were all activated via an app and would not be switched on until required. He had discussed these with Colonel Jiang, interrupters that would distort the transmissions from within the tunnel. He tested them beforehand on his own cameras and a few other devices that shared information and they worked. Of course, until the day, there was no guarantee that they would be as efficient in a tunnel with many Pods and cameras trying to transmit information. It was one of the risks that he had to take, just like walking into the tunnel on a Sunday morning.

His hunch and Colonel Jiang's guarantees seemed to come to fruition, the boxes were jamming the signals. The frustration at the Ministry was evident.

"What have we got in the area?" asked Hallam.

"I can get some drones there in a few minutes. We have patched through to the armed response unit; they are eighteen minutes away."

"What about local police? How fast can they get there?" she asked.

"Ten to twelve minutes," he said.

Gemma Laxton aka 'Alex', went around the roundabout and turned into the road coming out of the tunnel, heading down the wrong way. There were no vehicles there as nothing had left the tunnel for the last three minutes. She drove close to the tunnel exit and turned the car around. She had a flashing blue light on the roof and similar lights fitted on the front grill. To a casual glance, her estate car looked every bit a medical vehicle. She got out and opened the doors. She could hear gunfire from the tunnel getting closer. She glanced at her watch; it was two thirty-four. If everything was going according to the plan two figures should emerge from the tunnel in forty-seconds time.

Karam was also looking at his watch thinking exactly the same thing. He had no idea what was actually happening in the tunnel because the jammers would have blocked any cameras that he might have left or given to Sam and Oliver.

Sophie Hallam's frustration was clear, but she knew her team were doing all they could. Every available resource was being mustered, she knew that this was down to Karam Shahid, the man living in plain sight, but what was his purpose, what was he trying to achieve?

Emma Harrison approached her. "Ma'am, the Captain of HMS Dauntless, was a Charles Gray, he committed suicide four months after the sinking of the Aruda."

"Thank you Harrison, can you double check that there were no suspicious circumstances surrounding it, take a look at The Coroner's report."

"Of course Ma'am," she replied.

Simon and Tom were now clear of all the vehicles trapped in the tunnel. They walked around the van that Tom had thrown across the exit and headed for the daylight. Simon turned to Tom and punched him hard on the breast. There was a pop and a bag of blood burst inside the breast pocket of his uniform and began seeping out. Tom barely broke stride as he was aware of what Simon was going to do, this had all been in the plan that they had read earlier. As they approached the end of the tunnel, Simon put his arm over Tom's shoulder and started limping heavily, from the outside it looked as though Tom, dressed as a British firearms officer had been shot in the chest and that his partner was carrying him out of the danger area. Alex moved towards them, took a moment to look at the wound and then put her body underneath Tom's other arm. The two of them carried Tom to the estate car, by now Tom was dragging his feet and feigning unconsciousness.

They put Tom into the back, climbed in and sped off away from the Tunnel to the roundabout, blue lights flashing. As they reached it, they kept going, still no drones in sight, just a few Pods that they overtook. Taking the third exit, they carried along the dual carriageway, taking the next exit, and sped along for about a mile. This was a country lane which led to a small industrial estate with a handful of buildings. They pulled up to a roll shutter, as they arrived it went up and on the other side was Karam, but they had never met him and did not know who he was. He waved them in and closed the shutter behind them. In the dimly lit unit, he handed them fresh clothes, black motorbike leathers. Alex and Simon were given white helmets and high vis police bibs to wear. Anton and Tom had black helmets. They all changed in silence which was also in the instructions they had been given. Once ready, Karam raised the roll shutter, closing it again behind him. He beckoned them to follow him to the rear of the unit where four motorbikes were waiting for them. Karam had stolen these over the previous six months at different times, swapped the number plates and liveried two of them in police colours for Alex and Simon.

From leaving the tunnel and setting off on the motorbikes only nine minutes had passed. The police were just arriving at the Dartford Tunnel as people were starting to walk out and were congregating on the approach road. They were listening to the story of at least two gunmen trapping dozens of vehicles in the tunnel and then getting out and shooting at everyone, nobody had any idea how many casualties there were, exactly how many gunmen there were and who was still in there.

The police were ordered not to go into the tunnel but to wait for the armed response unit to arrive. They did however send Pods in from both ends to see what was happening but the cameras were still being jammed. They themselves could not operate any radios or cameras within four hundred metres of the tunnel. The armed unit was by now six minutes away.

In the café at Westminster, Charlie had a ping on his phone and saw a news alert of a suspected terrorist attack in the Dartford Tunnel in Essex. He did not think too much about it, there were constant false alarms at a time when everything was on edge anyway due to the war. He failed to notice that his phone was very low on battery.

The four motorbikes sped along the back roads bypassing Brentwood and joined the A12 dual carriageway past Margaretting. Five hundred metres along, Karam pulled into a layby, he and Tom drove to the end and dismounted. Alex and Simon pulled their bikes over at the entrance to the layby and removed their helmets. They went to the bushes at the side where they found hidden a dozen traffic cones and two folding metal signs with an arrow. A third sign said:

POLICE
VEHICLE DOCUMENT CHECK

Karam was checking his phone, he had been tracking two vehicles that had left Felixstowe docks. He knew that every other Wednesday each one would be carrying a cargo of thirty-five thousand litres of Benzene to CTM Chemicals in Guildford. Despite the lorries having self-driving capacity, due to the highly inflammable nature of the cargo, both vehicles had to have a driver by law. Karam had chosen this particular spot because there were no CCTV or traffic cameras, and it was an hour and twenty minutes from Guildford when the lorries would be expected to arrive. It was unusual to find many stretches of road that did not have cameras all the way along but during the cutbacks, once war had started, it was considered that in time Pod cameras would fill in all the blind spots. Karam knew that they would still be visible as Pods drove by, but he hoped that the Ministry would be busy with other things, after all they could only look for something if they knew what they were looking for. To all intents and purposes, this looked like a normal police check during turbulent times.

The lorries always left their yard at 2pm once the drivers had finished their lunch. It was one hour and two minutes to reach the layby. At two o'clock and one minute, Alex and Simon walked onto the edge of the A12 and waited. A minute later they could see a large lorry approaching. Three hundred yards away they could see the letters CTM on the front of it. As it approached, Alex stepped out into the road and began flagging the lorry to enter the layby whilst pointing at the sign about Vehicle Document Check. She left it late enough so that the driver did not have time to ring his office. As the lorry started to pull in, it revealed the second vehicle close behind which she also waved in.

The two lorries pulled up halfway down the layby. Tom approached the first driver, indicating for him to wind down his window, whilst Alex did the same to the second vehicle. In both instances they asked the drivers for their Flammable Goods in Transit Permissions which they both duly presented. They looked over the documents and said that everything was in order. The drivers both felt more comfortable, even if everything was in order it was still very unnerving during these troubled times to be pulled over by any of the Government agencies. Both drivers were then asked to get out and walk round their vehicles to check the safety issues and the relevant dangerous product signage.

They both got out from their drivers' sides at the same time and climbed down the four steps onto the tarmac and then following the officers, went around to the pavement side, blinded from the road. Once there the officers walked them, so they were closer together. Tom had started approaching from his motorbike and when the two drivers were within three metres of each other he pulled out a handgun as did Alex and Simon. Tom put his finger to his mouth to tell them to both be quiet.

"Do exactly as I say, and you will live, and this will be over very quickly, follow me and no heroics, we don't want to kill you, but we don't have a problem if we have to."

Tom led the way though the bushes into the trees behind the layby, and Simon followed with his gun trained on the two drivers, both in their fifties, the only age group with the skills and experience to drive lorries like this now, as nobody learned to drive anymore. Alex cleared away the cones and signage, dumping them back in the bushes, then joined Tom and Simon.

Tom led them thirty metres away from the road where they could not be seen, gagged them and tied them back-to-back, sitting against a tree trunk.

"We will be letting someone know where you are, they will be with you in a couple of hours." said Tom "and don't try to be heroes, we will be watching you" and he put a small camera on the branch of a tree opposite.

Whilst this was happening, Karam had climbed into the cab of each vehicle in turn and connected a device by Bluetooth to the lorry's software system. Karam had investigated all the lorries that CTM chemicals used that were of this size and they had two different makes, DAF built by the Dutch and Mercedes, the German company. Colonel Jiang's team was able to access the information they needed online, and the devices were pre-loaded with the required data, all Karam had to do was connect the two systems. He also left a satchel in each cab which contained a detonator provided by the Chinese, sufficient to create a reaction for the Benzene to ignite. By the time, the three of them returned from the trees he had finished his work. He acknowledged them and watched them mount their motorbikes and set off. He waited to see the two lorries start up and edge along the layby and pull out onto the A12, they had just over an hour's journey to make.

Charlie had another two news updates, when his phone battery died. He checked his rucksack only to find that he had forgotten the charger at home. He visualised exactly where he had left it on the bedside table and cursed himself. He asked Jasmin if she had a charger he could borrow, but she and her co-worker both laughed when they saw how old Charlie's phone was. He dropped an email to Emma in case she needed to contact him about Karam, to let her know that his phone was dead. He went online to try and find out a little more about the incident at The Dartford Tunnel. He glanced at his watch; it was three twenty.

At the Ministry, everyone was busy, analysing data, making calls, looking at screens, checking images. The armed response unit had arrived at the north side of The Dartford Crossing. They were being briefed and were preparing to enter the tunnel. All the people who had come out were held in one area and were being interrogated. For all the police knew, one or more of them could be the terrorists, hiding amongst them to escape.

The Armed response unit sent in two drones but could not get any images thanks to Colonel Jiang's transmitters which had worked very well. The Colonel was following events from his headquarters in Shanghai, it was eleven o'clock at night there, he was having all the newsfeeds sent through to screens in his comfortable office. The Colonel had been educated at Oxford followed by a Masters in America, and enjoyed many of the trappings of Western culture. He was drinking some fine Cognac as the events unfolded in front of him. Until now, he couldn't know for certain how things would pan out, he did not know much about this man Anton he had discovered via the Dark Web. He found himself sending weapons, money, diamonds, and technology with no guarantees that it would yield results, but he had a good feeling, only time would tell if he was correct or if he had been hoodwinked by criminals or The Ministry of Information. He was not concerned; his department had a huge budget and Anton's requests were small but might reap huge rewards.

So far everything was going according to Anton's plan. The images had come through from The Thames Barrier. Colonel Jiang had thought the Barrier to be an excellent target and had urged Anton to pursue this, but he had declined, suggesting it was too difficult to achieve, but could be used as a feint to buy time for the real mission.

The hardest part he said was avoiding detection in order to achieve their goal.

Jiang was now watching live news feeds from cameras positioned away from The Dartford Tunnel, and was watching the security services enter the tunnel. He had provided sufficient military hardware to cause carnage and he hoped that was what had happened.

Back at the tunnel exit, two armed teams of four were entering and progressing up to the van parked sideways across the tunnel blocking the entrance. They looked inside, there was nothing there except a folder. It was given to one of the armed officers and taken straightaway to whoever was in charge of operations outside.
Following their training, each team started to make their way into the tunnel, many of the structural lights had been shot out, but the lights on the Pods and a few vehicles illuminated where they went in a surreal half-light. There was no sign of any terrorists, and there were no bodies. Nobody had been shot. From time to time they came across a vehicle that still had its occupants hiding inside, terrified and crying, it had been a traumatic event for them.

The two teams kept going until they reached the other van. Looking inside there was nothing except for a file. This was gathered and another officer dispatched to take it to command. The team looked back up the tunnel at the hundreds of blocked cars. One of them wanted to move the van but was told to stand down until bomb disposal had been in case it was a trap.

The firearm teams made their way back out of the tunnel into the daylight. They had been seventeen valuable minutes. The leader approached the senior officer who was waiting two hundred yards back.

"Amhurst SO19, Sir" he said to the senior officer.

"Chief Superintendent Wallace," she replied. "What do we have?"
"Do you mind if I patch this call through to my senior officer at The

Ministry, I think it would save time," he said.

"No of course not, please go ahead," replied Wallace.

"Ma'am, Amhurst here, can you hear me?"

"Yes Amhurst, your comms have been down for quite a while, I am guessing the same thing blocking the cameras has been blocking all the communications?" said Hallam.

"I think so Ma'am, we haven't found out what it is that's doing it yet. I have Chief Superintendent Wallace with me, I was just about to explain what we found in the tunnel," he said.

"Hello Hallam," said Wallace.

"Hello Chief Superintendent," she replied, "Go ahead Amhurst."

"This was a highly organised event, prepared some time in advance I would guess. The devices blocking the signals may have been put there a while ago, we didn't find anything in the vans that would suggest differently. This was done with precision timing as well. The strangest thing is that from the cartridge shells everywhere, they had some serious firepower, but no-one was injured, let alone killed. I don't think it was ever their intention to hurt anyone."

"Any sign of how they escaped?" said Hallam.

"We haven't found anything to indicate how they got away, but we have a full alert here, we are searching everywhere within a ten-mile radius," said Wallace.

"Ma'am, we found two files, one in each van, they both had all the instructions for what to do, step by step. This was meticulously organised. Reading through I get the impression they did not know each other or the person organising. They were both given codenames. In the files it says that after leaving the tunnel they were to get inside an electricity van that would come down the tunnel approach from the north and escape through into Kent, taking the Channel Tunnel into France. Do you think this is anything to do with The Thames Barrier incident Ma'am?" asked Amhurst.

"I do, I think this is all connected to Karam Shahid, but I don't know what he is trying to achieve" said Hallam. We are checking all drone, Pod and gantry footage around the north side of the tunnel to see what we can find. We have input the facial recognition for the three ex-soldiers, let's see what that brings up," said Hallam.

"What about the escape route to France, we can catch them on the M2 or at the Channel Tunnel," said Amhurst.

"I don't think that is very likely. Consider how meticulously planned this has been, sophisticated technology to jam all the cameras, the perfect timing, years of organising and then they leave the plans in both vehicles? They wanted us to find them as another thing to throw us off the trail, Shahid has been doing that constantly". Alert the authorities at The Channel Tunnel, provide them with images of the three of them, but I think in the next twenty minutes we will be following them in a completely different direction. Chief Superintendent, can you have your staff question anyone in the area to see if they saw something, we might be resorting to some good old fashioned policework if we can't get the technology up and running there," said Hallam.

"Of course, we will keep you informed; we are at your disposal," replied Wallace.

"We need to find Harding, Laxton and Walker, but most of all Shahid. Concentrate on all Pods and cameras within a twenty-five-mile radius of the Dartford Tunnel, both sides of the river, it's possible that Shahid and his team went straight back over the bridge to the south side, but those files in the van tell me to look in the other direction, although of course it could be an elaborate double bluff. Look for any vehicle with three or four people in from two forty onwards within two miles of the tunnel exit on the north side, let's find these people," and Hallam was gone.

Harding, Laxton and Walker headed off in three different directions within five minutes of leaving Karam Shahid. They had stripped the police insignia from their bikes and removed their bibs and police markings from their clothes. Oliver Walker took the next slip road to the roundabout and started heading east along the A12 through Colchester, taking the back roads down towards Frinton on Sea. He had a map reference that Shahid had given him, he was told to be there at exactly four fifteen, his transport out of the country would only wait for five minutes. He drove along a narrow track off a country lane, carefully following his satellite navigation on his phone. When he was only a hundred yards away, he parked his bike and opened the five-bar gate to the field which was empty. He walked out into the middle and waited. It was twelve minutes past four. He looked very out of place in his biker's leathers stood in a field in rural Essex, but there were no drones or cameras around to see him and no Pods likely to come down that lane.

Looking around he saw nothing; the constant drizzle was not help visibility. He strained his eyes, something came into view, he could not tell what it was or even how big it was until it got closer. Fifty metres away he had a much better view of it, it flew overhead, banked on a tight curve, and came down to land within a few metres of him. It was like a small plane crossed with a rocket. It had a body and wings, but it was only three metres long and a metre high on its wheels. Once it had landed, the lid automatically lifted up on the body exposing a cockpit big enough for one person to lie down. He could see that the fuselage had a tiled pattern effect on it, and the whole craft seemed to be made from some kind of carbon. Unknown to Oliver Walker this was a Chinese made Stealth craft used to deliver special forces into combat zones. It was designed with the latest Chinese Stealth technology, using radiation absorbent materials, making it almost impossible to detect by radar. It was electric powered, the whole craft having hundreds of highly effective miniature solar panels that could convert even the dullest light into energy. Weighing only 250kgs and with an exceptionally sleek form it could cruise at four hundred miles an hour and land and take off in a space less than thirty metres long.

Walker climbed in and laid down in the cockpit. The lid closed and he heard a whirring sound, the whole craft started to reverberate. It began to move, picking up speed very quickly and within moments it was airborne and quickly rose high above the Essex countryside. A voice came though some speakers "Well done Oliver, a highly successful mission, and all exactly to the plan, this is Anton speaking. It's time to start a new life. We are flying you to Mauritius off the East Coast of Africa. It is firmly within the sphere of influence of our Chinese friends who helped with this mission. There is a file in the pocket by your left leg with all the information you need, your new home, contacts, and the details of your new bank account in which you will find fifty million renminbi. The bad news is that it is a long flight of sixteen hours and we can't stop, we want to get you there as quickly as possible. Sleep well my friend and well done. And as the message ended a gas poured in through the vents and sent Oliver Walker into unconsciousness.

Gemma Laxton and Sam Harding headed off to their rendezvous as explained to them in their mission files from Anton. Gemma rode her motorbike along the A12, picked up the M25 and headed for the Queen Elizabeth Bridge. As she approached, she gave a quick glance across at the police activity at the tunnel exit in the other direction. It was a fifty-five-minute bike ride to The Isle of Grain in the Thames estuary. Gemma's pick-up time for extraction was five o'clock. She arrived in an abandoned farmyard which Karam had scoped out before. The pilotless craft landed exactly on time and within a couple of minutes Gemma Laxton was fast asleep and climbing high over the English Channel.

Sam Harding's extraction point was in the Dengie National Nature Reserve on the Essex coast, a forty-minute ride. He followed the navigation on his phone to the Reserve car park, dropped off his bike and helmet and headed by foot, cross country. It was raining much harder now which was good as there was no one else around. After ten minutes he was out of sight of the car park and at the exact location given to him by Karam. He was ten minutes early and took the opportunity to finally breath and consider what he had done. It was extraordinary how everything had gone exactly to the plan he had been given, this strange thing that had happened to him, this man Anton he had met on the Dark Web. Was one of the other three Anton? Everyone had played their part, in complete silence. He could tell that two of them were ex forces, the third moved well, capable of handling himself, but did not seem to behave as though he had been in the military. He thought about the bag of diamonds in his pocket and what life had in store for him now. He had no idea what was coming next, he was just following instructions which up until now had worked out perfectly. Was this the point where it might go wrong? He had no means of escape if it was a trap, this is where it would end.

He heard a faint whirring sound and looked up into the rain to see a rocket shape approach, but he could tell immediately it was something being controlled as it slowed, turned and came down to land. He knew that if he got inside, that this may be the last time he ever sees England. He climbed in admiring the construction of this futuristic craft, it was snug for his powerful build, but he fitted, just. These things had been made for Chinese Special Forces, not for an Anglo Saxon frame. The view of the coastline was the last thing he saw as he went into a deep sleep.

Karam was checking his phone, he had sent Charlie a text, but he had not answered. He re-sent it and waited. His phone indicated that Charlie was not picking it up, so he decided to call. It rang a few times and then went to answerphone. Karam knew exactly where Charlie would be, why wasn't he answering? Perhaps he did not have his phone with him? Unlikely though, as long as he had known Charlie, he always had his phone with him, but it was possible it had broken or been stolen. He thought about calling the café, but that would seem too desperate and might make Charlie wonder why he was doing that. He could not leave him there, the wrong place at the wrong time.

Karam made the decision that he had to go to the café and warn him. This was not in the plan; in fact, it was the first and only deviation from a plan that had been years in the making. Karam put on his helmet and headed off along the A12 towards Romford.

At the Ministry, images were flashing across the screens, thousand upon thousand. Every eye in the room was strained at the vast amount of data coming through. One officer was tracking a paramedics vehicle around a roundabout. It had two people in the front and one in the rear, the images were not very good, but he cross referenced with the recognition software. The driver came up as Gemma Laxton. He shouted out "Got them!"

Sophie Hallam crossed the floor to the officer, standing close behind him and looked into his screen.

"Can we trace the journey?" she asked.

"Yes, on it now, here it is leaving the roundabout, we picked it up from traffic cameras going along the dual carriageway, they have now turned the blue lights off, you can see them coming off at the junction, this goes onto a B road, we can't find an image after this. We are creating a grid reference for the area without any camera coverage, we have drones entering the area as we speak," he said.

"No sign of the vehicles coming out of this blind spot later on?" Said Hallam.

"No Ma'am, the vehicle is within this area, it hasn't left," he said. On the screen, a map appeared with a red outline that was out of camera coverage. Data told them that no Pods had been within this area of three-square miles during this period.

"Get our two teams there, call Chief Superintendent Wallace, see how many men she can get on the ground to do a house-to-house search, it looks quite rural, shouldn't take too long. How are we getting on looking for Shahid?" she asked.

"We have managed to track him on the Piccadilly line, he got off at Cockfosters tube, we have images of him coming out of the there and walking, but then we lost him, we haven't been able to find him since," he said.

Sophie Hallam began pacing. "This guy is like a ghost, all of our cameras, and we can't pin him down. Keep looking, he is making fools of us," she said to the whole room.

Karam Shahid had now passed Newbury Park. He pulled into the side of the road checking there were no traffic cameras. Keeping his face away from the Pods that were driving along, he dialled a number pre-set in a phone he had wrapped in silver foil.

"Ministry of Information, how can I help you?" came the reply. Sophie Hallam had insisted that The Ministry had a switchboard staffed by bright intelligent people. Most organisations had an automated switchboard, press one for sales, two for accounts, but The Ministry relied heavily on the public for information and leads, and she wanted everyone who called in to be answered and encouraged.

"Sophie Hallam please," said Shahid.

"I'm afraid she is very busy at the moment, but I am sure I can help you?" replied the receptionist.

"I think she will want to talk to me," replied Shahid. "I am the one she is looking for right now."

"Of course, just a moment," she said.

There was a click then a voice

"Hallam speaking."

"Hello Sophie, I think you know who this is," he said.

"Hello Karam," she waved to officers in the room indicating to get a trace on the call. "That was quite a show you put on at the tunnel."

"Thank you, I think I have now demonstrated how serious I am, and what I am capable of."

"Yes, you have, I think we can all agree that you are a man who gets things done, but why? What is it you are trying to achieve?" said Hallam.

"I imagine you are getting pretty close. You probably know about Dauntless and my family?"

"Yes, we have found out that, I am so sorry for your loss," she said.

"Did you know I had a son?" he asked.

"No", she replied, waving furiously at her staff to start researching. There was a pause,

"It's the Houses of Parliament," he said. There was another pause,

"I don't suppose there is anything I can say that will stop you?" she asked.

"No, nothing at all, and it can't be stopped. You have thirty minutes to evacuate, get everyone out. You probably know this already, but Charlie Wilson knows nothing about any of this," said Karam.

"I know," said Sophie, "but Karam..." and the line went dead. Karam took the phone from his pocket, wrapped it back up in the foil and threw it in the waste bin on the pavement. He pulled his visor down and pulled out onto the road.

"Did we get a trace?" she asked.

"Only to East London. It was an unregistered phone."

"Let's look at all cameras in East London, I think he is heading into London," she said.

Hallam went downstairs dialling as she climbed the stairs two by two, it went straight through to a private number belonging to The PM. Siobhan Baillie became Prime Minister just before War broke out, benefitting from the disarray in the Conservative party in the mid twenty twenties. She had formed a cross party Government and was behind the creation of Sophie Hallam's Ministry of Information, hence the direct line.

"Prime Minister," its Hallam.

"Hello Sophie, how are things at the Ministry?"

"I am afraid to say we have a major terrorist incident. I believe the Houses of Parliament are about to come under attack. It's a long story but the perpetrators have proven themselves to be extremely capable. We need to evacuate immediately we have twenty-nine minutes. I know this will have political ramifications and we will need to manage the media, an attack like this on our homeland."

"Yes, I understand, go ahead and evacuate, I will get the private secretaries and press officers to start damage limitation," replied the PM.

Hallam headed back downstairs to the surveillance room calling the Executive Officer at Parliament who immediately put in place the evacuation protocol. Then she called the head of the Metropolitan Police who in turn called the active response unit who had been housed in Horseguards since the outbreak of War. They were instructed to make a sweep of the Houses of Parliament to look for explosives.

Parliament became a flurry of activity as staff were shepherded from their offices and taken outside and a register taken. The protocol was the same as it would be for a fire, accounting for everyone, the difference being that everyone was being gathered outside Westminster Abbey, well away from the Houses of Parliament. As the clock ticked, there was increasing urgency, MPs and three thousand staff were replaced by one hundred and fifty soldiers who were sweeping the Palace of Westminster, but there were eleven hundred rooms and three miles of passageways, and they were running out of time.

The officer in charge, Major Khan, was in constant contact with Sophie Hallam. With six minutes to go, the order was given for everyone to evacuate. The army personnel could be seen running from the exits.

Karam was working his way through the streets of The City of London and heading towards Westminster. He glanced at his watch, he had five minutes, he could not go any faster, the City of London has speeding alerts and he needed to try and slip in and slip out unnoticed.

The CTM chemical lorries were now separated, the second one had pulled into a charging station in Whitechapel and waited for ten minutes. The first lorry was now travelling along The Mall with Buckingham Palace in front, the steering wheel moving by itself, lights blinking on the Chinese device that had commandeered the computer system. The lorry turned left at the roundabout and pulled onto Birdcage Walk. At five hundred yards from The Houses of Parliament, the accelerator depressed, and the lorry picked up speed, thirty-five miles an hour, forty, forty-five, Big Ben came into sight, fifty miles an hour.

Charlie looked up from his ipad, and saw vehicles rushing along Westminster Bridge Road, Police and Army, whilst ordinary traffic was being stopped. Pods were turning around and speeding in the other direction. He looked at news feeds to see what was happening, but there was nothing. He leaned around to try and see Parliament Square, then he heard gunfire and saw a tanker come into sight, it was travelling way too fast, the bullets from the armed police were hitting the lorry, shattering the windscreen, but it wasn't stopping.
Fifty-five, sixty miles an hour, the speed limiter had been disabled, sixty five miles an hour, it adjusted direction and headed straight for the gates at the Cromwell Green Entrance. When it hit, it was travelling at sixty eight miles an hour, the gates collapsed and debris

was flying, the momentum hardly changed, such was the force of the impact, it hit the concrete barriers that had been installed back in 2003 to prevent a terrorist attack, crashing through the first row splintering fragments everywhere at high speed destroying everything they hit. Thirty metres into the entrance, the lorry came to a juddering halt as it hit the last barrier. Benzene was pouring out of a tear along the seam of the container, pooling on to the ground and spreading across the courtyard.

Charlie had seen all this happening from the café one hundred yards away, he could just see the lorry that had come to a halt inside the security ring of Parliament. The armed police who had dived to get out of the way of the lorry were picking themselves up, two of them had been hit by flying debris and were nursing wounds. As the dust started to clear they could see the damage that the lorry had made. Forty tonnes travelling at over sixty miles an hour, made quite an impact. The bollards and defences had been designed specifically to stop an attack like this and it looked as though it had worked, and then the tanker exploded.

The detonator Karam had left in the cab was on a delay, it was set to go off ten seconds after the lorry had stopped when there was no more motion. The reaction it triggered was designed to be sufficient to ignite the Benzene. The explosion was huge and could be heard four miles away. Everyone within two hundred yards was lifted off their feet and thrown back. Every window within five hundred yards was shattered and blown to pieces. The smoke plume could be seen across all of London and the sound of the explosion deafening to anyone unlucky enough to be nearby. The thousands of Parliamentary staff who were gathered around the corner outside the Abbey were shocked and panicked, they started running, causing a stampede as some fell and were trampled.

Charlie had seen the explosion, and then felt it, he was blown back across the café and knocked unconscious. The windows were all blown in and everyone was covered in glass. As he started to come round, his ears were ringing, he was completely disorientated, there was dust clouding the shop, he could feel shards of glass embedded in his arms and the trickle of blood, he had pain in his chest and arms.

As he lay there, he heard a voice whisper in his ear. It was distorted because of the deafness from the explosion, but he was sure it said, "Don't worry Charlie, I have got you".

He felt himself being picked up and put over a shoulder. He could see the floor beneath him changing from the shattered remains of the café to the pavement covered in glass. He could feel motion and then fresh air. He could tell they were walking away from the explosion as he drifted in and out of consciousness.

The images were coming through on screens in the Ministry, there was shock amongst everyone except for Sophie Hallam. She knew what Karam Shahid was capable of and this came as no surprise, but the magnitude of the event was not lost on her. It was not just the explosion, the damage and the loss of life, but an attack on the heart of Government whilst the country was at war and in a heightened sense of fear, this was just the start of it.

"It's him," said the voice in her earpiece, he is back on the phone.

"Hallam speaking."

"I hope you got everyone out," he said.

"We hope so, we can't be sure, you may have blood on your hands," she replied.

"I am not done," she could hear him straining, as though he were labouring, walking up a hill, exerting himself.

"There's more to come, get everyone away, no heroics, this can't be stopped, ten minutes," and he hung up.

Hallam addressed the room. "Get everyone away from Parliament at least 1000 metres, something else is going to happen, including military and police personnel, get everyone out, do you hear."

Phones were dialled and messages relayed. Back at Parliament the injured were picked up and carried away, the area cleared as quickly as possible.

Sophie Hallam was considering what Shahid would do next "Did we get any details from the tanker that crashed? Where was it from? Was there any writing on it?"

The officers in the room were busy on screens and keyboards. "Ma'am, it had CTM written on it, they appear to be a Chemical company in Surrey, calling them now."

Karam had been carrying Charlie over his shoulder around the corner and along the embankment when he called Sophie. He was dressed as a fireman, nothing looked unusual except for the fact that there were no other fireman in the vicinity. He carried Charlie three hundred yards and put him down on a bench. He looked him up and down and saw that all the injuries were superficial. "You will be okay Charlie. I will be in touch" and he walked off.

Charlie had been drifting in and out, he recognised the voice, but the face was different, smooth, no beard and blond hair, he was confused. Karam continued along the Embankment, threw the phone he had just used into a waste bin, then turned left and returned to the motorbike he had left parked. He had only quickly looked to see if there were any cameras. He thought he had parked in a blind spot, but could not be sure, he had taken a tremendous risk, none of this had been in his plan, Charlie was meant to have seen the text asking to meet him at The Borough so he could explain everything. Karam would not have been there but it would have got Charlie away from the danger. He put his leathers back on over the fireman's uniform, put on his helmet and pulled out onto Whitehall heading up to Trafalgar Square.

"Ma'am, CTM said they were expecting a regular delivery of Benzene this afternoon, two lorries, each with thirty-five thousand litres, they aren't due at their yard for another half an hour, they are ringing the drivers now," said the officer.

"I doubt very much they will get an answer," said Hallam. "There's another lorry heading for Parliament, get everyone out of there. Let the armed police units know, see if they can disable it before it arrives. Someone find out if Benzene can explode or if it needs to be detonated." Hallam was thinking about the moral hazard. The lorry did not explode with the impact, it blew up ten seconds later, she thought it must have been detonated.

"Ma'am, Benzene won't explode without something triggering it," said the officer who had quickly Googled the information.

"Tell the armed units not to fire, we can't afford to stop it anywhere that hasn't been evacuated, loss of life would be too great, at least Parliament is now empty."

The second CTM lorry pulled onto Birdcage Walk and like the first tanker started to pick up speed. Soldiers, police and armed officers watched as the lorry sped along driverless, instructed not to try and stop it. In the Ministry of Information Sophie Hallam and her officers watched on various screens as the lorry headed towards the fire that was already burning, engulfing the entrance to The Palace of Westminster.

The tanker carried along the road, everything was motionless, as though the earth was stood still. They all watched as it disappeared at speed into the smoke and fire, ploughing into the last of the bollards that were still intact, smashing through them and ploughing on to the buildings where it finally stopped. Hallam and her staff all watched the bomb that had been planted in plain site at the heart of the British Constitution, the home of Democracy and one of the most iconic buildings on the planet. There was silence in the surveillance room even though there were fifty people there by now. The seconds ticked down and then it exploded, another mighty explosion that rocked the centre of London. The fire that engulfed the buildings was now licking at the base of Big Ben, it was intense and was being filmed by hundreds of drones that now filled the sky above Parliament Square and Westminster Bridge, many belonging to news agencies. People all around the world had watched a bomb driven into Parliament through a police and military cordon as everyone watched on helplessly. It was not a good reflection on the British Government.

Karam heard the explosion and saw the plume of smoke rising in his wing mirror as he crossed Vauxhall Bridge. He hoped that there were not too many casualties, it was never his intention to cause deaths and injuries. He knew that what he had done would have reverberations, but he still had things he needed to do and had to concentrate. He could only hope that he was not spotted in Westminster. He carried on his planned route to the south coast, pulling over momentarily to send an email to the offices of CTM Chemicals informing them where their missing drivers were tied up. His journey to Birling Gap near to Beachy Head was over two hours, plenty of time for Sophie Hallam to find him if she was able to track him. His extraction point was also meant to be in Essex, but he had been forced to change his plans because of Charlie. He had sent a message to Colonel Jiang informing him of the change of co-ordinates. Karam has found a few places suitable for extraction over the previous twelve months, all close to the coast. Although the pilotless planes were fast and difficult to see on radar, they could be seen by the human eye, so the less time spent over land the better. He had to get there before Sophie Hallam could track him down. He had received notice that Harding, Laxton and Walker had been picked up and were already well on their way.

Charlie was thrown off the bench when the second tanker exploded. Even though he was at least four hundred yards away and behind buildings, he was still affected by the force of the blast. It was another twenty minutes before an ambulance arrived and took him to St Thomas's Hospital where he was treated for his injuries, mostly cuts and bruises although he also suffered a broken wrist, ribs and concussion. It would take a few days before his hearing returned to normal.

Sophie Hallam had learnt that Karam Shahid was an extraordinary man, who despite the resources available to The Ministry somehow stayed one step ahead. Had he made any mistakes that might lead her to him?

"Check out all the cameras within two thousand metres of The Houses of Parliament. The detonations may have been remote, or he may have done them himself which means he would have needed a line of sight. He could have been in one of the buildings overlooking Parliament Square, check everything you can find," she said.

Fire engines and crews were now attending the fire at Westminster. The Houses of Parliament had not even finished their refurbishment which had been delayed and did not start in earnest until 2023. It had been slow and had split the country due to its spiralling costs coinciding with the brutal austerity measures introduced after the great Covid Depression. Work had ceased when war broke out, which meant the Palace of Westminster had been covered in scaffolding and tarpaulins for the last twelve years.

It was an extraordinary sightseeing hundreds of firemen and dozens of engines, working round the clock to dampen the fire. Water was pumped from The Thames to keep the supply going, but even the relentless rain that was pouring down could not stop the fire that ripped through the ancient buildings. It was a terrible sight, and the images were being beamed live around the world.

The fire had quickly taken hold once it was in the building and had started to rip through Westminster Hall, the damage was devastating and would take years to repair. It took two days to dampen the fire and what was left was just the shell. Incredibly nobody had died, with only a few dozen injured, mostly from glass fragments and cuts. One of the most extraordinary images was of rats and mice running in huge packs across Parliament Square as the fire disturbed their home under the floors of Parliament, not an image that the Government wanted the world to see.

All the buildings within a couple of blocks had lost their windows and there was some superficial damage, but as Sophie Hallam and the

Prime Minister knew, the damage was not to the buildings but to the confidence in the Government and the Security Services. Fortress Britain had been penetrated and this could deal a fatal blow to the resilience of the British people.

"Find me Shahid," shouted Hallam at her team. Her phone was ringing constantly from all Whitehall departments including The Home Secretary and The Prime Minister, but she knew she had one specific thing to do, to catch Karam Shahid.

Everyone in the surveillance room pored over footage from hundreds of cameras, internal security from inside office buildings, traffic cameras, congestion charging cameras, shop security, CCTV, a few Pods, but not many as they had been excluded from the area. Time was not their friend and it was ticking by, with every minute Karam was getting closer to safety.

"Ma'am, we have some images we think you should see," said an officer looking at her screen. It had been over an hour since the second explosion.

Hallam walked across and saw a frozen image of a fireman carrying a man over his shoulder along the embankment. The time at the bottom of the screen put it two minutes after the first tanker and before the second. It seems strange that a fireman could have got there that fast. The image was from behind now, showing the back of the fireman, and the head and shoulders of the man being carried. His head bobbed up with every stride.

"Hold it there, go back, show his face, the man being carried," said Hallam.

The officer pressed a button and took the images back a few frames at a time.

"There hold that." Sophie leaned into the picture and turned her head upside down to get a better look. "Emma, Emma Harrison, where are you? come over here and look at this."

Emma came across and looked up at the screen. "Oh my God, its Charlie," she said, and held her hands up to her face.

"I thought it was," said Hallam, "You can see he is moving; he is ok. Do you recognise who that is carrying him," she asked.
"A fireman, I don't know any firemen," she replied.

"Can we get another angle, another camera?" she asked.

At that moment with his other hand, the fireman took something from his pocket and held it to his ear. She looked at the clock in the corner it was nine minutes and twenty-eight seconds past four.

"What time did the last call come in from Shahid, the second warning?" she asked out loud.
After a momentary pause a voice came back "nine minutes and twenty....."

"That's him, that's Karam Shahid, track him, where does he go next?" she asked.

They fast forwarded and watched Shahid lay Charlie Wilson down on the bench, and then walk on. He turned left down a road, where there were no cameras, and unfortunately no Pods were driving past, having evacuated the area automatically. They fast forwarded again but did not see anyone emerging.

"Where does that road go?" asked Hallam.

"Through to Whitehall," came the reply.

"Get me footage from Whitehall from four ten to four fifteen," she said.

The screens flickered and new images appeared along Whitehall in different locations and different angles.

"This screen is where that road come out onto Whitehall," said the officer.

The images blurred as it was fast forwarded. At four eleven, a motorbike pulled out and turned right onto Whitehall heading towards Trafalgar Square. She looked across at the clock on the wall, it was five twenty. He had more than an hour's start. They took a note of the number plate and tracked it back to a motorbike stolen five months previously from the Brixton area. The officers tracked the bike over Vauxhall Bridge but then lost it when the bike went under the railway bridge where there were not any cameras.

"We seem to have lost him, unless he has stopped under the bridge."
"Can we get a drone there or a Pod?" said Hallam.

"Doing that right now, image coming up"

A camera was panning round the area under the bridge. There was nothing parked there and no entrances or exits. He seemed to have disappeared.

"Go back to the footage. Show him entering the bridge area. Look at the time thirteen minutes past four. Let us concentrate on all the exits for the next three minutes."

They watched the screens as they fast forwarded showing various vehicles entering and leaving.

"What about that motorbike?" said Hallam.

"Different jacket Ma'am, different numberplate, different coloured helmet, no panier on the bike," said the officer.

"Get the drone back underneath the bridge, I want a closer look."

The officer tapped some keys, the screen changed, and an image appeared of the area underneath the railway bridge. It was quite large as there were several rail lines going overhead that were coming into

Waterloo Station. Sophie Hallam was looking very carefully, scanning the pavement areas.

"Get closer there, that pile of rubbish, can you zoom in there?" she asked.

"Yes Ma'am."

The drone moved closer and the zoom lens brought a pile of newspapers and discarded cardboard into focus.
"Probably where someone has been sleeping rough Ma'am, they use the cardboard to stop the cold," said the officer.

"What's that just behind the cardboard, its blue and shiny, you can just see a little bit sticking out. Do we have any operatives close by?" she asked.

"Yes, there are two police officers five hundred yards away."

"Get them there to take a look," she said.
Valuable minutes ticked by whilst the police officers made their way to the bridge. They came into focus and were asked to pull back the cardboard. There behind it was a motorbike panier, inside was a black jacket and a black helmet.

"He has changed jacket and helmet and got rid of the panier. Track that motorbike we saw leaving," said Hallam.

The team were now pulling up every image looking for the new target. The number plate was scrutinised, it had been reported stolen some months before, all the new data was being input into the system. It took another ten minutes before images started appearing showing that Karam was travelling south down the A3, but that image was at four twenty-nine, it was now five thirty-five.

"We need to find him and fast, he has got a big lead on us, get our teams on their way down through South London," said Hallam.

Karam was now traveling down the A23, he knew that The Ministry would be tracking him, no matter how many red herrings he threw at them, he would not be able to lose Sophie Hallam. The motorway had cameras every five hundred metres and there were Pods driving up and down. He pulled off at Hickstead, onto the roundabout and stopped in the underpass. This was his last opportunity to throw them off. He took a spray from inside his jacket and applied it to the cowling. It was a bright green. It was a shoddy job, but hopefully good enough to avoid suspicion. He used it all then hid the empty can behind some weeds that were growing.

He reversed his jacket, which now became bright green. He had stickers for his helmet to match the jacket that he roughly applied, and he put a new magnetised number plate over the existing. The transformation was complete, as best as he could do in a few minutes. He went round the roundabout and started heading cross country on A roads.

There was much less traffic and hardly any traffic cameras, the opportunities for him to be seen were far less. Taking this route was going to add precious minutes to his journey, but he knew that staying on the fast roads was too risky and he could not speed anyway as that would be too obvious.

Things were fever pitch in the surveillance room, bit by bit, Karam Hashid's journey was unfolding, he was spotted along the A3, then joining the M25 and coming off onto the M23 heading for Brighton, but it was all taking time. Drones were being commandeered from Amazon and other delivery companies to be the eyes of The Ministry, there were now hundreds of them looking for Shahid on his motorbike. It was five thirty-five, the last sighting was on the Motorway at Hickstead. They worked on the premise that he must have come off there. Did he go East or West? The Armed Response Unit was now in hot pursuit in four vehicles, but they were at least fifty minutes behind. Hallam gave the instruction for the nearest police officers to go and check out the Hickstead junction as well as drones to scan the area.

Shahid was working his way through the Sussex countryside. His navigation on the phone told him he was thirteen miles away from Birling Gap as he passed through the village of Rodmell. He had not seen any drones overhead for ten miles, but he knew he could not be complacent. He accelerated, pushing the bike harder desperate to reach his destination before Sophie Hallam could catch him.

A patrol car arrived at the Hickstead underpass. The two officers got out and started looking around. They did not find much. They radioed in reporting as much. Their call was patched through to the whole floor.

"Did you find anything at all?" asked Sophie Hallam.

"No, nothing really, empty crisp bags, a few empty tins, a paint aerosol, some fast-food wrappers," said the police officer.

"A paint aerosol? Is the nozzle still wet?" asked Hallam.

"Not to the touch, but if I push my nail in it, it is soft, its fast-drying paint, probably used in the last hour or so," said the officer.

"What colour is it?" asked Hallam.

"Green, quite a bright green," he replied, and he focused his police camera onto it to show the colour.

"Our suspect may have changed the look of himself and his bike again, let's look for a motorbike with bright green paintwork along the roads east and west from the Hickstead roundabout," she said. It was now five forty-five.

Karam was six miles from his rendezvous and was starting to take risks along the country lanes. He was not an experienced biker and was pushing himself as far as he might dare. He knew that if there were any cameras or any kind of surveillance then his speed might trigger some alarms, his rendezvous was for five fifty-five with a five-minute window of opportunity. It was going to be very close.

He passed through Piddinghoe, Bishopstone then Exceat when a speed camera flashed. He looked at his phone, he was four miles away, he accelerated further pushing the motorbike to eighty miles an hour. That speed camera would have picked him up and may have triggered an alert, but he only had a few miles to go.

"Ma'am, we have had a camera alert on the A259 in Sussex, we have an image, coming up now. It's a motorbike".

 "Anything we can do about the resolution?" asked Hallam.
"Enhancing now," said the officer.
As the image sharpened, so did the colouring. The rider was wearing a green jacket

"That's him, that's Shahid," said Hallam. "Get everyone we can into the area as fast as possible, I want drones there right now."

Phones and keyboards went into overdrive, every possible asset in the area was called upon. Within minutes drones, Pods and Police were converging on this quiet little part of East Sussex.

Karam could see drones approaching in his mirror as he sped down Birling Gap Road. At the bottom he took a sharp right along the South Downs Way and carried along for three hundred yards. His navigation told him he was only fifty metres away from the rendezvous and it was in less than one minute. He stopped the bike, jumped off, letting it fall to the ground and climbed over the fence. He had visited this place before, to set it up as his extraction point. He put his arm into the back of the hedge and felt for a canvas bag. He found it and pulled it out, undoing the tie string. He pulled out a machine pistol and began running towards the edge of the cliff.

He could hear drones closing in behind him. He turned and saw two of them within twenty metres of him; they were stationary, watching him, their electronics flashing in the light drizzle.

He could hear another drone approaching, but this was heavier and noisier. He looked back and out to sea, it was his rescue craft, coming in at speed.

Sophie Hallam and her team were watching all of this unfold via the cameras on board the two drones. They could see the rocket shaped aeroplane approaching.

"It's a rescue craft," she said. "Get the drones to attack Shahid, we need to stop him."

The officers started typing instructions furiously into their keyboards. The two drones got louder as they powered up and tilted downwards to launch themselves at Shahid. He knew what they were doing, looked up and opened fire. Karam was no expert shot, having the weapon was always going to be a last resort. His aim was wild, and the drones were unaffected, they were aiming straight for him, he kept firing and then simultaneously, they exploded. The Chinese drone had an armament and shot the two drones out of the sky, the remains of them came crashing down in the field embedding in the wet grass.

The Chinese craft swept round and landed a few metres from Shahid. The canopy went up and he got in, throwing away his weapon. The craft powered up and started accelerating just as four more drones approached the field.

Sophie Hallam now had eyes on the situation again. She could see the small rocket like plane taxiing across the field

"Attack that, stop it taking off," she shouted.

Instructions were typed, and the drones turned to aim at Karam, but his craft was military grade and much more powerful, in only a few seconds it had picked up speed and was airborne, Hallam's drones never got close and all they could do was watch it as it rose into the sky and disappeared out of sight, Karam giving a farewell wave as it climbed into the clouds.

"Shall we scramble the fighters?" asked an officer.

"I don't think there is much point," she said "that thing will be miles away before we can even get into the air. We will have to think of another way to catch Karam Shahid," she said.

For Colonel Jiang, his job had only just begun. The success of Karam Shahid's plan was beyond his wildest dreams. His social media technologists started developing all kinds of conspiracist theories surrounding the attack, and there were so many visuals being used by every media agency that their job was quite simple. The Houses of Parliament burning, the lorries crashing through the anti-terrorist defences, it could not be any better. Jiang and his team were able to sow so much doubt amongst the British people as to the efficacy of their leaders and agencies to keep them safe. Thereafter Prime Minister Baillie and her Government were on the back foot. The Home Secretary and the head of The Metropolitan Police were both forced to resign. There were question marks surrounding Sophie Hallam's position and the future of the Ministry of Information.

At the Public Enquiry she and the Ministry were exonerated, it was accepted that they had done everything that they could, but with Chinese interference and support, the terrorists had succeeded by the narrowest of margins. The Public considered this to be a whitewash and questioned the security of the United Kingdom. The Chinese continued to undermine the British Government, who could never shake off the stigma of abject failure.

Karam Shahid's pilotless plane landed on a Chinese military airbase in Mauritius at two o'clock in the afternoon having slept almost the whole way. He had also been subjected to the sleeping gas, the Chinese scientists knew that a journey of that length in such a small craft and confined space could lead to extreme claustrophobia and anxiety. It was Chinese military policy that any flight longer than two hours should have enforced sleep.

When Karam awoke, he was lying in the craft in a hangar, with the canopy raised. As he regained consciousness there was a round of applause and cheering. Sam, Gemma and Oliver were there with a hundred or more Chinese military personnel. They helped him out, introduced themselves and the party carried on all night.

CHAPTER SEVEN

MONDAY 19TH JUNE 2034

Charlie arrived at the café and ordered his usual. Jasmin was no longer there; she had moved to Liverpool when things became very difficult in London. Charlie and Emma had also considered moving away but they knew they could not sell their flat, at least not without a big loss, and they probably could not rent it either.

Emma had struggled to find work when The Ministry closed, but she had now found something, it was not ideal, but it helped pay the bills whilst she retrained as a programmer.

Charlie took his seat by the window. The café had been rebuilt, almost from scratch, but it still had a familiar feel to it. The view was completely different, the Houses of Parliament were a hollow ruin.

He unpacked his bag, laying out his iPad, telephone, notepad, pencil and a book. He sipped on his coffee and looked out of the window. The sun was shining, and people were going about their business, life seemed normal, but everything had changed.

He looked down and turned the book over. There were not that many books printed these days, and Charlie had to persuade his Publisher to get some hard copies made. Ordinarily the Publisher would have said no, but they were extremely pleased to have been given this book to launch. Seven publishers had entered a bidding war to get what was considered the hottest book of the year. Five copies had arrived that morning by drone. He had already sent two on to his Mum and Dad, and his brother. Charlie looked down at the title, 'How I helped end the War – The Life and Times of Karam Shahid' by Charlie Wilson. Charlie held it up in his hands. He opened it to the first page. 'To my friend Karam, who gave me the honour of telling his story'.

It had taken a few days for Charlie to recover from his injuries before he could leave hospital. He had been visited by Emma and family as well as by Sophie Hallam and various officers from The Ministry.

Hallam had told him that she knew he had nothing to do with the plot to blow up the Houses of Parliament and to destabilise the country, but she still asked him plenty of questions. She seemed extremely interested in trying to find out what kind of man Karam Shahid was.

Charlie suffered from some post-traumatic stress after the attack but as time went by, his wounds healed both physically and mentally. He returned to University life and continued with his journalism. There was plenty to write about.

Charlie looked at the book again. Two months after the attack on Parliament he received an email from Karam. He explained everything and apologised to Charlie for keeping him in the dark. He hoped that they might meet one day, but understood it was unlikely. There was an attachment to the email, containing the story of Karam's life, as a child growing up in Damascus, the Civil War, meeting his wife, his children, coming to England, the attacks he orchestrated, everything in exquisite detail.

After losing his wife and daughter, he had sunk into despair and wanted to kill himself. He felt he had nothing to live for. He had stood on the platform at The Elephant and Castle for over an hour waiting to throw himself under the train, but he could not do it. He was not afraid; he had lost his faith and did not believe there was anything on the other side of death, but he worried that if he ended it all here, he would have wasted an opportunity. He did not know what that might be, but he felt there was something he had to do.

He kept himself to himself, not revealing anything that had happened and gradually formulated a plan. The death of his son, wife and daughter had all been unnecessary and avoidable. Why had Syria been at War? Could it have been avoided? He then thought the same about the Third World War. Was there anything he could do that might help to change things.

Having studied and taught International Relations and socio-economics, he knew better than most the way modern societies were structured and what their Government's had to do to stay in power, he understood the importance of propaganda and story-telling to keep populations subjugated and in agreement, so he also understood how this could be compromised. That was how he started on his plan. He had the patience and intellect to prepare over several years. He knew he would have to do something so impactful that it would potentially change the course of history.

As Charlie finished reading it, he came to the final paragraph:

'Charlie, I hope you know what to do with this information. I give you my blessing to turn it into a book. I have read so many things online about the terrorist Karam Shahid, now is the time for my side of the story, to let the people know what the Governments of the world have been doing to them, and I know you are the man to write it. I understand that times are still difficult and dangerous, but perhaps the war will end, and freedom of speech will return. I leave this with you as my gift and hope that one day my story will be told'.

Charlie had received the email in April 2032, the war was continuing, the Wall was being built and personal liberty was being squeezed by The Ministry of Information. That was not the time to be trying to publish this account of Karam's life, Charlie knew it would be taken down as soon as it was published. He was even wary about starting to write the book in case he was taken into custody. Sophie Hallam had told him that she knew he had nothing to do with Karam Shahid's plan, but a change of personnel at The Ministry and the case being re-opened could see Charlie having to answer questions all over again which would mean them going through his personal life. He downloaded the file on to a memory card and hid it behind a cupboard at his parent's house.

The war ended five months later, and things started to change quite quickly. the Ministry of Information was closed within a few months as the people clamoured that there was no need for such an authoritarian and intrusive body now that we were no longer at war. Charlie doubted that the whole edifice was entirely closed, and part of it was probably moved to GCHQ.

He continued to teach at the LSE, and wrote articles, his reputation building all the while. In August of 2033, he and Emma married, Sophie Hallam attended, they enjoyed a honeymoon in Italy, the first time they had been abroad together. By June 2034 Emma was six months pregnant. Charlie was delighted but the pregnancy did cloud his judgement about writing Karam's story. He had thought long and hard and had spoken to Emma and his parents about the risk that the authorities might come for him, but they allayed his fears and encouraged him to write it. The UK was a different country now, the war was behind us, all Coronavirus restrictions were lifted, there was talk of some of the SAGE scientists and immunologists facing criminal trials for the fabrication of data. None of that was true, they had only been delivering the facts and information to Government, but that did not fit current policy and scapegoats were required to turn around public opinion. After fourteen years of fear, it would take someone to fall on their sword to change the way that people thought.

In March, Charlie had retrieved the file and had started working on the book. He contacted a few Publishing houses who all knew it would be a best seller; it was so explosive. Charlie agreed a deal and a substantial advance which meant that Emma could give up work and concentrate on the pregnancy. They were also now able to move out of London. They put their flat up for sale but had to reduce the price significantly to get a buyer. Property outside of London had started rising, but fortunately the pre-sales of the book were staggering, and another large payment came Charlie's way.

When he had finished writing the book and knew it was ready for publication, he put a paid advert in The New York Times reading "Five aside football kit for sale, no longer required, please call CW for further information". Karam had asked him to post this advert if he was ever ready to publish the book. Karam had an alert if such an advert was ever printed.

As Charlie sat in the café pondering everything that had happened, he received an email from Karam. It had a picture of Karam with a beautiful woman stood on a beach. He was holding a baby in his arms and smiling.

'I hope you get a buyer for your football kit Charlie, I don't suppose you will get much time to play now that you and Emma are having a baby, congratulations to you both. This is my son, three months old, his name is Nazrim and this is my wife Sannika. Thank you for writing my story. Perhaps we will be reunited one day after all. Your friend Karam.'

Charlie did not try to write a reply, it was unlikely that he would be able to do so anyway, Karam was very careful, and he did wonder if somebody somewhere was still watching him. How did Karam know about Emma and the baby? Nothing that Karam did would ever surprise him.

Charlie packed away his things, put on his rucksack and left the café saying goodbye on his way out. The sun was still shining, the weather seemed to be improving since the co-ordinated efforts on climate control, certainly the rain had started to reduce and there were the occasional bright days. He put on his sunglasses and started walking along the Embankment thinking about his future, Emma and the baby. He was glad to be leaving London, it had changed so much and was not the City he had grown up in.

As he passed The Embankment Tube station, he picked up a copy of The Standard, one of the last printed newspapers left in the UK. He read the headline 'First case of Cannibalism found in Hackney''. He folded it up and put it back on the stand. It was time to leave.

EPILOGUE

After the attack and the ensuing fire, almost the whole of the Palace of Westminster was destroyed. It was considered too dangerous to do anything with it, and it was debated whether to demolish it or not. Parliament had been split with some of it meeting in Portcullis House close by, and the remainder moving to a new building in Leeds and linked by video, but it did not really work, and everything was moved north. The House of Lords had already moved a few years before to sit in York as part of the Johnson Government's initiative to level up the UK. The cost of the refurbishment had been put at twenty-four billion pounds which was an impossible sum to contemplate after the cost of the war and Britain's financial crisis. It was agreed that the site would be left as it was as a memorial, like the Kaiser Wilhelm Memorial Church in Berlin. It was illuminated and sat on the banks of the Thames in an Orange glow, a reminder of the war, Big Ben had been fully restored as the fire only damaged the lower half.

After the attack, the impact from social media had an effect on the support for the War. The British Public talked more about peace and were less inclined to be compliant. The Government knew this and began to worry. In the summer of twenty thirty-two, President Trump died of a massive coronary and his daughter, Vice President Ivanka Trump became President. Within a fortnight, there was a coup at the Chinese Communist Ruling Party and President Xi was imprisoned. There were charges against him, embezzlement, murder, torture, a whole litany of things.

The Chinese Government had lost the support of the people over the war. At the start, China had done very well politically, but over the next few years, the fundamental weaknesses of their economy were laid bare. It was not yet a sufficiently developed economy driven by domestic demand, but one still heavily reliant on exports. The first couple of years had been fine as those supine countries that had capitulated and supported China, helped drive the Chinese economy, but as their own economies started to implode, it affected China. Losing the two markets of Europe and the United States proved a drag and Chinese living standards lowered. President Xi had hoped that the emerging middle classes in Africa would drive a new export boom for China, but his policy of destabilisation and using Africa as a proxy was so successful that the whole continent went into steep decline. The Africans blamed China for their predicament and had no appetite for Chinese made goods which were boycotted by everyone. For all the banner waving and rhetoric, the Chinese people were feeling it in their pockets. By twenty thirty-two there were food shortages and people began to starve. President Xi would not entertain an end to the war, but by the summer, the moderates in the party were sensing that something had to be done.

It was dangerous for anyone to be discussing overthrowing President Xi who had absolute control over The Ministry of State Security which was the eyes and ears to everything in China, but the leaders had the support of the Army. On July twenty third, President Xi was arrested in his Summer Palace in Beijing and a temporary military Government installed. Within a month there were new elections, and a transitional Committee for Global Peace was formed.

Ivanka Trump, equally keen on an end to the war offered a fig leaf to the new President Chen, and on August 31st 2032, an armistice was signed quickly followed by an all-encompassing peace agreement that included a new framework for global trade and an emphasis on climate change. All the G12 nations signed and the world quickly moved to a period of co-operation.

The United Kingdom had been instrumental in the negotiations from behind the scenes. Prime Minister Baillie knew that she could not hold the UK together, that internal tensions were running too high, the war had to end and some normality resume. Despite its weakened position economically and militarily, Great Britain still had some standing politically in the world. Baillie turned out to be a good mediator and could sense the mood music. It helped that there had been many changes of leadership around the world over the previous two years with the overthrow of Vladimir Putin by the opposition party of Alexei Navalny. Putin had been in power for thirty years but eventually the claims of corruption and his ostentatious lifestyle had caught up with him. By 2029, Putin was no longer the strongman of ten years previous with diminishing health and presence. Navalny welcomed the British Prime Minister, it seemed as though all the major players were ready for peace.

The internationally agreed end of the war at midnight, September 16th, 2032 was greeted with joy around the world. There had been frank and open discussions with the emphasis on the future rather than blame and recriminations. China acknowledged its introduction of the Covid28 virus into Africa and immediately shipped three billion vials of the antidote. By March the following year, the virus was under control and borders began re-opening. Of course, life could not resume as it was when Charlie was growing up. Nothing was the same as then, after the long-term impact of Covid19 and Covid22. The vaccine rollout of 2020 had been haphazard, with some developed economies like Israel, the UK and Switzerland inoculating a large proportion of their population quickly, but the rest of the world struggling to build any kind of critical mass despite a promising start.

It was the inefficiency of the mandarins at the European Council and the failure to get on top of the Pandemic there that really led to schism that broke the European Union into two. The financial and economic collapse had fractured the belief in the project, but it was the failure over the vaccination programme especially measured against Great Britain that started the rioting across Europe's major cities.

Britain had fared well in 2021, getting to a critical mass of vaccinations by mid-summer, and re-opening large parts of the economy, but the variations in the strains that reared their head by autumn meant that Covid was always present. The weakened Government of Boris Johnson remained in the thrall of scientists who fed data suggesting that the virus would always be with us and that varying levels of protection would have to be maintained. Charlie became part of history although he did not know it at the time. He had been in the stands and watched Arsenal beat Chelsea on the 16th of October at The Emirates, which turned out to be the last game of football played in England with a crowd watching for 12 years. The last concert took place on the same day, thereafter no gatherings were allowed apart from funerals and weddings which could have a maximum of twelve people. Masks and social distancing became a normal part of life, people settled into the routine of working from home which only hastened the shrinking of London. It also had a huge impact on society, marriages collapsed to less than fifty thousand a year and the birth rate fell as it became exceedingly difficult for couples to form relationships, such was the fear generated by the media and Government agencies.

Fines were replaced by custodial sentences for any illegal gatherings, but they happened all the same. A whole new black market grew up of clandestine clubs where people could go, hold hands, hug, and even have sex. As time went on though, people got used to the isolation. Although Covid deaths hovered around one hundred thousand a year throughout the twenty twenties, the actual population of the UK shrunk by seven million as immigration and birth-rates collapsed.

The message of 'Stay Home, Protect the NHS, Save Lives' morphed into 'Be Aware, Mix Less, Keep Everyone Safe'. Scientists dominated the TV channels with one or two, hour long briefings daily, but after a while people stopped watching them, resigned to their new lives, where there was less to do and more to fear. The Covid22 outbreak, engineered by the Chinese State only intensified the reaction of Western Governments. Temporary laws introduced to tackle Covid19 continued and became established in statute. Societies became dominated by the fear of Virus's throughout the 2020s changing the way we lived our lives.

In September 2032, the peace negotiations were not only held at Government level, but also at corporate level. The boards of the five largest companies in the world met with the political leaders to plan the way forwards. For the first time in years, there was an optimism and pragmatism about the future.

The largest corporations had become much more powerful than countries themselves and were now embedded in the matters of state. In the UK, after the shambles of PPE and the logistical shortcomings of the vaccine rollout, Amazon were invited by the Government to look at an overhaul of procurement and distribution for the NHS. Despite the best efforts of Public Health England to thwart them, within twelve months, they had reduced costs by fifty five percent, streamline purchasing, warehousing and distribution, making savings of over twenty billion pounds. This led to Amazon becoming a key partner for the British Government, embedded in every aspect of Government business.

Environmental issues by now were playing a significant part that could no longer be ignored. The extreme weather conditions increased during the decade, with floods, fires, and droughts, leading to mass migration. The Great Flood of 2026 alone had left five hundred thousand people homeless as rivers burst their banks all over the UK flooding homes and businesses the length and breadth of the country. The Hurricane season of the following year left almost eight thousand dead in the USA, whilst a quarter of Sydney was burnt to the ground from a wildfire that could not be brought under control that same year. Natural disasters were happening all over the world and it was clear than man was no match for the wrath of mother nature.

It was agreed that nation states competing for resources and political dominance was not in the interest of the planet and the future of Homo Sapiens and all other species. A committee made up from the five largest companies and members of the UN would co-ordinate global policy on energy, food production, and ecology. The Israeli

Philosopher Yuval Noah Harari and a group of eminent thinkers including ethicists and moralists were invited to join the committee which was finally able to formulate a holistic policy going forwards, driven by the need to save the planet and benefit all of mankind, rather than the pursuit of profit benefitting the few.

Although the war had been a terrible thing, it had not been the blood fest of the previous two World Wars. None of the super-powers had considered using nuclear weapons, when it came to it, the notion of mutually assured destruction acted as the ultimate deterrent. There had been a scare in 2029 when an offshoot of ISIS had captured the families of some of the Pakistani Nuclear Scientists and some of those who sat on The National Command Authority and attempted to detonate a nuclear device, but Chinese Special Forces were flown in and the threat diffused.

The new period of co-operation generated some extraordinary forward thinking and big ideas, there was a new air of optimism.

In the UK, Prime Minister Baillie went to the polls on a ticket of restoring normal life in the UK by encouraging its citizens to live with any new virus as they came along. She won a landslide with a Commons majority of three hundred and eleven seats. Everyone had had enough and wanted the return of some kind of normality. The opposition parties had failed to read the mood of the British people.

Immediately after the attack on the Houses of Parliament, the Mayor of London put forward the proposition that London should be better protected from threats, suggesting that it was too important, that if London fell the United Kingdom would fall. His ideas gained some support from Parliament. MPs from the South were annoyed at having to travel to Leeds to sit and debate and wanted London strengthened so that Parliament could return. The Mayor had some influence with the London newspapers who promoted the idea of a security fence around the Capital, as the only way to protect Londoners, The City, Government and UK sovereignty. This was being debated whilst the UK was still at War, when it was narrowly passed in a heated Government debate, and work started almost immediately. The attack had rocked the UK, the images and press coverage that went global had terrified everyone, but this was on the back of a decade of fearmongering and suppression of the population by the Government and media. The constant drip of messages of fear had kowtowed the population, with freethinking consigned to the waste heap. It really was not that difficult to persuade the nation, that building a protective cordon around London was a good idea.

The five-metre-high solid structure was pre-fabricated and erected within the boundary of the M25 ring road that ran around the city. It was an enormous project covering one hundred and eighty-eight kilometres, but due to simple methods of construction it was completed within a year. At one stage there were thirty thousand people working on it, and on one day alone, two kilometres of wall was erected. It was hard to imagine that only a few years previously there had been outrage at the notion of Donald Trump wanting to build a wall between America and Mexico, and here in the heart of England a wall was being built to separate the Capital from the rest of the country.

Once up, all roads in and out had checkpoints, where documents were presented and scanned. It became difficult to enter and there were many unintended consequences. The population of London used to swell by two million people a day before Covid 19 but that was already changing with Parliament moving outside of London. The policies of 'levelling up the country' in the 2020s had led to an economic boom in the Midlands and the North which had attracted younger more mobile workers who could get a better standard of life with bigger and cheaper housing and the countryside to live in. The wall became another reason not to live in the Capital and the exodus continued.

There were fewer migrant workers living in London as a result of the War, internment and emigration which meant a shortage of labour which in turn drove up wages. The comfortable life the middle classes had enjoyed for the previous twenty years started to suffer as cleaners, builders and even the Baristas commanded higher wages. Inflation was also eroding their wealth at the same time as the value of their property declined. This was not a good time for the professionals and intelligentsia who found life to be getting much harder.

The rest of the country looked on bemused as the wall was erected. So much power had moved from London to other parts of the country by the 2030s that London was no longer regarded as the economic and political powerhouse that it used to be. There was so much material for comedians who asked whether the wall was to keep everyone else out or to keep Londoners in.

Charlie wrote several pieces about this and built a reputation as an authority on the subject introducing it as part of his classes at the LSE with comparisons to the Berlin Wall, and the Great Wall of China, and their socio-economic impacts.

Inward investment in London had been steadily collapsing. Property prices were in freefall and the wealthy of the world no longer saw London as a safe haven. The two attacks on the Dartford Tunnel and then the destruction of the Houses of Parliament battered the confidence of the wealthy International Elite. London had been for decades an open City that was happy to turn a blind eye as to the source of any money that might come and buy assets, especially prime London real estate. The introduction of The National Crime Agency and its ability to seize assets of money laundering had started very slowly but after picking up momentum, begun to stem the tide, but the economic decline of the 2020s and then the attack on Parliament, power-charged everything, the super wealthy were selling up and helping to drive prices down even further in London and the population continued to shrink.

Restaurants and bars began to close as customers dwindled. This had started during the Covid-19 Pandemic, but as habits changed, fewer people ate out and went out. The young and mobile continued to move to other parts of the country that offered more opportunities. As economic activity moved to the north and London became less important, suppliers were keener on serving the markets of the booming northern cities. Incomes continued to fall, and poorer

Londoners were forced to grow vegetables in their gardens and every open space was given over to allotments by the local Councils, and of course it was the poorest who were the least economically mobile.

It all seemed so sudden for those living there, but this had been coming for a few years, this was just the culmination of events. The population of London had shrunk by 20% before between the second world war and 1992 and had gone into terrible decline in the 1970s and 1980s, but this felt different. The wall did not make Londoners feel safer, they were not being protected from the outside, they felt as though they were being kept inside, prisoners in their own city.

THE END

ABOUT THE AUTHOR

Grant Williams was born in Hampstead, North London in 1963. An extraordinarily varied career has led to a lifetime of experiences and helped develop both a vivid imagination and an insatiable curiosity. The success of his first novel World War 2 Survival, which became an Amazon International Best Seller was the springboard to further creativity. 2034 was born of the global Pandemic and the changes to society. The author is now pursuing a full-time writing career with forthcoming books utilising his observational skills as well as a critical mind.

OTHER BOOKS BY GRANT WILLIAMS

World War II Survival: The epic story of Leonid Aleksandrov's journey from Russia to Normandy and Berlin
Available on Amazon: http://getbook.at/WW2survival

Printed in Great Britain
by Amazon

82100912R00144